A Tim

D0838447

"Grabbed my attention on page one. A psychic mayor who finds lost things—and dead bodies? A secret room locked for decades? Puzzles are unraveled and secrets spilled in a fast-paced paranormal mystery full of quirky characters you'll want as friends."
—Elizabeth Spann Craig, author of *Pretty Is as Pretty Dies*

"A delightful yarn! Few amateur sleuths are as charming as this psychic mayor sleuth in a small coastal town where murder stalks the dunes and ghosts roam the Outer Banks. Kept me turning pages until it was done."
—Patricia Sprinkle, author of *Hold Up the Sky*

"Filled with likable (if eccentric) characters and boasts a vividly realized small-town setting." —*Booklist*

"A quaint setting and leisurely pace make this a fun read. The characters' interactions reflect the intricacies of small-town living. The mystery unfolds cleverly with a well-rounded group of suspects." —*Romantic Times*

"This opening act of a new amateur sleuth is a wonderful mystery due to memorable eccentric characters including Duck. The whodunit is complicated enough to keep readers entertained and stymied . . . The heroine is sassy and spunky . . . Joyce and Jim Lavene have . . . another hit series." —*Midwest Book Review*

"A leisurely mystery that had me guessing almost 'til the very end . . . It was fun and the characters were likable . . . I could almost smell and feel the salty sea air of Duck as I was reading. The authors definitely did a bang-up job with the setting, and I look forward to more of Dae's adventures and the hint of romance with Kevin." —*A Cup of Tea and a Cozy for Me*

"The Lavenes have launched a wonderful series, with a great deal of opportunity for future books . . . All of the characters in this book . . . are delightful. This is a mystery with strong characters, a vivid sense of place, and touches of humor and the paranormal. *A Timely Vision* is one of the best traditional mysteries I've read this year." —*Lesa's Book Critiques*

continued . . .

Fruit of the Poisoned Tree

"I cannot recommend this work highly enough. It has everything: mystery, wonderful characters, sinister plot, humor, and even romance."
— *Midwest Book Review*

"Well-crafted with a satisfying end that will leave readers wanting more!"
— *Fresh Fiction*

Pretty Poison

"With a touch of romance added to this delightful mystery, one can only hope many more Peggy Lee Mysteries will be hitting shelves soon!"
— *Roundtable Reviews*

"A fantastic amateur-sleuth mystery."
— *The Best Reviews*

"For anyone with even a modicum of interest in gardening, this book is a lot of fun."
— *The Romance Readers Connection*

"The perfect book if you're looking for a great suspense."
— *Romance Junkies*

"Joyce and Jim Lavene have crafted an outstanding whodunit in *Pretty Poison*, with plenty of twists and turns that will keep the reader entranced to the final page."
— *Fresh Fiction*

"Complete with gardening tips, this is a smartly penned, charming cozy, the first book in a new series. The mystery is intricate and well-plotted. Green thumbs and nongardeners alike will enjoy this book."
— *Romantic Times*

Perfect Poison

"A fabulous whodunit that will keep readers guessing and happily turning pages to the unexpected end. Peggy Lee is a most entertaining sleuth and her Southern gentility is like a breath of fresh air . . . [A] keeper!"
— *Fresh Fiction*

"A fascinating whodunit with unusual but plausible twists and plenty of red herrings."
— *Genre Go Round Reviews*

A Touch of Gold

Joyce and Jim Lavene

BERKLEY PRIME CRIME, NEW YORK

THE BERKLEY PUBLISHING GROUP
Published by the Penguin Group
Penguin Group (USA) Inc.
375 Hudson Street, New York, New York 10014, USA
Penguin Group (Canada), 90 Eglinton Avenue East, Suite 700, Toronto, Ontario M4P 2Y3, Canada
(a division of Pearson Penguin Canada Inc.)
Penguin Books Ltd., 80 Strand, London WC2R 0RL, England
Penguin Group Ireland, 25 St. Stephen's Green, Dublin 2, Ireland (a division of Penguin Books Ltd.)
Penguin Group (Australia), 250 Camberwell Road, Camberwell, Victoria 3124, Australia
(a division of Pearson Australia Group Pty. Ltd.)
Penguin Books India Pvt. Ltd., 11 Community Centre, Panchsheel Park, New Delhi—110 017, India
Penguin Group (NZ), 67 Apollo Drive, Rosedale, North Shore 0632, New Zealand
(a division of Pearson New Zealand Ltd.)
Penguin Books (South Africa) (Pty.) Ltd., 24 Sturdee Avenue, Rosebank, Johannesburg 2196,
South Africa

Penguin Books Ltd., Registered Offices: 80 Strand, London WC2R 0RL, England

This is a work of fiction. Names, characters, places, and incidents either are the product of the author's imagination or are used fictitiously, and any resemblance to actual persons, living or dead, business establishments, events, or locales is entirely coincidental. The publisher does not have any control over and does not assume any responsibility for author or third-party websites or their content.

A TOUCH OF GOLD

A Berkley Prime Crime Book / published by arrangement with the authors

PRINTING HISTORY
Berkley Prime Crime mass-market edition / March 2011

Copyright © 2011 by Joyce Lavene and Jim Lavene.
Cover illustration by Robert Crawford.
Cover design by Annette Fiore Defex.
Interior text design by Laura K. Corless.

ISBN: 978-0-425-24024-3

BERKLEY® PRIME CRIME
Berkley Prime Crime Books are published by The Berkley Publishing Group,
a division of Penguin Group (USA) Inc.,
375 Hudson Street, New York, New York 10014.
BERKLEY® PRIME CRIME and the PRIME CRIME logo are trademarks of Penguin Group (USA) Inc.

PRINTED IN THE UNITED STATES OF AMERICA

10 9 8 7 6 5 4 3 2 1

We'd like to thank our editor, Faith Black,
for her help and understanding. We'd also like to thank
the rest of the team of editors and artists who made
this book better. You guys are great!

Chapter 1

"On a dark night in 1812, the schooner *Patriot* vanished with all hands onboard, never to be seen again."

The story always started the same way when Max Caudle told it. Any story that had to do with dark and stormy nights and the sea had particular appeal for this group of first-graders. They lived on the Outer Banks of North Carolina, an island with the Atlantic Ocean on one side and the Currituck Sound on the other. They knew how bad and scary storms could get.

"Theodosia Burr Alston was on that ship, trying to reach her father, the infamous Aaron Burr, in New York. She'd sailed from her home in South Carolina during the war with the British. The soldiers let her ship pass because she had a special letter from her husband, the governor of South Carolina. But it might have been better for her if the British soldiers had captured her. Because right after that, a terrible gale hit and the *Patriot* was assumed lost at sea."

1

"Was Theodosia Burr killed in the terrible gale?" The little girl's eyes were wide in her pretty, tanned face. "Or was she killed by pirates?"

Despite the fact that all of these children had heard the tragic tale of Theo Burr the way most kids on the mainland listened to "The Three Little Pigs," there were always questions.

"Dae, maybe you could take this question." Max smiled at me.

It was unusual for him to step out of his tale. Max was a master storyteller and loved the tales of the Outer Banks' dark past—pirates, marauders and gold—better than anyone else I knew.

"Miss Dae is the mayor of Duck, North Carolina, our hometown," Max continued, probably trying to prompt a response from me.

I was fairly sure the kids knew who I was since this was Walk to Story Time with the Mayor Wednesday, but I played along.

Twenty pairs of eyes all turned and stared at me as though they'd never seen me before. I smiled back (my big, friendly mayor smile) and jumped right into it. "Well, kids, we all know the terrible things that can happen at sea."

"Pirates!" one little boy blurted out, grinning despite his teacher's reprimand for speaking out of turn.

"Hurricanes!" another little girl (I recognized her as the granddaughter of Vergie Smith, the Duck postmaster) yelled out, causing a loud rash of talking.

Both teachers that had accompanied me to the Duck Historical Museum stepped in at that point to calm the group. When the kids were quiet again, they nodded at me to continue.

"In this case, Theo Burr wasn't killed by the pirates who attacked her ship or by the terrible gale that came up that January." I glanced at Max to see if he wanted me to go any further.

All the kids had already turned back, owl-eyed, to face Max again. The two teachers with me were probably as anxious to hear the tale continue as the children. Even as adults, we never tired of the story.

Those of us who grew up in Duck know about how our Banker (our term for the people who lived here) ancestors survived by picking up cargo from ships that went down close to the Outer Banks. Be it pirates or storms, they didn't call this area of the world the Graveyard of the Atlantic for nothing.

Max began his tale again. His curly brown hair and cheerful red face that matched his red suspenders seemed unlikely for a man who could impart such gloom and doom. He'd been the curator of the museum for as long as there had been a museum. He knew every ship's relic, barnacle and cannonball better than most people knew what was in their closet at home.

"It's true. Theo Burr wasn't killed by the pirates who captured her ship. But she was forced to walk the plank, and the pirates thought she was dead just like the rest of the *Patriot*'s crew."

The voice and inflection were perfect. The children were wrapped up in the story just as I had been at their age—and was now. I could remember sitting on this floor listening as Max told his tales of woe and privateering with style and sufficient substance to cause fear to creep into my heart.

For other children of this age, this might seem too frightening, but Duck children knew the terrible truth of the past. They respected it and learned to live with it.

"But you said Theo Burr wasn't dead," the first little girl said accusingly.

"Aye, and she wasn't," Max confirmed with a squinted left eye. "Old Frank Burdick, the pirate, confessed on his deathbed that he had held the plank for Theo Burr. He said the crew and passengers of the *Patriot* were all murdered. The pirates plundered the ship, then abandoned her under full sail."

"But what about Theo Burr?" the little girl demanded. "Was she dead or not?"

"People tell different tales. But an old Banker story says that Theo made it to shore around Nags Head. She was picked up by a family who made their living salvaging from wrecked ships. They say she couldn't tell them who she was but that she carried a small portrait that was later identified as one Theo Burr had painted for her father."

"But did she die?" a little boy asked in a shaky voice. "My dad says her ghost walks the beaches looking for her dead baby. She has to be dead to be a ghost, right?"

Max laughed and pulled at his suspenders like he always did. "That's right, young man. But that was a long time ago. No matter what, Theo Burr would be dead by now. But there are plenty of people who believe she lived the rest of her life on the Outer Banks. They say she couldn't remember who she was and started a new family with a man from Duck."

"So she *is* a ghost and walks around looking for her dead baby," Vergie's granddaughter said in awe. "What about the pirate gold?"

"She didn't have any pirate gold," Max replied with infinite patience. "But the real treasure is finding out if Theo Burr really lived here the rest of her life. If she did, one of *you* might be related to her. Now that would be something, wouldn't it?"

The kids looked around at each other. One little boy stuck his fingers in his ears and shook his head. "Tell us about the curse of the pirate captain," he pleaded. "Talk about his ghost coming back to look for his hidden pirate treasure."

They all agreed with that idea, and Max told the story about Rafe Masterson's curse, which had been a legend in Duck for more than two hundred years.

I left the group to go over and help Agnes, Max's wife, who owned the Beach Bakery. She always brought treats on story time days. She was unwrapping brownies and cupcakes while I took out all the tiny boxes of juice.

"He loves when the kids come," she said with a smile at her husband. "He worries they'll forget, you know? They don't teach our history in school anymore."

"I don't think he has to worry about that. I'm sure everyone over the age of twelve can recite the tale of Theo Burr word for word. I know I can."

"But things are different now with all the gaming and such." Agnes sighed as the last of the cupcakes was laid out. "There might be a time when all of the legends are lost. I hate to think of it, but sometimes I can feel it sliding away."

I agreed. With corporations fighting to see who could buy out more of the older homes in Duck for condominiums, I didn't know if there was hope for the future or the past.

But not today. The Duck Historical Museum might be small, but you couldn't stand here without feeling like you were in the heart of Duck, past and present.

I glanced down at the floor and saw a gold coin. Probably from the display in the glass case across the room, I thought. Agnes had already gone to tell the kids it was snack time. Max was still answering questions about ghosts and pirates.

I bent over, picked up the coin and flipped it over in my

hand. It was a dull gold, burnished by sea and sand. Unlike the recovered treasure often shown in movies, none of the old gold that washed up here was ever shiny.

I knew the tale of how the Duck Museum came to have that pirate treasure as well as I knew the tale of Theo Burr. This one was closer to home. Max had found the gold early one morning. It was in an old wood chest that had washed up on the Atlantic side of the island. This was years before, when Max was a young man. He'd received a finder's fee from the government and had donated the gold to the museum.

I looked closely at the coin in the palm of my hand. Max would certainly miss it if it was gone when the museum closed. He might even come to me since I'd been Duck's unofficial finder of lost things since I was a child.

At one time, when I was a teenager, I had big dreams of saving the world using my special abilities. When I was alone, I even dared to call them my *powers*. There were things I could do that other people couldn't do. I was very impressed with myself.

But time had given me better perspective and honed the abilities I was born with. I might not ever save the world by finding everyone's many sets of lost keys and misplaced TV remotes, but I helped the people I cared about—the same reason I had become mayor of Duck.

I slipped the gold coin into the pocket of my jeans. I didn't want to interrupt Max's enjoyment of talking to the children. I wasn't surprised to see the coin out of place. How many times had I visited the museum to find cannonballs where they didn't belong or an old ship's compass taken apart on a table? Max was a good curator, but he was far from neat.

Around the cupcakes and apple juice, the talk was still of Theo Burr and other ghosts that inhabited the Outer

Banks. Max was juggling questions between bites of Agnes's delicious cupcakes and glances at his watch.

"Hot date?" I asked when I could get close to him.

"What?" He pushed his glasses back against his face and smiled as he understood the humor in my words. "You might say so. You won't believe what's happened, Dae. I think I finally have a real lead on someone in Duck who's related to Theo Burr."

"That's wonderful!" I gave him my full attention, which wasn't easy since the cupcake in my hand was really good. "I know you've been looking for proof that Theo lived here rather than died as soon as she washed up on shore."

"All of my life," he agreed with a seriousness only dedicated historians can muster. "If I'm right, it will rock the historical world. Not to mention my intense joy at flaunting it in Sam Meacham's face!"

I knew how much that meant to him. Sam Meacham was the curator of the Corolla Historical Museum. He believed Theo Burr had died when she reached shore, in the arms of one of the Bankers who'd stolen her personal possessions once she was dead. His proof was a portrait that was widely recognized by historians as Theo. It was found at a Banker woman's home in Nags Head in 1869. While the painting was never definitively identified as being a portrait of Theo Burr, most historians agreed with Sam.

But not Max. "I'm trying to convince a man who claims to be a relative of hers to give me a sample of his DNA. He's meeting me here in a little while. If his DNA matches the DNA from Theodosia's hair samples, it will be the first real proof of what happened to Theodosia Burr in the winter of 1812. Don't forget, her husband never sent a search party here to look for her. He and Aaron Burr looked everywhere but the Outer Banks. She was here all the time, not knowing who she was or where she belonged. A tragedy, to be sure."

I knew Max's strong feelings on the subject. There weren't many who agreed with him. I also knew he might never find out the truth. But it made him happy to tell the story. I loved Duck history. I hoped Theo Burr survived the pirates and the terrible gale. It would be another feather in the Duck historical annals to say that she spent her last years here.

"Be sure to let me know what happens." I smiled and ate more of my cupcake. "The kids always love your stories."

"We both know they're so much more than stories," he said with another glance at his watch. "They keep the history of Duck alive, Dae. Without our past, we have no future."

One of the teachers saved me from an intense lecture on the importance of Duck history by coming over and thanking Max for his program. She was a newcomer to Duck, one of many who came for a vacation one summer and decided to stay. They added to our increased population of almost six hundred full-time residents.

It may sound small, but for a scrap of land hemmed in by water that could rise up at anytime and wash us all away, it was a lot. It was the largest population Duck had ever known. The town was becoming more popular as a tourist destination every year. We didn't have the wild horses of Corolla or the lighthouse at Hatteras, but we were sandwiched in between on the one-hundred-mile stretch of land, brought together by a narrow ribbon of road.

Some people liked the growth. Others were unhappy about it and wanted things to stay the same. The one thing

I'd learned in my thirty-six years was that nothing ever stayed the same.

It was almost time for the story adventure to be over. The teachers gathered the kids together and thanked Max for his time. They were equally enthusiastic in their thanks to Agnes for her cupcakes. I knew Agnes enjoyed these moments as much as Max. Their daughters still lived in Duck, but neither of them were married yet. No grandchildren.

As the teachers took the kids to the bathroom before leaving to walk back to Duck Elementary School, I helped Agnes throw away the cupcake wrappers and empty juice boxes.

Max paced the floor, continually looking at his watch. He was obviously nervous about meeting what could be an ancestor of Aaron Burr. It would either validate his life's work or turn into another joke that Sam Meacham could throw at him in the bar at night. I supposed that would be enough to make anyone nervous.

"He's got everything riding on this DNA," Agnes told me when we walked out to the trash cans. "Damn fool went ahead and told Sam about the whole thing, of course. He'll crash and burn for sure if it isn't true."

"Let's hope it works out then." I took the lid off the trash can. "He and Sam really like to argue about Theo Burr, don't they?"

"And everything else." She stuffed the trash in the can. "They argue about which town was settled first, Duck or Corolla. Which museum has the oldest artifacts. Honestly, they act like little kids with their toys."

Before I put the lid back on the trash can, I bent down and picked up a scrap of paper from the ground. It was one of the coffee cards they punched at the Coffee House

and Book Store. It seemed odd to me because Max and
Agnes didn't drink coffee. As I tossed it into the can and
put on the lid, I decided it was probably something a visi-
tor had left.

As Agnes and I walked back around the front of the
plain little building that had been donated to the Duck
Historical Society, I recalled the old store that had been
here, a place where we used to buy chips and soft drinks.
Someday no one would remember that little store. Agnes
was right. Everything was changing too quickly.

Near the front door of the building, a large statue of a
duck that had been used to promote tourism stood beside
a statue of a horse. Both had become animal icons in this
area. There were two rusted cannons legend said had
washed up on Duck's shore back in the 1700s. Several
cannonballs were stuck in concrete around them.

The old museum was cool and musty smelling when
we went back inside. The light was too dim to really see
everything the historical society had managed to piece together through the years. But I was proud of this little
place anyway. It represented the heritage of everyone
who'd been born here. From pirates to wild horses, all of
it was part of our past.

The teachers were getting the kids lined up to go outside. Agnes kissed Max good-bye and told him they were
having his favorite, tacos, for supper. She reminded him
not to dawdle after his meeting and come right home.

I smiled, seeing them together. I hoped someday there
would be someone who looked at me that way. Right now,
I was kind of stuck waiting for that person, wondering if he
would ever blow into town on the right breeze and decide
to stay. I'd given up on the indigenous male population.

Once the kids were in their semi-straight lines, the
teachers led the way down Duck Road. There were a few

backward glances and shy waves at Max, who returned them with gusto.

"Let me know how your DNA meeting goes," I said to him before I followed the kids outside. "It would be something if you could really prove your theory about Theo Burr. That would put Duck on the map historically."

"It'll happen, Dae. I know I'm right. Wait until you see Sam Meacham's face when I do it. Take it easy. See you later."

Outside, it was a beautiful day and traffic had picked up on Duck Road. Probably a few early tourists. People who lived here were used to walking under the puffy white clouds and bright blue February skies. Some of the cars sped by, making me a little concerned for the large group of kids on their way back to school.

I'd had a few rainy days since the Walk to the Museum program started, but in general the weather had cooperated. I enjoyed helping the kids with their history lesson. I liked being the mayor of Duck and doing all the things that went with it. It took some time away from my thrift store, Missing Pieces, but sometimes that was a good thing.

Business was slow, as usual, after the crowds of summer. I usually collected more than I could sell over the winter. It was a bad habit that had filled the house I shared with my grandfather until he encouraged me to open the shop and sell the odds and ends I found.

I reached into my pocket as my cell phone rang and realized I'd forgotten to give Max the gold coin I'd found on the museum floor. I signaled the closest teacher that I had to run back to the museum. "I'll catch up," I yelled over the traffic passing us.

Kevin Brickman was on the phone. My heart did a little dance at the sound of his voice until I sternly reminded it that we had no real inkling of his intentions. Brickman was new to Duck, less than a year. He'd refurbished and reopened the old Blue Whale Inn and, so far, had been very successful in the undertaking.

"I was wondering if you'd like to take a break from the store and get something to drink, but I see you're busy being the mayor," he said with a smile in his voice.

"Where are you?" I glanced around but didn't see his red Ford pickup. I was only a few steps from the museum door. "I'm almost done here. I could meet you somewhere." I tried not to sound too eager to see him even though I'd spent a lot of time thinking about him.

A car full of laughing tourists went by as I waited for his reply.

Suddenly, the whole world exploded into a ball of fire with such force that it blew me backwards into Duck Road. I heard the screech of brakes around me, and everything went black.

Chapter 2

Brickman was crouched beside me, my head cradled on his arm. He was looking down at me, his face black with soot.

"Are you okay?" He sounded scared. "Stupid question. Sorry. Not what I meant. Do you hurt anywhere? I had to move you. I'm sorry. The ambulance is on the way."

I realized then that I'd lost consciousness. "What happened?" My voice was rough and hoarse. I coughed and choked, thick smoke coming from somewhere around us, making my eyes water. My throat and lungs burned.

"The museum blew up. I don't know why yet. Don't worry about it right now, Dae. Focus on staying awake. Stay with me until they come for you."

I was so tired. My head and right leg hurt. "Kevin, I don't know if I can."

"You can." His face came closer to mine. "Stay with me, Dae. Come on. Stay awake. You might have a head injury. It would be a miracle if you *don't* have a head injury."

"I'm too tired," I whined, despite myself. That's when I knew *something* was really wrong. I never whine.

"You can do it," he coaxed, despite my whining. "Come on, Dae. Do it for me. Look at my face. Tell me about Duck. Tell me about the pirates and all the things you've collected in Missing Pieces. Don't close your eyes, sweetheart. Stay here. Focus on me."

Despite the fact that most of me seemed to be lying on pavement littered with debris, it was easy to do as he asked. I liked the sound of his voice. It made me feel warm and wanted. I tried to smile and reassure him that I was all right, that he didn't have to stay if he needed to be somewhere else. But the words wouldn't come, and slowly he faded from my vision and everything went dark again.

I was dreaming about Theodosia Burr. She was wearing white, just as the legends describe, and she was being forced to walk a rickety plank of wood that led off of an old ship. It rocked at its anchor, causing her to reach out to the closest pirate to keep her balance.

"Let 'er fall!" one of the pirates yelled and the rest agreed.

The man Theodosia reached out to kept her steady, but he couldn't save her from her fate. He moved away from her, and I could see his face. It was Kevin Brickman with long hair and gold coins that made a chain around his neck. He wore brightly colored clothes and tall, leather boots.

Theodosia stood at the edge of the abyss, her snow white slippers clinging to the plank that had become her doom. Her lovely face turned toward the men as she begged them to carry news of her death to her father and her husband. "I only ask this of you. Please do not make them suffer wondering what became of me."

The men surrounding her laughed again and pushed at the wobbly plank with their boots. For a moment, she put out her arms again, as though someone would be there for her. Then, as though resigned to her death, she crossed her hands over her heart and plunged down into the cold waters of the Atlantic.

But one man was missing from the pirate crew. The Kevin Brickman pirate had lowered a long boat, unseen by his peers. As the pirates finished laughing and turned away to other chores, Brickman was fishing Theodosia out of the water. She lay in the bottom of the boat, shivering and coughing, as he rowed toward Nags Head.

I woke with a start, sitting straight up in the hospital bed. Alarms went off and tubes flew around me.

"Take it easy!" Gramps warned, getting to his feet. "You'll pull all this paraphernalia out of you, and they'll have to put it all back in."

I lay back against the pillow and looked around the room. It was dark outside. The tiny window near my bed showed the street below.

The last thing I remembered from real life was Brickman asking me to stay awake and calling me sweetheart. Though my head was pounding with pain—it felt like thousands of miners were chipping away at something in there—I could still feel the warm glow from those words.

"What happened? Is Kevin all right? How long have I been here? Did the museum *really* blow up?"

Gramps sat back down in the chair beside the bed.

"Let's start with you, if that's okay. How are *you* doing? You had a lot of us worried."

Kevin? Was he worried? "I'm fine except for this headache. I hope they have some Tylenol. When can I go home?"

"I think the doctor expects you to spend the night. You probably have a concussion. You were only a few feet from the museum when it exploded."

"Gramps! Are you trying to make it worse? Why did the museum explode? What happened? How is Max taking it? You know how his life is wrapped up in all that history."

Gramps bowed his head, then looked back at me. "Max is dead, Dae."

"What? What do you mean? He can't be dead. I just saw him at the museum. He was waiting for his ultimate proof that Theo Burr lived on the island for years after everyone thought she was dead."

"I'm sorry. He wasn't as lucky as you, Agnes, and the kids. He was still in the museum when it exploded. Cailey Fargo is working through the debris with the new arson investigator from Manteo. It'll be a while before we know what happened. But they called me a few hours ago about Max."

"But if there was an explosion, how can they tell for sure? Everything must be all over the place. Even if they think Max is dead, he might not be. They make mistakes about these things in the early parts of an investigation. I've heard Chief Michaels talk about it before."

I knew I sounded a little hysterical, but there was that jackhammer going off in my head and I couldn't believe Max was dead. My mind raced away from that reality and wondered how our little museum could explode. It seemed impossible, but I knew if Gramps was telling me, it must be true.

"I shouldn't have told you," he said. "I'm sorry, honey. You have to get better, and then we'll worry about the rest of it, okay?"

"Okay." I bit my lip to keep myself from becoming a sniveling, whining mass. I had to get myself together and get out of the hospital so I could find out how this could happen. "Is everyone else okay?"

"You were the closest one to the scene. There were a few accidents when you flew out into the street. Some debris hit a few cars and caused some problems. But all of the kids and their teachers were far enough away. I haven't talked to Agnes yet, but Ronnie said she was okay physically. I wouldn't want to imagine how her mental state is."

I stared at all the little plastic tubes around me. Some of them were plugged into me while others seemed to be waiting for their opportunity. The doctor came in and told us that I was banged up a little but essentially whole. He wanted me to spend the night but said that as long as there were no changes in my condition, I could go home in the morning. He told me a nurse would bring me something to help me sleep since it didn't look as though I had a concussion after all.

He sounded like some bad TV show. Even his smile seemed off to me. Gramps waited until he was gone to tell me again how happy he was that I was okay. He reminded me how important it was that I spend the night in the hospital since the doctor thought it was necessary. "I don't want to wake up in the morning and find out you sneaked back during the night. This is for your own good, Dae."

"You don't have to convince me," I assured him, settling back against the pillow again. "Don't worry. You can go home and get some sleep. I'm going to do the same."

"I'll be here for you in the morning." He stood up and kissed my forehead. "I love you, honey. We'll get to the bottom of what happened when you're feeling better. You'll see."

After he was gone, I stared at the blank white ceiling for a long time. I drifted in and out, thinking about Max and the explosion. It didn't seem real. My mind rejected it like a bad dream.

A nurse came in and gave me a pill along with a pep talk about going home in the morning. The pill helped the jackhammer in my head, but it couldn't quiet my restless mind. The pep talk didn't affect me. Of course I was going home tomorrow. With everything else that had happened, the idea seemed trivial and stupid.

I went over and over everything that had happened at the museum and afterward. I saw Max waving to us from the doorway as he always did. We all began to walk away, and I answered the phone call from Kevin as I started back to the museum after realizing that I still had the gold coin.

The gold coin. It seemed to whisper to me from across the room. I wondered if the doctor was wrong and I had a head injury after all. While I had strong feelings for certain objects, I'd never experienced anything like this before. It was as though I could hear a voice calling me.

I tried to ignore the whisper and closed my eyes for a while, only to have them pop open again. But my gaze continued to go back to the bag that held my clothes. My jeans and the Duck T-shirt that I'd worn that day were in there—along with the gold coin from the museum.

I wanted, *needed*, to see the gold coin again. I told myself it was because it might be the only piece of the museum still left intact. But it was more than that. There were voices inside me. I pulled up the white blanket and sheet, covering my head. But it was no use. Seeing the coin, feeling it in my hand again, had become an obsession.

Another nurse came in and checked my pulse and temperature. "Would you like some more ice water, honey?"

"No. I'm fine, thanks." I rustled up a smile. "I'm trying to get a good night's sleep for tomorrow."

"That's right." She beamed. "You'll be going home in the morning. Who's the lucky girl?"

I might've objected to her patronizing tone, but I was too focused on getting her out of there so I could find some way to reach my clothes. It seemed to take her forever to straighten the sheets and check the IV. *Why didn't she leave?*

Once she was gone, I quit asking questions about why I wanted to see the coin again. Instead, I worked on how to get over there. It wasn't that far. But I was surrounded by so many tubes and wires, I wasn't sure I could manage to get away from them without alerting someone who might stop me.

I sifted through the medical spaghetti and realized only one tube was actually attached to me. The only thing I had to worry about was that one line, which led to a bag of glucose hooked up to a tall, stainless steel pole. I moved across the narrow bed carefully until I could throw my legs off the side next to the pole. I used one hand to propel myself off the bed while the other hand held onto the glucose feed and moved the pole closer to me.

The tile floor was cold under my bare feet, and my knee, which hadn't hurt since I'd woken up, started hurting again. It was my storm knee. It always hurt right before a storm. Gramps said that was because I'd injured it surfing in the rough waves off the Atlantic side of Duck.

He said it was my weak knee because it was my favorite to injure.

Ignoring the pain, I rolled the pole closer to me as I got off the bed and struggled to keep my hospital gown from exposing my rear. Why did they always show people in the movies with the backs of these stupid gowns closed? Why did they create them that way in the first place?

The voices from the coin kept me on track, whispering their secrets as I gingerly began to cross the room. Looking back on it, I wonder why I didn't think I'd lost my mind. Maybe being raised as a finder of lost things made anything seem possible. Whatever the case, I didn't question my thirst for the coin's knowledge, and kept moving slowly across the tile.

I was nervous that one of the nurses would come in and check on me again. They might keep me from reaching the coin and that wouldn't do. It was the only thing in my mind, and the closer I got to that bundle of clothes, the more important it seemed.

One of the wheels on the pole squeaked at every other revolution. I cringed each time. What would happen if I couldn't reach the coin? What if someone else got to it before me? My brain buzzed with the whispers coming from it. What were they saying? If I held it in my hand again, would I be able to hear them more clearly?

I could always say I was trying to reach the bathroom, I realized. They didn't have to know my real purpose. If I never told anyone about the voices in the coin, I'd never have to share it with anyone.

I finally reached the chair and ruthlessly shoved the bag of clothes on the floor so I could collapse where they'd been. I hadn't known it would be such an ordeal moving a few feet. I was exhausted. Apparently being partially blown up took a lot out of a person.

But there was the coin to consider, with all of its secrets to learn. Carefully I lifted the bag from the floor with
my free hand. I could smell smoke even before I took out
the clothes. As I reached in and touched my Duck T-shirt,
my fingers began to tingle. It was the same feeling I always experienced when I first touched someone to help
them look for something. But I'd never felt it this strong
when touching an inanimate object. What was going on?

My jeans and T-shirt, even my underwear, were full of
tiny holes. The sensation of touching all of them at once
made me drop them on the floor. The feelings were over-
powering, threatening to swamp me with emotions I
couldn't control.

But I had to have the coin. I put my hand more firmly
on my jeans, forcing myself to ignore the sensation, focusing on the coin that was still in my pocket. I never
stopped to think it might not be there. I *knew* it was there.

I grasped the coin and let the jeans drop. They didn't
matter. The dull gold coin gleamed in the palm of my
hand, the bathroom nightlight illuminating it. I held it for
an instant, admiring its form and weight, and then my
head exploded with a thousand images.

I saw everything from the moment the coin was made,
hundreds of years ago. It was stamped and put into a
wooden chest with hundreds more like it. The chest was
sealed and put on a ship. The rough seas scraped the chest
back and forth across the bottom of the ship. It seemed as
though it might be lost to the Atlantic in a terrible storm.

But other hands took it away from the ship it had sailed
on. Rough fingers moved through the treasure, counting
and admiring. The gold was new then, shining brightly
even in the dull lantern light.

That wasn't the end of its journey. The storm that had
ravaged the coast caught up with the buccaneer who'd

stolen the chest, sending the groaning vessel into the unkind embrace of the icy sea.

The currents and the years moved the partially raided chest closer and closer to shore. Once again the sun shone on the coin, now crusted with saltwater and seaweed. Still locked in the chest, it had finally reached land and waited to be found by the next person who would admire and covet it.

A man approached it on the sandy beach, stopping to look at the treasure that waited for him that morning. He glanced around, and seeing only gulls as his company, he picked up the treasure chest and stalked down the shore to his home.

I gasped for air and opened my eyes, almost drawn into the history of the coin so far that I was afraid I would never find my way back. The voices were those who'd touched the gold, caressed it, desired it to the point that they would kill for it.

I was sitting on the cold floor, the hospital gown not covering my icy butt as I held the coin in front of me like an icon. It was morning, sunshine streaming in through the window near the bed.

I realized I'd have to get off the floor and at least sit down in the chair unless I wanted the hospital staff to think I was crazy and keep me another night searching for head injuries.

I pushed up on the chair and finally reached my feet. My knee ached from the cold and the position I'd been in on the floor for God knew how long. I managed to hobble back to the bed, the coin still in my hand, and was waiting for the morning nurse when she arrived a few minutes later.

The coin that had seemed so important that I would've happily risked my life to hold it again was dead in my grasp. It was as though I'd absorbed the voices inside of me once I'd seen its story.

I was freezing, exhausted and terrified as I gazed out of the hospital window. The young nurse chatted about breakfast coming, a doctor visit and the trip to the front door in a wheelchair. I nodded, made the right replies, my mind focused on what had happened with the coin.

What *had* happened? Nothing, maybe. It might've all been a trick of the injury. And maybe everything. I couldn't ignore the strange feel of things around me—the bed, sheets and blanket. I was scared to lay my hands on any of it. There was a residual energy to everything I touched. Or I'd lost my mind.

"Dae?"

I didn't even notice Gramps had come in until he was standing at my bedside, frowning at me. "Are you sure you're okay? I called your name twice and you didn't respond. Should I get the doctor?"

"I'm fine." I smiled and touched the fresh bandage on my wrist where they'd removed the IV needle. "Ready to go home. I'm glad you came early."

"I brought some clean clothes for you." He put a green, cloth Harris-Teeter shopping bag on the bed next to me. "I'll have the hospital throw away the other things you were wearing. I don't imagine you'll ever wear them again."

"No!" I protested at once, then justified my too-frantic outburst with an explanation. "The fire investigator might want to look at them. I was the closest one to the blast. There might be some residual evidence on them."

The frown between his eyebrows didn't go away, but he nodded. "All right. I guess watching all those police shows on TV is good for something after all." He paused and put his callused hand on my cheek. "You're sure you're okay?"

"Of course." I climbed out of bed, holding the stupid hospital gown closed. Gramps might've changed my diaper a few times, but that was no reason he should see my backside again. At least I could use both hands this time. "I'll get changed and we'll go home."

I picked up the cloth shopping bag and gasped, disguising it as a cough. I could feel the history of the bag, from when it was made somewhere in China to when it came to the U.S., where it was counted and sold.

"Dae?" Gramps was staring at me again.

"Sorry." I thought fast. "It's the old storm knee. A little stiff and sore this morning after the fall."

My green shirt and pink skirt were in the bag. Bless his heart, Gramps couldn't color coordinate himself out of a fishnet if his pants were on fire. The clothes gave me the same reaction as the Harris Teeter bag.

I reached for the faucet on the bathroom sink, the flush handle on the toilet, even the toilet paper; all showed me where they started and how they came to be here.

What was I going to do? I rested my head against the cool, drab tile in the bathroom where no one could see me. How could I live this way? I was overwhelmed by the minute details of all the everyday items that made up life.

Touching people and helping them see what they'd lost was one thing. It had been a choice to learn to use my gift. The discipline not to see things when I casually met people had become part of me when I was a small child. It was so incorporated in me that I took it for granted. I didn't remember how I'd learned to do it. My grandmother also had the gift. My mother had learned from her and helped me along, even though the gift had passed her by. There was no one in my life like that now. I felt lost and alone as I stepped out of the bathroom.

"Ready?" Gramps asked with a wide smile.

"We'll have to take a little ride in the pink wheelchair," a nurse's aide told me. "Pink is for girls, you know, hon."

I had to touch the arms of the chair to sit down. Immediately, I saw the chair being made at a factory in Toledo, Ohio. But that wasn't all. A strong emotional surge wrenched through me and I knew the last woman who'd ridden in the pink wheelchair was going home to die. She'd fought lung cancer for two years. There was nothing more that could be done for her.

I bit my lip to keep from crying out at the strong emotions left behind. Then I folded my hands in my lap and tried to ignore the sensations that buzzed through me. It was going to be a long day.

Chapter 3

We had no choice but to pass by the museum on the way home. There was only one, two-lane road that ran the whole length of the Outer Banks. It connected the hospital in Kill Devil Hills to our home in Duck.

"It's a wreck," Gramps warned before he got there. "I'm sure you can imagine what it's like."

I couldn't really. Everything had happened so quickly. It was like one minute I was looking at the museum and the next I was in the road. Even the trip to the hospital seemed surreal.

As we came around the curve in Duck Road, the sight was even worse than anything I could have imagined. It looked like a scene from some TV-news war coverage. The area where the blue museum had once stood was now flattened, filled with ash, parts of the building and other debris. The whole corner was gone; an old picnic table was the only structure still standing.

"Stop the car, Gramps!" I had to see it. I wanted to look at it up close. "Please, Gramps. If you take me home now, I'll be back up here in five minutes."

"You can see the fire chief and the county arson investigator are here with their people," Gramps said. "Maybe later might be a better time, Dae. The doctor said you should go right home and get in bed anyway. Leave it for tomorrow, honey. It will still be here."

Those might've been my thoughts yesterday before the museum blew up. Everything in Duck stayed the same, didn't it? Nothing ever changed that drastically. Only now we knew that wasn't true.

"Please, Gramps." I saw Cailey Fargo, my fifth-grade schoolteacher who was now Duck's fire chief. I also saw some of the volunteer firefighters raking through the debris. "We can go home after we stop for a minute. It won't take that long."

"Okay. All right." He gave in and turned the car into an open space across the street. "But only for a minute. I know how you are, Dae, but this isn't the time to snoop around. Leave it to the experts."

There was nowhere close to the museum that wasn't covered with tarps and crime scene tape. We had to wait for traffic to pass before we could cross Duck Road. I stared at everything that was left, wishing I was brave enough to pick all of it up and find out what it had to say to me. Maybe this newfound ability would tell me what had happened without the months of investigation that I knew would come.

I winced as we crossed the road and I saw all of the black skid marks, shattered glass and pieces of someone's bumper. I realized that most of the accidents these parts represented were caused by my abrupt appearance in the middle of the road.

Kevin looked up at me as we reached the scene. He'd saved my life yesterday. I didn't know what I was going to say to him. Everything seemed unreal right now. My heart was pounding in my chest, and it was all I could do not to break down and cry like a baby. Maybe Gramps had been right about going home first.

Kevin stopped what he was doing and came across the debris field like a man on a mission. His eyes were intent on mine in a way that would've made me happy a few days ago. It made me cringe now.

"Dae!" He put out his arms as we got a few yards from each other. I knew he meant to hug me. There was a warm, expectant smile on his handsome face.

I took a step back and put my hands in the pockets of my familiar green skirt. "Kevin." I smiled back but looked away from his puzzled expression.

He glanced at Gramps. "Should she be here?"

Gramps shrugged. "Try to keep her from it. I wasn't any good at it."

"I'm fine," I assured them both. "You don't have to talk about me like I'm a child."

"She wanted to see it," Gramps continued.

"Maybe she should've waited." They both turned their heads to stare at me.

"Hey! I'm right here!" A little anger made me feel better as I reminded them both of my obvious presence. "Yes. I wanted to see it. I don't think that's so unusual, do you?"

Both men backed off.

"Do they know what caused the explosion yet? Or if it really was an explosion?" I tried to sound like the mayor of Duck who was interested because it happened in my town. It was that too, of course, but so much more. I focused on a piece of the yellow duck statue that had stood outside the museum for as long as I could remember. It helped me keep myself from falling on the ground and blubbering like Gramps and Kevin obviously expected me to.

"Why don't we go say hey to Cailey and that young arson investigator over there," Gramps suggested. "Dae's minute is almost up and we still don't know more than when we stopped."

At last, someone was taking me seriously.

"You'll have to put shoe covers on to walk across the debris field," Kevin said. "You don't want to contaminate the crime scene."

He went to what looked like a command center set up near the old picnic table and brought back green cloth booties for us to wear, along with gloves. Gramps started putting his booties on over his worn tennis shoes.

I bent over to pick up one of the green booties, but the exertion caused immediate jackhammering in my head. I couldn't bend my sore knee to put them on that way. I tried to shove my foot into the covering without using my hands, but it was useless.

"Let me help you." Kevin crouched down in front of me. "Headache, huh? Head injuries will do that."

"I don't have a concussion, if that's what you mean." I lifted my foot anyway. I couldn't do it by myself, and I wanted to talk to Cailey about what happened.

The first foot went fine, but I lifted the other foot too high and almost lost my balance. I reached out and grasped Kevin's shoulder.

The touch raced through my brain, showing me all aspects of creating the blue T-shirt he wore. My hand jerked back as though he were on fire. It was what I'd feared when he'd wanted to hug me. It wasn't the history of the shirt that bothered me. I was scared of what I'd see if I touched another person.

"Dae?"

I opened my eyes to see Kevin's concerned expression. "Sorry."

"Are you sure you're up to this? Maybe you should let everyone report to you. Isn't that what mayors do?"

"Maybe. But I want to know what they know *now*, not next week."

Gramps had already started walking toward Cailey and the new arson investigator. Kevin put out his arm. "At least let me walk with you."

It struck me that the terrible green gloves he'd given me might be useful in this exchange. I didn't want to take a chance on seeing anything else by touching him. I put on the gloves and went through their manufacture and shipping process. It was kind of drab and unexciting except for a dead mouse someone had found in the box of gloves before it was sealed.

When it was over, I put my hand on Kevin's arm with all the insecurity of someone grasping a hot poker. But there was nothing. I tightened my hold on him. Still nothing. This was good. I could manage this way.

"Look, I'm taking you home right now." His voice sounded tough, the way I imagined he might've sounded when he'd worked for the FBI before coming to Duck. "You're not all right. If you fall over out here and we have to take you back to the hospital, what will that prove?"

I smiled my big, bright mayor's smile at him. It's the one I had practiced to use when I took office. "It's okay now, Kevin. Really. I had a bad minute there, but I'm fine now."

He stared me down, but I didn't blink. It really was better . . . with the gloves on. Maybe this would give me a chance to get over this new ability or at least learn not to let it take over my life.

"Okay," he said, giving in. "But if you look at me again like that, I won't be responsible for my actions."

I caught my breath. "Like what?"

"Like there's nothing in your eyes. I've only seen that kind of blankness once. That person had lost her mind."

That was a sobering thought. I didn't respond to his promised threat. Instead, I started walking across what remained of Duck's history, and Kevin kept pace with me.

Cailey and the new arson investigator were already giving Gramps the lowdown on what they knew so far. We went through the whole round of Cailey asking me how I was and if I should be there. Duck Police Chief Ronnie Michaels joined us, and Cailey introduced Brad Spitzer, the Dare County arson investigator.

"Brad, this is Dae O'Donnell, the mayor of Duck," Cailey said. "She was here at the time of the blast yesterday."

"Mayor O'Donnell." Brad held out his hand. He was a very ordinary-looking man: brown hair, brown eyes, no distinguishing features. He had a touch of gray at his temples that probably put him in his forties. He was only about as tall as me, not muscular, but medium build.

"Mr. Spitzer." I acknowledged him, forgoing the handshake he offered. I didn't know how far I could push the insulating quality of the gloves.

"I know you're not feeling quite right yet, Mayor," Chief Michaels said in his usual abrupt manner. He always reminded me of an old marine drill sergeant with his flat-top haircut and immaculate police uniform.

There was an awkward moment as Brad put his hand back at his side after I declined to shake it. Chief Michaels *humphed* and cleared his throat. "I think I should debrief you as soon as possible. You may have seen something important and not realized it. When you're feeling better, that is."

"I'd like to be there as well, Chief," Brad added. "It would save us a lot of time on the investigation if all of us

knew what the mayor saw yesterday before she was injured."

Cailey agreed this was an excellent idea. *Great!* I really
needed to think about an audience wanting to hear how I
was thrown into the road and left with an odd backlash
that made me able to glimpse how everything in the world
was manufactured and shipped to stores and warehouses.

"Sure," I said, hoping they wouldn't notice my lack of
enthusiasm. I raised as much of a smile as I could muster.

No one said anything for a few seconds. I could feel
them all looking at me and wondering if something was
wrong that hadn't been made right by my brief hospital
stay.

I knew I had to say something or I'd end up going
home without any information and all of this would have
been for nothing. "So, what do we know so far?"

Cailey blinked a few times, adjusted her helmet and
looked at Gramps before she said, "Dae, maybe we should
talk about this later, honey."

Sometimes it's hard when your fellow town officials
remember when you learned to ride a bicycle. It's not that
they don't respect me, but they get this protective, paren-
tal attitude that drives me crazy. I had to assert myself. I
was the mayor of Duck, and I deserved answers. "I'd like
to know what you have so far," I told her. "I'm sure you'll
have more later and we'll talk again. But I need some
answers for our citizens right now."

I could see my tone reassured them a little. Cailey took
out her notes, hastily scribbled in a tiny, sooty notebook.
"We found some human remains that we assume belong
to Max. We can't find any record of him having had an
X-ray in the past that we could use for comparison. We
won't know for sure until the DNA tests are finished."

"That could take a while since we'll have to send it to the state lab," Brad explained. "It could be weeks before we know for sure."

Chief Michaels agreed. "Depends how far they're backed up right now."

I swallowed hard on their objective details of Max's death and held a little tighter to Kevin's arm. "What do we know for *sure* right now?"

Brad cleared his throat. I thought for a minute he might be a little irritated by my demand. But he resumed his smile and nodded toward where the museum building had been. "If you'd like to come this way, Mayor, we'll take a look at the epicenter of the blast."

We followed Brad as a group even though I felt sure Chief Michaels and Cailey had already been given this information. Everyone was careful to walk around or over debris waiting to be collected by the firefighters. There were pieces of chairs and tables, shattered glass from the showcases that had once held Duck's treasured past, and an old microfiche machine that had essentially melted as if it was made of wax.

A few things seemed to have been left intact—one of the old cannons, some musket balls, the anchor from the *Helena*, a ship that went down off the coast in the early 1900s.

I noticed two firemen carefully bagging a charred tennis shoe and thought about Max dying here. I fought back tears, reminding myself that I could cry later. I was pretty sure the whole group would cheerfully drive me back to the hospital in Kill Devil Hills if I became emotional.

"We believe this is where the actual blast occurred," Brad explained, pointing to an area right outside of where the building had been. The old concrete was now blackened and buckled. "You can see the concussion marks here. We think this is where the cannonball hit the large propane gas tank that fed the stove in the museum."

"Cannonball?" Gramps, Chief Michaels and I asked at the same time. Kevin looked surprised but didn't say anything.

Brad nodded, a bewildered expression on his face as though he hadn't considered until now that we would all think this was odd. "There's no doubt about it. We have the pieces of the ball right over here."

"But there were dozens of cannonballs in the museum," Chief Michaels said. "It probably got in the way of what really blew this place up. A cannonball couldn't lob in here and cause an explosion. Anybody seen any pirate ships that might be attacking Duck?"

Chief Michaels was obviously making a joke, but Gramps looked serious. "Are you saying a cannonball was dropped or thrown into the propane tank?"

"No, sir." Brad cleared his throat. "I'm saying a cannonball was *fired* into the propane from a few hundreds yards away." He looked to the south of the museum site. "Maybe from that hill over there. There's a residue on the surviving pieces of the cannonball suggesting it was fired from a device."

"You mean a cannon?" I pitched in.

"Exactly, Mayor," he concluded. "It would take that kind of firepower to make the gas tank explode."

"I don't want to second-guess you, son." Chief Michaels looked at Brad and Cailey. "But are you sure about this? Isn't it possible the tank blew up because of the fire and whatever caused the explosion? Have you checked this out, Ms. Fargo?"

Cailey shrugged, almost apologetically. "I know it

sounds unbelievable, Chief, but I agree with Brad's assessment. We won't know absolutely until the tests come back from the lab. For right now, this is our working hypothesis."

I was having a hard time believing it too. Or maybe I didn't *want* to believe it. How was I going to tell people that a cannonball had been blasted into the museum? "Chief Michaels, has anyone been up there yet to look for a cannon?"

"No, Mayor," he answered smartly. "This is the first I've heard of it. But I promise we'll look into it." He got on his radio as he walked away from the group, probably calling for a few of Duck's finest to come and take a look.

I turned back to Cailey and Brad. "You're saying someone purposely shot a cannonball into the museum and blew it up?"

Brad kind of glanced at Cailey. "All we can really say at this point, Mayor, is that it appears that a cannonball was fired at the museum, which caused the propane tank to explode. This is only our preliminary finding. We don't know if there was intent to do harm as yet. Maybe it was an accident."

"If it turns out someone did it, one way or another, that makes Max's death a homicide," Gramps said.

"It would," Cailey agreed, pushing back her graying brown hair.

"Are there any working cannons around here?" Kevin asked. "It seems to me that most of these old weapons I've seen are rusted and unusable."

"I don't know," Cailey answered. "I've never even considered it. Max would know—"

There was no way any of us could finish that statement. Max *would* know, no doubt. The only expert around here was dead.

"What now?" I had to clench my teeth to keep them from chattering as I asked the question. I was freezing.

"We investigate," Cailey said. "Chief Michaels looks for the cannon or maybe tracks of some kind that show a cannon could've been there. When we have more answers, we'll let you know. My guys have been out here all night, Dae, and not because I told them they had to be here. We're doing the best we can with the situation."

"I know you are." I put my hand on her sooty shoulder, glad the gloves prevented me from getting impressions from her jacket. "You know people are going to want answers right away. The idea of someone blowing up the museum is going to be hard to swallow."

As if to punctuate my words, two TV crews rushed up to the curb and began heckling the firefighters who wouldn't let them on the crime scene. Duck police officers probably should have been on the job, but something this big was going to be hard for our handful of officers to cope with, even if we called in the part-time officers.

"I know." She shook her head and had to adjust her helmet again. "I'm sorry we can't do more. We all loved Max."

"No good jumping to bad conclusions anyway," Gramps added. "We'll have to let the investigation run its course."

"We'll do our best, Mayor O'Donnell," Brad assured me. "I know this isn't easy for anyone."

I don't know why exactly, but I lost it then. Maybe it was these hardworking firefighters that had been out there working all night. I knew Cailey was as close to Max, or closer, than I was. I knew all of these people loved Max. No one wanted to think his death and the destruction of the museum could be anything but a terrible accident.

I took my hand from Kevin's arm. He started to walk

with me when I moved, but I shook my head. I couldn't stop the tears from streaming down my face. I left abruptly and went toward where the side of the museum had been. I stripped off the dirty gloves to wipe the tears away.

I needed a few minutes alone. If that looked crazy or weak, so be it. Max was dead. He had always been there for the town and for me. The horrific truth of it settled on me like a cloud of the greasy black soot from the fire.

I kicked something and looked at it. It was the trash can I'd helped Agnes with yesterday. Somehow it was still in one piece. All of its contents were on the ground, but that appeared to be the result of someone accidentally knocking it over. It didn't look like the fallout from a cannonball ripping into a propane tank and blowing up the museum.

Even through my tears that strange twist hit me as amazing. It was like that time a bad hurricane blew through Duck, demolishing one house while leaving the one right next door completely untouched.

"Are you okay?" Kevin came up behind me anyway. "I could take you home if your grandfather wants to stay."

"I'm fine, except that Max is dead. The whole museum is gone. But this stupid trash can is still here. Someone could take it home and use it. What a world, huh?"

I could tell by the look on his face that he wasn't really getting what I was saying. That was okay. It actually made me feel a little better saying it.

I reached down without thinking and picked up the coffee card I'd put into the trash yesterday. I don't know what possessed me to touch it after my recent experiences.

It was dripping wet, probably soaked by the high-power fire hoses. For a second, I didn't feel anything from it. I thought maybe my new ability had left me, gone as fast as it had come, like a storm at sea.

Then suddenly it all rushed in, filling my mind with information that choked me. I dropped to the wet ground as I heard Kevin call my name.

Chapter 4

It was as though I was standing at the end of a long tunnel. I was engulfed by the vision from the card. I could still hear Kevin calling me but I couldn't answer.

I saw Max arguing with the man who had the coffee card in his pocket. The man slammed the door to the museum when he went outside. He glanced at the coffee card as he took it out. All of the numbers were punched on it. He shrugged and hurled it toward the trash can before he got in his car and drove away.

I couldn't really tell anything about what was said. It was enough to know that he and Max were both extremely angry. That didn't surprise me once I realized that Max was speaking to Sam Meacham from the Corolla Historic Museum.

The intense feeling from the argument between the two men dissipated as rapidly as it had come to me. I gasped for breath and found Kevin with both arms around me, holding me up.

"Someone call 911," I heard him yell. "Get an ambulance over here!"

"No!" I put my hands on his chest, feeling the familiar energy from his jacket. "I'm okay. Really."

"The hell you are," he growled.

"It's not what you think."

His eyes stared into mine. "Then what is it? What's going on, Dae?"

I showed him the soggy coffee card. "Something's happened. I feel—some kind of energy from things since the explosion. Everything I touch: my clothes, your jacket, *everything*. I don't know what to do about it."

There! I'd said it out loud. It was a relief.

Two firemen I recognized as paramedics ran over to us, emergency medical bags in hand. They both looked bone weary, the kind of exhaustion where your eyes are dull and your skin looks gray. "What's wrong? You need help?"

"No. I guess not." Kevin shrugged. "It's fine. Sorry. Thanks."

Surprised, I moved away from him as the paramedics gave us an annoying glare before returning to their grunt work sifting through the debris that had been the museum. "You believe me?"

"Of course." His tone was matter-of-fact. "Your abilities probably changed when you underwent the shock from the explosion. I've seen it before."

Of course, my inner critic mocked him, *it's rather commonplace*. "Great! Maybe you can tell me what to do about it." I was being sarcastic. How would he possibly know what to do?

He glanced around. "Not here. I know your abilities

aren't a secret, but maybe now isn't the right time to talk about them with the media."

I followed his gaze and noticed the TV crews fanning out around the debris field, trying to find someone to pounce on for information.

I wasn't ready to be recognized and go through an interrogation about what happened. Maybe it was a non-mayorlike attitude, but I didn't want to blurt out something that I'd regret later. I needed time to decide what my statement was going to be.

"Missing Pieces." I put the coffee card into my pocket with the gold coin. "Let's go there. I don't want to tell Gramps about this yet. I don't want to worry him any more than I have already."

Gramps didn't protest the fact that Kevin was taking me to the store. He was surprised but recovered quickly with a pleased expression on his face. He loved the idea of me having a relationship with almost any local man. Kevin was icing on the cake since Gramps liked and respected him.

Kevin and I managed to skirt around the reporters as Cailey took off her helmet and walked toward them as if she was going to give them a statement. The reporters moved toward her like sharks to a chum bucket. Maybe she did it on purpose. As soon as we were away from the scene, she left them angrily demanding to know what was going on.

Kevin helped me into his pickup. I cursed my awkward, injured storm knee for making me look like an old lady. Then I dealt with the new sensations of manufacturing and distribution coming from the truck. I rubbed my hand on the worn red seat.

"What are you seeing?"

"You got this truck at an auction. Before you had it, a man in Virginia used it to haul tobacco and, occasionally, moonshine."

He raised his eyebrows. "I knew he was a farmer. I didn't know about the other part."

Sensations like those I felt from the truck were already becoming almost second nature. How something was manufactured—even how it was used—was easy to absorb and ignore.

But the coffee card and the gold coin, the pink wheelchair at the hospital were so excruciatingly different. It had to be the emotional quality to the items. I could feel the strong emotions like they were my own. A second aspect to this new and scary ability.

The coffee card emotions felt new, as though the argument between Max and Sam had happened yesterday. "I've been completely crazed by all of this," I said as he started the truck. "I tell you and it's no big deal. Why aren't you upset about it? Why don't you think it's crazy?"

"I told you I knew people like you when I was with the FBI." He pulled the truck out into traffic. "One of them was a psychic who was able to track down kidnapped children. She found them in half the time we could with conventional means."

"And she was blown up?"

"No. She was shot by a kidnapper and almost died. It changed her. She started hearing the children's voices as well as being able to tell where they were. She could hear their cries for help when they were being tortured. It made her even more effective at her job. It also drove her crazy."

We'd reached the parking lot for the Duck Shoppes on the boardwalk, where Missing Pieces was located conveniently close to town hall. Everything looked so normal, as if, a quarter mile down the road, the museum was still there and Max was still busy sorting artifacts.

"I don't know why, but I sense a lesson here." I turned to him as he parked the truck. "What happened to your friend?"

He shrugged as though it didn't matter, but I didn't have to be a psychic to see it did. "She lost herself. When I finally quit last year, she was being transferred to a psychiatric facility. She couldn't cope with all of it. It was too much."

"She was your partner, wasn't she?"

"Is that from your new ability?"

"Nope. A lucky guess. I'm sorry. Is that what made you quit the FBI?"

"It was the end of twelve years of events that made me realize it was time to leave," he admitted. "Sometimes, it's just time to go."

I unbuckled my seat belt and urged my sore knee out of the truck. I hoped this was a cautionary tale because it didn't make me feel any better. On the other hand, I knew a little more about Kevin. It seemed to come in small bursts. He obviously didn't like talking about his time in the FBI. "So this is where you get your insight into what's wrong with me?"

"There's nothing wrong with you, Dae. At least nothing that a little rest won't help. Besides being too close to the explosion, your abilities are natural to you. My friend refused to give herself time to adjust to her new abilities. She couldn't control it, so it controlled her."

I looked across the parking lot at the Coffee House and Bookstore. I had a powerful urge to go in and question Phil, the owner, about Sam Meacham's recent visit there. The energy left in the coffee card was like the demanding energy left in the gold coin—pushing me to act. I had no way of knowing whether the feeling was something important or not.

But like so many businesses in Duck, the coffee house was closed until mid-March. I couldn't find out any information about the card until Phil came back.

People hailed me then rushed over as Kevin and I walked by the shops on the boardwalk overlooking Currituck Sound. Everyone wanted to make sure I was okay— and find out the latest gossip about the museum. Everyone in Duck would've heard about it by now. It had probably made the news last night and this morning. Not a lot happened here that made it to TV.

My friend Trudy Devereaux, the owner of Curves and Curls Beauty Spa, which was right next door to Missing Pieces, stopped talking and cutting Ellis Walters's hair when she saw us.

She hugged me tight and cried. "Oh, Dae! I was so worried about you. Don't you ever do that to me again! Sometimes trouble seems to find you like a lure attracts fish."

We commiserated for a few minutes, her green smock feeling familiar even to my heightened senses. Trudy and I had grown up together—there wasn't much we didn't know about each other. We were wiping away tears by the time Ms. Walters came out to ask questions about the museum.

"You call me or come by when you can," Trudy said, urging Ms. Walters back into her shop. "And be careful. You could've died yesterday."

I promised that we'd talk and Kevin and I went next door to Missing Pieces. I played with the key in the lock like I always did to get the door open. Visions of a few former tenants rushed through my mind at the touch of the key to the lock. But they were like ghosts—no substance or emotion. Maybe I'd been there long enough that their energy was starting to fade.

I didn't open the blinds or turn on the lights, as I usually did. Normally I would've been hoping for a few winter visitors who wanted to buy my treasures. Today I felt like skulking around, hoping that no one would wander in.

Kevin locked the door behind us, and I sank down with a grateful sigh onto my burgundy brocade sofa. I closed my eyes and let the familiar energies from my shop lap around my disturbed senses like a warm bubble bath.

"Tea?" Kevin held out a box of orange spice chai. "Or coffee?"

I grimaced. "I've had your coffee, thanks. Tea, please."

"What's wrong with my coffee?" He busied himself putting water in the little pot on the hot plate. "It kept me awake plenty of nights when I was on a stakeout."

"*That's* what's wrong with it!" I smiled, very happy that he was here with me. Since we'd met a few months ago, we'd developed a nice friendship. I felt like I'd known him forever. There was nothing more to it than that. Not for my lack of imagining more, however.

Kevin had proven to be an easygoing, steadfast kind of person. He was good-looking, hardworking, and every woman in Duck was interested in gossiping about him. And those were just the married ones.

"When did you first notice the change?" he asked as the water in the pot began to get hot.

"At the hospital last night. It started with the gold coin I picked up at the museum."

"What gold coin?"

I explained about finding the gold coin before the museum blew up and then told him about its effect on me. "I thought I was going crazy. I'm still not too sure."

"Maybe not crazy," he remarked. "It's not that much of a stretch from your natural abilities."

"Maybe not to you, but it's a big stretch for me. Seeing where everything was made is one thing, but feeling what the people who owned it or touched it felt, is another."

"Such as?"

"Just now, opening the front door, it was like a mild reaction. But the coin and the coffee card were like emotional hurricanes blowing through me."

"What else?" He put the tea bag in the pot and took out a cup and spoon.

"It's mostly shipping and manufacturing."

He looked up at that. "Come again?"

"Where and how things are made, the people who made them, and seeing them shipped out to places. It's kind of crazy."

"That's why you wouldn't take Spitzer's hand."

"That's why I didn't hug you when I first saw you." The words tumbled out, then hung there like yesterday's laundry.

"Sugar or honey?" he asked in a suddenly polite tone.

We were obviously both embarrassed by my revelation. "Honey. Thanks."

He finished making the tea for me, then grabbed a Cheerwine out of the fridge for himself. I smiled as he got it and sat down beside me. Kevin, new to the South, was obsessed with drinking Cheerwine. I wondered what would happen if he ever tried Moon Pies.

"You should start a journal," he said, snapping the top from the bottle. "It might help if you can compare things that happen to you."

"How long do you think it will last?" I held my tea and tried to sound as if it didn't really matter. But it did. It was frightening, too different from my usual ability to help find things.

"It might not go away. This new ability might take the place of the old one, or it might add to it. That's why it's important to get on top of it."

That idea was a slap of cold water. I put my tea on the little side table I'd acquired at an auction over the summer. I looked around my shop, all my carefully gathered treasures. I had feelings for most of them, but I never expected to know what they were feeling in return.

"I guess you haven't tried to find anything yet," he said. "Maybe you should. It would tell you if you've traded abilities or if you've enhanced the original."

That sounded like a good idea. It was something positive and concrete to do. I still felt kind of shaky, but I was curious to find out what was going on. "Are you volunteering?"

"Sure. Why not?" He put his Cheerwine down and stuck his hands out toward me. "I've been trying to find a missing case of wine at the hotel. Maybe you can help me with it."

To say I was nervous about touching him was like comparing a dingy to a sloop. I was terrified of what I might see or feel. I wished I'd brought the evidence gloves with me to protect me from something I couldn't even name.

"Okay." I had started to reach toward him when someone began pounding on the shop door.

I could see my friend Shayla Lily trying to sneak peeks inside the shop. "I know you're in there, Dae!"

I gave Kevin an apologetic look, not sure if I should murder Shayla for wrecking the moment or be happy it hadn't gone any further. There had been something in

Kevin's tone when he'd told me about his FBI partner, the psychic. I'd gotten the feeling that they'd had more than just a working relationship. I might have been on the verge of finding out why Kevin had resisted the advances of all of the women in Duck.

Not me, of course. I'd been careful not to put myself in that position with him. If all he wanted from me was friendship, I was happy to give it. Well, maybe not *happy* exactly, but I thought he might come around in time.

When I opened the shop door, Shayla burst into the room as she always did. Her black hair was drawn back from her cocoa-colored face, showing off her finely drawn brows. She always dressed in black, probably part of her mystique as a tarot card reader.

"What the hell is going on here?" she demanded.

Another reason I hadn't pushed hard to have a romantic relationship with Kevin is that he'd dated Shayla for a short while. She has a long memory.

"Nothing." I glanced at Kevin, hoping he would back me up.

"Thirsty!" He drained his bottle of Cheerwine.

"Dae—Oh my God! What have you done to yourself? Your aura is all over the place! Girl, you have either been cursed or you've had a near-death experience. I'm thinking it must be a curse because I'd know if you almost died, right? My tarot cards have been telling me something was up with you. I didn't think it was this bad."

Shayla sat down on the burgundy sofa, wedging herself between me and Kevin. She was probably the only person in Duck who didn't know about the museum. She knew everything about the spirit world but hardly anything about the real world. "Okay. I'm here now. Tell me all about it."

Shayla was also known as Mrs. Roberts, Spiritual Advisor. She'd inherited the shop next door from a previous palm and tarot reader and kept the name. We'd been friends since she'd come to Duck from New Orleans a few years back. I'd gone to her, hoping she could help me contact my dead mother since she was also a medium. There was no luck on that front, but she'd been a good listener.

"I'm going to get back to the museum and see if I can help them finish up." Kevin got to his feet.

My heart said, *No! Please stay!* But my mouth said, "Thanks for giving me a ride over here. I'll see you later."

He smiled, hesitated as though wanting to say something else, but then said good-bye and left the shop. As usual, there seemed to be more left unsaid between us.

"I'm glad he's gone." Shayla let out a deep sigh. "The air was so thick in here. It's that tension between him and me when we get together. There are too many unresolved issues between us, but until he takes a better look at it, there's no helping him."

Shayla was a *wonderful* medium, but sometimes she could be a little thick.

"I'm glad you're here. A lot has happened." I swallowed my disappointment that Kevin was gone. It was probably for the best anyway, like Gramps always said.

"Let me make some tea," she interrupted before I got started. "Do you want something?"

I told her everything, and she listened while she buffed her nails and drank her tea. When I was finished, she shook her head. "No wonder you're such a mess! You should've come to me right away. You need your energies balanced. It's a good thing I stopped by."

She took my hands before I could stop her. There was nothing to it. She closed her eyes and advised me to do the same. I drifted into that special spot where I could see if someone has lost something. I saw Shayla's gold charm bracelet behind her desk and smiled.

My ability to find missing items through simple human contact was still part of me. My new gift seemed confined to my getting information from inanimate objects when I touched them. How these things could have such exacting specifications was beyond me. Maybe later when I understood the new ability better, it would make more sense.

"There now!" Shayla raised her head, opened her dark eyes and smiled. "How do you feel?"

"Better. Thanks." I was able to answer honestly. "And I know where your lost bracelet is."

"I guess you can still find things then. I've been looking for that since last Sunday."

"You should've asked me."

"I should've. It would've saved me from tearing my place apart. That bracelet belonged to my grandmother. And you knew where it was all the time."

"We always seem to help each other."

"I'm glad I could help out." She stared hard at me. "Your color is a little better, but your chakra still needs some work. Let's schedule another session at my place tomorrow. I'm gonna have to charge you for this one, Dae. A girl has to pay the rent, you know."

That was Shayla. I smiled as she put the appointment into her BlackBerry. She glanced up at me. "So, what exactly did Kevin say about me while you all were talking?"

"He didn't mention you," I answered, hoping it wouldn't hurt her feelings.

"See? That's what I'm talking about. The man can't stand himself without me. I have to wonder how long he can take the torture." She sighed, said she'd see me later and click-clacked out of Missing Pieces on her high-heeled sandals.

When the door closed behind her and I was alone, I was scared. I hadn't been scared like this in a long time.

Everyone in Duck pretty much knew and accepted that I could help them find things by touching them. It wasn't a secret. I'd been doing it since I was a child.

This new talent was something else. I knew Kevin was right. I had to conquer it or at least get it under some kind of control. I couldn't go around the rest of my life almost fainting every time I touched a high-energy item like the coin. The manufacturing and distribution I could handle. Even what I felt in Kevin's truck was okay. The rest would take some time.

Since I was so familiar with everything inside Missing Pieces, I decided to try an experiment. I'd already touched the brocade sofa and the teacup. I'd experienced only a residual kind of awareness from them. I didn't know for sure how old either one of them was, but maybe age wasn't a factor as much as intent.

I mean, the gold coin in my pocket was much older and had brought me to my knees. On the other hand, the coffee card was much more recent, but its energy was just as strong. It was confusing—and frustrating.

I tried to focus on other items in the shop. I touched my teapot clock. Nothing much there. The mirror with the delicate carvings I'd found in Cape Cod was barely a buzz. Some clothes held nothing beyond the creators and a little about the people who'd worn them.

I was about to give up when I saw the miniature portrait I'd been harboring for a few years. It was tucked into a quiet corner of the shop, away from the regular traffic. No discerning customer had ever managed to find it.

I'd had it appraised after I got it at an estate sale. The appraiser was unsure about its origin. It was definitely by an early 1800s artist who was renowned locally for painting portraits. No one famous, but everyone from around here recognized his name.

We'd both speculated on who the lady in the portrait was. She was dressed in white with a small white veil on her dark hair. Her eyes were luminous, but her pretty face looked worn.

I'd shown it to Max once, wondering if it could be a lost painting of Theo Burr. I thought it looked like her. Max didn't. That was the end of that discussion.

I approached the portrait carefully, as though I could sneak up on it—like it wouldn't notice until it was too late. My hands trembled as I reached for it, uncertain of what I'd feel.

Chapter 5

Touching the portrait brought a bright flood of light and pictures cascading through my brain. It was like newsreel footage on steroids. I could barely keep them straight.

The woman in the picture was sad and tired. She was alone on a dark beach, not sure where she was. She met a man who took her home, and she stayed with him, though she knew she didn't belong there.

She had another life far away, but she didn't want to go back. There was too much pain and loss. The man who'd found her was good to her, and they lived together for several years before her death.

I moved my hand away, tears in my eyes. The portrait *was* of Theo Burr even though she'd used another name while she lived in the Outer Banks. Max had been right about her. She hadn't died at the hands of pirates. She'd

lived a second life here, but not because she didn't remember who she was and what she'd left behind.

"Max." I thought of him and how much I wished I
could tell him what I'd found. No one else would appreciate it the way he would. I cried when I realized there was
no one else to tell. Max was gone forever.

After my complete emotional breakdown, I left
the shop and headed home, not up to facing a regular
workday. I slept the rest of the day and through the night,
despite crazy dreams about Theo Burr, pirates and exploding cannons.

I woke up early the next morning, and I felt a lot better.
Maybe I didn't have all the answers, but I was learning. It
was a brand-new day and I was ready to go.

"I'm making pancakes," Gramps offered from the
kitchen as I came downstairs.

"I'll take some." I flipped through the newspaper on
the table. "Are we in the paper?"

It was kind of a joke in Duck about us making the
news. Since the *Duck Gazette* closed its doors a few years
back, there had been only a handful of times when the
town was mentioned in any of the surrounding newspa-
pers. We made the TV news a lot less often.

"Yep. We didn't make the front page, but it's a good
piece about the museum."

I looked at the article. It was fair and unemotional. The
kind of story someone who wasn't from Duck would
write. "I miss the *Gazette*," I told him as he brought a
huge stack of pancakes to the table.

"We all do." He kind of hovered there, not sitting
down.

"What's wrong?"

"Nothing." He shrugged.

I knew better. While he went back for coffee and syrup, there was a knock at the front door.

"Who could that be this early?" he asked.

"Like you don't know."

"I didn't invite him. You know how people around here show up all the time."

I went to answer the door while Gramps fiddled with the silverware and got out cups for coffee. It was Kevin, looking freshly showered, his dark, still-wet hair neatly combed. "I'm only here for the pancakes. Your grandfather didn't call me because he's worried about you."

"Thanks for the heads-up. The pancakes and Gramps are in the kitchen."

Right behind him was Officer Tim Mabry in his Duck Police uniform. "Morning, Dae."

"Is this an official visit?" I asked him.

"Sort of." Tim had a sheepish look on his lean face. "The chief wanted me to remind you that they all want to question you sometime today about what happened to the museum." He smiled at me, waiting until Kevin went into the kitchen to say, "Why didn't you call me, Dae? I had to hear what happened to you from the chief. I thought we knew each other better than that."

In actuality, we had *no* relationship beyond a longtime friendship, but Tim never wanted to hear that. We'd gone to school together since first grade, and he had proposed to me in high school. He'd always thought we should be linked romantically and continued to try and convince me of that through the years. Of course, this was between other girls he dated and proposed to. But he always came back to me.

"Come on in and eat some pancakes. Gramps made a ton of them. I'm sorry no one called you to tell you I was okay. It was very confusing when everything happened. And it all happened so fast."

He leaned his lanky, six-foot-six frame inside the doorway, a smile on his clean-shaven face below carefully cropped blond hair. "Thanks. I hope you're feeling better. Did someone call Brickman?"

"I don't know, Tim. He was there when I stopped at the museum on the way home." I knew that would make him sulky, but it was no good lying about it. He'd find out one way or another. This was Duck and everyone knew everyone else's business eventually.

Though Kevin and I had certainly never been linked romantically since he'd come to Duck, Tim thought of him as a rival for my affections. Maybe he was a tad psychic because he was right about my feelings for Kevin. I was glad he didn't make his assessment common knowledge.

"Of *course* he was." Tim's lips turned down at the corners like when he pulled someone over for speeding. "Why is he *always* around when things happen, Dae? Have you ever wondered about that? Two murders this year and *Kevin* has been there for both of them. That must be some kind of record."

"Are you saying Chief Michaels is calling Max's death a murder?" I latched on to his words, not their intent.

"Well." He sniffed and hitched up his pants. "I think it's likely, don't you? I mean someone doesn't get blown up accidentally, right?"

"Did you ever find the cannon or any sign that a cannon had been around before the explosion?" Gramps joined us at the doorway. "Thought I'd see what all the whispering was about. The two of you come in and eat before everything is cold. That way, we can all hear what you're saying."

"Not a cannon." Tim did as he was told and we walked

into the kitchen. "But we found some wheel marks that could fit a cannon frame and a set of truck tire prints from the vehicle that may have delivered it."

"Both of them overlooking the museum on the hill?" Kevin asked as he helped himself to maple syrup.

"That's right." Tim took off his hat and sat down at the table. "These pancakes smell great, sir."

"Thanks." Gramps smiled at me and put out another plate and cup. "Dig in."

"How are you feeling, Dae?" Kevin asked as we ate.

"I feel fine," I answered, actually meaning it. "I'm going to open Missing Pieces today and check in at town hall. Maybe the chief and whoever else can question me there."

"Are your hands cold?" He nodded significantly at the gloves I was wearing.

"Yes. I guess it's the injuries from the explosion." *That's it! Nothing more. I don't want to discuss it right now.*

"It's been a mild winter," Gramps reminded me. "You're sure everything is okay, honey?"

I glared at Kevin for bringing it up. He knew it would cause trouble. I assured Gramps that I was fine, then Tim started wondering if I should go back in for a checkup.

I changed the subject by talking about the fishing trip Gramps had booked today on his charter boat. Tim changed it again by telling us (me) that he was thinking about buying his own place with his overtime pay.

"You already live in your parents' old house," I said.

"Yeah." He grimaced at Kevin, who wasn't looking at him. "But I'm thinking about moving. I'm starting to think about my future now, Dae. I'm not a kid anymore."

I agreed with that, but I knew he'd never sell his parents' house. He'd marry someone from Duck, and they'd have a family right there. Not that there was anything wrong with that idea. I wished I felt that way about him and everything could be wrapped up nice and neat between us.

I glanced across the table at Kevin, who was still talking about fishing with Gramps. I didn't want to fall in love with someone who wasn't from here and probably couldn't appreciate the way we lived. I wasn't even sure if Kevin would stay in Duck.

Gramps asked how the Blue Whale, Kevin's hotel, was doing. "It's been slowing down after tourist season, like everything else around here. It's nice after being so busy at the end of the summer. I can appreciate the downtime. That's what I was looking for when I came here."

Kevin had purchased the old Blue Whale Inn, sight unseen, after leaving the FBI. He'd been an agent for twelve years. He'd said from the beginning that he didn't want that life anymore. Sometimes at night it drove me crazy thinking he might go back to it anyway.

"After being closed for thirty years, there must be plenty to do anyway," Gramps remarked. "It looked like it caught right on again once you got it open. People always loved that old place."

Tim's radio went off, calling him to an accident on Duck Road going toward Sanderling. He wiped his mouth, gulped his coffee and thanked Gramps for breakfast. "Can I drop you at Missing Pieces?" He was asking *me* but glaring at Kevin over my head.

"That's the wrong way," I reminded him. "But thanks, Tim. I appreciate the offer. I'm actually looking forward to walking down like I usually do."

"All right. I'll see you later, Dae. Take it easy. Don't try to do too much like you always do. But make sure you give Chief Michaels a call." He nodded at Kevin. "Brickman."

Kevin nodded back. "Officer."

When Tim left, the conversation around the table went

with him. Gramps needed to get to his boat, and I was anxious to get on with the day. I helped clear the table, hoping Kevin wouldn't ask anymore leading questions. Maybe he thought I'd told Gramps about my new abilities.

"I'll see you at supper." I kissed Gramps's head with its thinning white hair before he put on his straw hat. "Have a good trip today."

"Don't forget tonight's bingo night. I won't be here for supper." He nodded toward Kevin. "Make some plans of your own. I won't be home until late."

He winked at me as he began gathering up his lunch and other items for the trip. I knew what he was thinking. He used to be the same way with Tim. Maybe I was more transparent than I thought. Was it obvious to everyone that I had feelings for Kevin?

I grabbed my purse and headed for the door.

Kevin was right behind me. "Gloves?"

"I have to get through this," I explained when I was sure the door was closed behind us so Gramps wouldn't hear. "I don't know exactly how to do that yet. I thought I could wear them for a while. They seem to help."

"You can't figure it out that way." He followed me down the steps and into the sandy street. In Duck, everyone walks everywhere, but we still don't have any sidewalks. Sidewalks were on my agenda as mayor. "You have to keep working with it. What did Shayla say?"

"She said my chakra was messed up. She's going to try and realign it again today."

"I thought she might be more help. That's why I left yesterday."

I smiled at the threads of sunlight that touched the edges of his dark hair. The sun peeked through the heavy shrubs that grew all in one direction along the edges of Duck Road. His eyes were like the Atlantic side of Duck, more gray than blue. I felt like I could walk with him forever.

"Dae?"

"Uh-yeah? Sorry. Shayla's trying to help. I guess she's not sure what to do with someone who falls over when she touches the wrong things."

"You have to keep trying, keep working with it," he urged as we walked and avoided the few cars that passed us. "You can't shield yourself from it with gloves."

"I touched most of the stuff in Missing Pieces before I left yesterday," I added, sounding like a child trying to impress a favorite teacher.

"And?"

A stubborn, demanding favorite teacher. "Most of it seems to come in fragments that aren't very strong. Not like the coin and the coffee card. Only the miniature had that kind of energy."

"Miniature what?"

I explained about the portrait, trying to keep the excitement down but failing. Though I was still sad about losing Max, I couldn't help but be thrilled to find out he'd been right about Theo Burr. "Max thought he had DNA evidence that Theodosia lived here and had a child. He was right, although he was wrong about her not knowing who she was. She didn't want to go home again. She created a new life here and never told anyone who she was."

"You saw all that from touching a tiny picture?"

"Some of it was like connect-the-dots and intuition. It was like I could feel what she was thinking when that portrait was painted."

We walked along the road toward the Duck Shoppes and Missing Pieces. Town hall was on the boardwalk too. Traffic still wasn't very heavy. As Kevin had said, most of the tourists had gone home, leaving the 567 full-time residents here for the coming winter. We had some Canadian visitors in the fall and winter, but mostly, they went to Myrtle Beach. It was good to have the revenue that the crowded streets and restaurants brought in the summer, but I was always glad for the quiet of winter.

"Did you start writing anything down yet?" he asked.

"Sort of. I'm trying to understand what's happening and why. Do you think there's a connection between the coffee card, the gold coin and the miniature? Is that what I'm feeling when I touch those things?"

"I don't know," he admitted. "You're going to have to learn to sort through these feelings you have and see where they take you. Have you tried to see if you can find things yet?"

"Yes." I didn't want to talk to him about seeing Shayla's missing bracelet. I didn't like talking to him about Shayla at all. There was always that awkward moment where I wasn't sure how he felt about her and I was afraid I'd say something wrong.

"Want to come over tonight and have dinner? We can try to find that cask of wine again." He smiled at me like it mattered to him. Or was I reading those emotions into it? Maybe he just wanted to find the missing cask.

"I appreciated all your help yesterday. I'm sorry about what happened when Shayla got there," I blurted out. "It's not that I didn't want you to stay. But you and Shayla in the same room—"

"Yeah. I know." He put his hands in his jacket pockets. "I take it she wasn't looking for anything?"

"She didn't say."

He stopped walking as we reached the Duck Shoppes parking lot. "Just there for girl talk?"

"Yeah, I guess." I scuffed the toe of my sneaker on the

sandy pavement. "She wanted to examine my chakra." Was he pumping me for information about her?

He nodded. "I understand. Shayla is Shayla. No one is quite like her. She's a force of nature."

"Yeah." Now I felt lame for saying anything. "Well, I should go. Where are you headed?"

"I actually have some business at town hall. Something about a new permit that restaurants need." He looked away as a school bus passed us. "So, how about tonight? No chakras. We'll see if we can find the wine and drink some of it. What do you think?"

With thousands of tiny zings of pleasure racing through me, I answered, "Sure. What time?"

I danced up the stairs to the town hall with him, hoping I wasn't talking too much and wondering why what I felt for him made me feel like such a kid. A thirty-six-year-old kid, I reminded myself, sobering as we reached the town clerk's office.

Nancy Boidyn, Duck's town clerk, looked up from her typing and gave a little screech before she leapt to her feet and hugged me. "Dae! It's so good to see you! Oh my God, I've been so worried since I heard what happened. I couldn't believe it. You were so lucky that you weren't hurt any worse."

I hugged her back. Kevin kind of wandered away to look out the window at the Currituck Sound that flanked the boardwalk.

"Do you need anything? Should you be working?" Nancy fluttered around me with compassion. "Sit down. You probably shouldn't be on your feet."

"I'm fine, really. I'm going to check some email while you help Kevin with his permit. Is there coffee?"

Nancy fussed and put coffee in my seashell-shaped cup. She made coffee for Kevin too. I closed the door to my office and leaned against it as they started talking about filling out his permit.

Was I reading too much into Kevin asking me to dinner by myself? He'd invited me to dinner and asked for my help looking for the wine again, but did that make it a romantic overture? I'd had dinner at the Blue Whale a dozen times since it opened.

But not alone with him.

That was true, although I felt silly even thinking it. Usually there was a crowd of us when we had dinner at the inn because Kevin wanted to try out some new dessert or sauce. He loved to cook.

I need something new to wear.

Okay. Maybe I didn't *need* something new to wear, but I wanted something new. Was there anything wrong with hoping he might see *me* as a force of nature someday as he did Shayla?

It might take a new dress and shoes, and maybe something different with my hair. I didn't want to miss the opportunity to have him look at me in a new light.

I had hundreds of emails, of course. Most of them were well-wishers hoping I was recovering. Some were trash that I deleted. Some, like the one for the mayor's conference we would be hosting in Duck right after the first of the year, had to be answered.

I could hear Kevin talking to Nancy at first. Then it grew quiet in the outer office. He probably had finished up and left. The knock on the door startled me, and my finger slipped over a key, causing T's to go running across the page.

"See you later," Kevin said with a smile. "I hope we can get those gloves off of you tonight."

I swallowed hard and nodded. "See you later."

Nancy's face replaced his at the door, but all I could hear was his voice saying he wanted to get my gloves off. There was something sexy in the way he said it.

". . . and the chief will be here later to talk to you," Nancy said. "He'll call first. Dae?"

"Hmm? Oh, right. He wants to talk about what I saw at the museum before it exploded."

Nancy shut the door and sat down in one of the chairs that faced my desk. "What *did* you see?"

"Nothing, as far as I know. But he and Cailey and that new arson investigator from Manteo think there might be something important that I don't realize I saw."

"Did you"—she gulped—"did you see Max explode?"

Chapter 6

"*No!* He was in the museum. I didn't really even see the museum explode. It happened so fast. One minute I was at the door, the next there was a flash of light and I was in the street."

"Oh, Dae. How *awful!*"

My throat felt tight and I knew if I said anything else about it, I'd start blubbering again. Instead, I looked around my little office that had once been a storage closet. It had a window overlooking the sound, and I had put all the sea paraphernalia I could find in it. I had a ship's bell from a freighter that went down in the early 1800s and seashells I'd collected. I'd left my white oak desk the way I'd found it so that it looked a little banged up and unfinished.

Nancy came around the desk and hugged me. "It's all gonna work out, sweetie. You'll see." There were tears in her brown eyes, but her smile and resolve didn't waver.

"Thanks," I whispered.

"I'll make sure you aren't disturbed for a few minutes." She walked out and closed the door.

My mother's face stared back at me from a barnacle-encrusted picture frame. She'd been dead thirteen long years. Like Max, she was gone too soon. I'd lived with her death on my conscience every day since she'd gone off the bridge coming back from the mainland. Her body was never recovered.

It was my fault because I was a stupid, young, know-it-all in college. We'd argued when she came to see me. My last words to her were said in anger, carelessly flung like sharp stones, meant to wound.

I came home from college after she died and had prayed every night since then to see her ghost, to have a chance to say good-bye and tell her that I was sorry. But though I could find things with my special abilities, I couldn't see spirits like Shayla could. She'd tried to help me contact my mother, but it hadn't happened.

I looked out of the window at the sun-kissed, sparkling water. Sniffling, barely in control of my emotions, I knew I had to get out of there. I couldn't dredge up all the old, bad memories again to heap on the new, bad memories. I had to do something constructive.

I waved to Nancy as I left town hall, not trusting myself to speak. I headed down the gray boardwalk to Missing Pieces. I wanted to recapture the excitement I'd felt about going to Kevin's for dinner. It wasn't easy.

Then I remembered a dress I'd taken in early September. I'd picked it up and admired it twice since buying it with a group of other clothes from a woman in Grandy. I'd even thought about keeping it for myself, but I couldn't imagine where I'd wear it.

With the shop door open and the blinds pulled up on the sunny day, I walked to the back of the shop where I kept the clothes. There were only a few racks since clothes weren't my principle sales. Customers came in and bought them randomly, so I purchased with care.

The dress was still there. It was a simple, elegant creation of blue silk with a knee-length skirt and a low neckline that would be perfect for my grandmother's pearls. I tried it on and decided it looked nice with my blue eyes and sun-bleached brown hair. I still had my summer tan, and thankfully, my bathing suit top had extended low enough that my chest had no white areas—at least none that the dress would reveal.

I twirled around in front of the mirror, feeling pretty and a little fragile. I smiled at myself and messed around with my hair, holding it back from my face on one side and simpering, "Oh, Kevin. I love it when you look at me that way."

Someone cleared their throat behind me, and I prayed with hastily closed eyes that it wasn't Kevin.

"I have some packages for you," Stan, the UPS driver, said, his voice a little choked.

"Thanks." I scooted up to the front of the shop feeling stupid, my cheeks burning. But Stan was okay.

"You look good in that dress, Dae." He smiled as I took the last of the packages from him and signed for them. "I don't know who Kevin is, but he's a lucky guy."

Stan is married and has several children, so I got through it. More to the point, he lives in Whalebone and so was unlikely to run into Kevin. At least I hoped so.

He waved good-bye as I checked my packages. I'd become the only UPS dropoff last spring, and it had proven to be lucrative. It wasn't a fortune, but every little bit helped pay the rent on Missing Pieces.

With Stan gone, I spun around in the blue dress again, a little more cautiously.

I never stocked shoes, but I thought Darcy at the Sunflower Fancy across the road might have something strappy and sexy for me. They would cost the earth, and I'd probably never wear them again, but I was in the right mood and ready to take my chances with Kevin.

I looked at myself again in the mirror. Gramps was right when he said I look like my mother. Her hair had been different—darker—but our faces were similar—heart-shaped with wispy eyebrows and a slightly pointed nose.

I took off the dress and put it behind the counter as my first customer came in to look around. I'd forgotten to move the miniature I believed to be Theo Burr, but I went and got it before the woman noticed it. I wouldn't part with it for anything, but I was glad I was still wearing the gloves when I touched it.

The woman, who said she was from Charlotte, was looking for antiques for her new house. She had a good eye. There was an old ship's compass from the *Emulous*, one of the more famous Outer Banks wrecks. I'd had it a few years, but it didn't work. Lots of hands had touched it and put it back down. It was too banged up for most people.

"I'll take this," she said when she came up to the counter with it.

"Do you know what it is?" I asked. Though sales were slow, I couldn't let my true finds go without making sure the right person was getting them.

"I do!" She proceeded to tell me how she'd read about the wreck but had never dreamed she'd be so lucky to find something from it for her house. "How much?"

That was always another aspect of my prizes. They were expensive. Either people wanted them or they didn't. It was part of the package. I named my price and she took out her wallet. "Do you take Visa?"

It was a good sale. I rang it up, boxed the old compass, and smiled. "Thanks for coming in."

"Thanks for having this here," she said enthusiastically. "I didn't want to tell you because I thought it might drive up the price. My great-great grandfather was the captain of the *Emulous*. This is very dear to me."

Actually, I probably would've charged her less, but I didn't say so. I was almost too sentimental to have the shop when it came to things like that.

It was a good thing I made that one big sale because it was my only one that morning. I closed for lunch and went across Duck Road to Sunflower Fancy to look for shoes. Darcy found me a perfect pair that I could afford and thanked me for my business.

"Terrible thing about the museum," she said as she boxed my shoes. "Everyone's talking about it. I hear the police are looking for Sam Meacham. If anyone *human* killed Max, I suppose it was Sam. Those two were always going at it."

I kind of agreed, especially since I knew Sam had been there earlier in the day before the explosion. I'd known Sam all of my life, just as I had Max, only we weren't as close. I couldn't imagine him killing anyone.

Then the word *human* filtered through my brain. "What do you mean, 'human'?"

"Some people think it's the old pirate curse," Darcy continued.

"You mean they think a pirate's ghost killed Max?"

She shrugged her thin shoulders, her lavender dress almost matching the highlights in her gray hair. "You've lived here your whole life, Dae O'Donnell. You know that Duck was cursed by Rafe Masterson. He swore he'd come back, and some of us think that's *exactly* what's happened."

* * *

I left Sunflower Fancy with more than a pair of shoes. I hadn't thought about people believing that the pirate curse was on us again. I don't know why not. There were still the occasional tales of finding a mermaid, and we had our share of ghost stories that everyone believed were true.

I remembered hearing about the pirate curse before I ever went to school. We repeated it over and over once we all gathered in school, especially around Halloween. Rafe Masterson was long dead, but his spirit lived on in Duck.

Rafe was one of the pirates who had been a scourge of the Graveyard of the Atlantic for many years in the late 1700s. He was finally captured by an old Banker trick of tying a lantern to a horse and leading it up and down the shore. Many rich merchant ships were lured to wreck on the coast this way, believing they saw safe port. This was primarily used before the advent of lighthouses.

Rafe believed it too, and his ship was wrecked. The other members of his crew, all scurrilous hellions, were killed as they washed up onshore. Rafe, however, was saved for a more grisly fate.

He was hanged, drawn and quartered, his remains put out on wrecked timbers embedded in the beach to dry, as a warning to other pirates. His last words before he was torn apart by four strong horses were a curse on the people who lived where Duck is today: "My ghost won't rest until your village is destroyed. Look for me by moonlight with my bony skull laughing as you die."

As curses went, it was a really good one. People were truly terrified for a very long time. Many fires and other catastrophes were blamed on the curse. Even as recently as twenty years ago, the fire that destroyed the original fire station was blamed on Rafe. It was easy to imagine that the museum filled with pirate paraphernalia could be one of his targets. Even easier once everyone found out that a cannonball had been fired into the museum.

"We have to call an emergency town meeting," I told Nancy when I got back across the street. "How much notice do we have to give?"

"Twenty-four hours," she replied without hesitation. "I can post it on the Web site this afternoon and outside town hall. Why? What's up?"

"I think we should address what happened at the museum," I answered without getting into the gory details. "Can you call the council together for a meeting tomorrow night at seven P.M.?"

"You got it! I think this is a good idea. There are a lot of worried people out there."

I went back to Missing Pieces while she answered the phone. I wasn't exactly sure how to address the curse of Rafe the pirate at the meeting. It was bound to come up. I hoped something would occur to me before then. Nancy was right too. It wasn't only Rafe we needed to talk about. Max's violent death in our peaceful little community would have shaken many residents.

When I got back to the shop, I tried on the blue dress with the shoes and decided it would do. I'd wear Grandma's pearls and matching earrings and use the new perfume I'd bought a month ago. It was called Mystique, and it came in a sleek, black bottle that seemed both elegant and decadent.

All right. I was sold by the advertising. I'm sure I wasn't the only one.

The afternoon dragged on as I got more and more nervous about being alone with Kevin that evening. Not that we hadn't been alone before—but this seemed different.

Intent, I suppose. Knowing that I had a plan in mind to make him notice me as a woman and not a science project.

Sometimes, especially now with all the talk about my abilities changing, I felt more like a puzzle he was trying to piece together in his mind. Added to that was the new speculation about his partner in the FBI. He might be avoiding the idea of a romantic relationship with me because of what happened to her. It seemed to me Shayla would fit that profile too, but I had no way of knowing how he was looking at it.

Before I could drive myself crazy wondering and worrying about what the night would bring, I closed up for the day and went next door to Curves and Curls to get a pedicure to go with my new shoes. It made sense, I thought, since Kevin would be able to see my toes. He'd seen them all summer in my sandals, but that was different.

I wore the blue dress and the shoes so Trudy could give me her opinion. After spending a few minutes talking about everything that had happened and catching up with each other, I twirled so she could tell me what she thought.

"You look awesome! I love the gloves!" She looked me up and down with a critical eye. "This has to be a hot date outfit. Are you finally going to take Tim up on one of his many offers?"

Sometimes I felt as if Trudy had known me *too* long. "No. And what do I have to do to convince everyone that Tim and I will never be more than friends?" I sat down in the chair and hugged my secret to myself. "This is something different."

"A new man?" she guessed, taking off my expensive shoes. "Is there a new man in town? I haven't heard about anyone."

"He's not *that* new."

She narrowed her green eyes. They were a different

color almost every day thanks to her contact lenses. "You're talking about Kevin Brickman, aren't you? All of this is for him?"

"He asked me over for dinner tonight. *Alone*." The secret spilled out of me without much coercion. I'd make an awful spy.

Trudy shook her platinum blond hair that never looked less than perfect, framing her pretty, tanned face. She'd never even had a zit all the way through high school. "He's not over Shayla yet, Dae. If he *is* looking at you, it's a rebound thing. You don't want that."

"Please! No cynicism. I've seen you go after a man for a lot less reason."

Her eyebrows rose after she put cotton balls between my toes. "Dae, it's the museum, isn't it? You had a near-death experience and it's warped your brain. Take a minute to think about this. You don't want Shayla's leftovers."

"That's not it." I argued with her, although I had to admit the reason for the dinner might be different for me than for Kevin. Would he have invited me over if he wasn't trying to analyze my new abilities?

"Dae—"

"I won't listen!" I closed my eyes as she applied polish to my toenails. "I'm going tonight no matter what."

My phone rang. It was Nancy reminding me of my appointment with the chief. "When?" I asked, something like panic building inside of me. I didn't know if I was ready to discuss what had happened in the graphic detail Cailey and Chief Michaels were looking for.

"They're here right now, waiting for you. ASAP, I guess."

I turned off my phone. "I have to go," I told Trudy. "The chief wants to talk to me about the museum. Sorry."

"That's okay." She pulled out the cotton balls and used

a hair dryer to dry the polish quickly. "What *did* happen over there, Dae? People are saying it's the pirate curse again."

"I know. Darcy told me. That's where I got my shoes."

"The shoes are perfect," she remarked, then added. "It's crazy. But who else would want to hurt Max or blow up our little museum? Nothing makes any sense about it. Kind of like you going after Kevin."

I ignored the last part and told her about the town meeting tomorrow night. "I'm going to find some way to talk about the pirate curse without sounding stupid. I hope Chief Michaels will be there with Cailey to discuss what they can with everyone. I really don't think Rafe is back to kill people and blow things up, Trudy. There's a rational explanation for what happened."

Chief Michaels wasn't going to like that I'd promised a news briefing of sorts for him. He never shared information with the public if he could help it. The investigation might be ongoing, but so were panic and fear. We had to nip the pirate-curse rumors before they became what would pass for the truth.

The new people to the community, like Brad Spitzer and Kevin, might think it was crazy to believe in such things today. But I'd found that people will believe anything in the absence of the truth.

Feeling a little overdressed, I made a grand entrance into town hall, where the group was waiting for me. Nancy, looking stressed, was doling out coffee and sodas. Cailey and Brad were talking together quietly in one corner of the room while Tim and Chief Michaels were whispering in another.

When they saw me, everyone got to their feet and stopped talking. It was a little nerve-wracking. Were they all talking about me?

"Let's go in my office," I said with as much calm as I could. "Nancy, please hold all calls."

She nodded, plainly glad to see us go into another room. "Would you like me to take notes?"

"That shouldn't be necessary since we're all *finally* here," Chief Michaels assured her, his hat tucked under his arm.

I took the dig about being late in stride. After all, his reference to a meeting "sometime" today had been a little vague. I tried to take into consideration that he'd probably not slept much since the explosion happened. He and Max weren't close friends, but everyone knew everyone else in Duck. He was bound to be as affected by it as other town residents.

Tim brought in two extra chairs, which made my office feel much smaller. As he passed me going in, he whispered, "Big date tonight, Dae?"

I ignored him too. This wasn't a good time to argue about much of anything. Our long-standing disagreement about our relationship would have to wait. I knew it didn't make it any easier for him that everyone in Duck expected us to end up together. Everyone, of course, except me.

I sat down behind my desk, hoping the chief wasn't wasting his time with me. Someone else probably had a better vantage point. There were all those people in the cars and walking down the street at the time of the explosion. I assumed he was either in the process of finding and interviewing them or he'd already done it.

Despite not knowing what I could say to help, or maybe because of it, the meeting made me as jittery as ten double-shot lattes. I was already overwrought about Kevin, my night in the hospital and Max's death.

Taking a deep breath and anchoring myself with the familiar surroundings in my office, I put on a grim smile and addressed them. "I don't think I saw anything that could be helpful to your investigation."

"There might be something you saw that you don't realize is important," Cailey countered in her old fifth-grade-schoolteacher's voice.

"Start at the beginning, Mayor," Chief Michaels urged as they all took out notebooks. "We know you were at the museum with the kids. What happened then?"

I told them about the program with Max and the kids, about how I walked out with everyone else.

"What made you turn back?" Brad, the arson investigator, asked.

I hadn't wanted to share the existence of the gold coin with them. It seemed I had no choice. I pulled it out of my purse and showed it to them.

"This is evidence." Chief Michaels had Tim put on gloves and take the coin from me. "You should've told us sooner."

"I didn't think it was important." I gave up the coin reluctantly, still feeling attached to its individual energy. I knew everything about it anyway. I just liked having it with me. "The coin didn't cause the explosion. What difference does it make?"

"No, it didn't *cause* the explosion," Cailey agreed. "But it might be part of the motive for what happened. Dae, all the rest of the gold coins were stolen from the museum. This is the only one left."

Chapter 7

"We believe the explosion may have been to cover up the theft of the coins," Chief Michaels explained further.

I glanced at him in total disbelief. "As valuable as the coins may be, there were only a few of them. Max added fake coins to the display to make it look more impressive. Museums up and down the coast have the same coins. Why our museum?"

"We don't know yet," Cailey said. "But we know the coins are gone. They would've melted in the heat and we would've found what was left of them. Anything else you took from the museum, Dae?"

The question sounded more like an accusation—as though I'd stolen the coin. Or maybe my guilty conscience just made it feel that way. "No." But I couldn't explain what made me put it in my pocket either.

I thought about the coffee card from the trash that was

in a plastic bag in my purse. Would they have the same reaction if I shared that information? I wasn't sure, but I realized it *could* be evidence. "I found a coffee card in the trash outside if that counts for anything."

They all exchanged glances and shifted in their seats.

"Does it have a name on it or something useful to the investigation?" Brad asked, a little impatience in his voice.

"Well, only the Duck coffee shop name." I realized I couldn't tell them how I knew it belonged to Sam. They wouldn't believe it. I had no proof to back me up.

"That's irrelevant," Chief Michaels said. "But please don't take anything else from the crime scene. This is a serious matter, Mayor."

Even though I reminded myself that it *wasn't* a crime scene when I found the gold coin on the floor at the museum, I still felt fully chastened. I folded my hands on the desk. "I don't know what else I can tell you."

"You didn't see anything unusual when you turned back after leaving the museum, right?" Brad demanded. "Any detail that could help us determine what happened and who was responsible would be helpful."

I thought back again to that instant before the explosion. The door to the museum had been closed. That was the only detail I could remember, except for that brief flash of light. It hadn't come from the museum building, as I thought back on it. Instead, the burst of light had flashed close by—close enough to catch my eye.

I couldn't be sure what the flash was, maybe just a glint of sunlight reflected off of one of the cars going by. After my coffee card was summarily dismissed as unimportant, I didn't feel much like sharing another ghost of a thought, but I told them anyway. "I saw a flash of light."

"It's possible she caught someone lighting the cannon," Brad theorized.

Cailey agreed, sitting forward in her seat. "Are you sure you didn't see anything else with that flash of light, Dae? A face or a car? Anything could help us."

"No. I'm sorry. I wish I could help. It all happened so quickly," I explained.

"We understand." Cailey patted my gloved hands and smiled. "If you think of anything else, let us know right away. You're lucky to be alive. It could've been so much worse if everyone else had still been in the museum."

Everyone in the room agreed. A few minutes of dead silence followed as we considered the wider tragedy that had been narrowly averted. It made me wish I could say something about the coffee card belonging to Sam, even though I didn't believe he had anything to do with Max's death. The two men may have disagreed, but that's a long way from murder.

"Thank you for your time, Mayor O'Donnell." Brad broke free from the trance we all seemed to be in. He got to his feet and offered me his hand. When I didn't offer mine in return, he frowned. "I'm sorry. I forgot. I hope your hands weren't too badly injured. We'll update you when we can about the situation. Everything we've found at the museum will have to be shipped to the lab and analyzed, including your coin. The process will be slow but thorough."

I realized he'd given me the perfect excuse for wearing the gloves until I found a way to handle my new abilities. No one had to know the real reason I was wearing gloves—except Kevin. "Thanks. I set up a special town meeting for tomorrow night at seven. If all of you could be there to answer as many questions as you can, that would be great."

The chief and Cailey kind of hesitated but eventually said they'd attend, barring emergencies. Brad kind of grunted and walked out of the room. I wasn't sure if that meant he'd be there or not.

"Now all we have to do is deal with all the pirate curse rumors," Cailey said. "It's amazing how long people will hold on to something like that."

"I plan to address that tomorrow night." I smiled at both of them. "Someone needs to set the record straight."

Cailey looked at Chief Michaels and they both laughed. "Good luck with that, Mayor," Chief Michaels added. "I suppose you think you're the first person who's tried to lay the ghost of Rafe Masterson to rest."

Tim cleared his throat. "It kind of makes sense. I mean, someone fired a cannon at the museum."

"Which should not be common knowledge yet," Chief Michaels reminded him with a stern expression. "We haven't said anything about a cannon to the press."

His reprimand slid off of Tim like rain off a fisherman's slicker. "Maybe Rafe came to get his gold back. He vowed revenge, don't forget, and we don't know whose gold it was that Max found."

We all stared at Tim and he shrugged. "That's what people will say when they find out what happened."

"Which they won't find out from *this* office," Chief Michaels said pointedly.

"What's next?" I asked to change the subject. This was getting us nowhere. "Where will the investigation go from here?"

"It's hard to say." Cailey hedged, obviously not wanting to share. "We'll look into all the leads we have and analyze the fire."

"You'll have to talk to Sam Meacham too." Tim echoed what I was thinking. "Everyone knows what went on between him and Max. Besides Rafe, Sam is the most likely suspect in this case."

When Cailey and the chief didn't disagree, I knew they were thinking the same thing, probably minus Rafe being the top suspect. I didn't believe a pirate ghost caused the explosion that killed Max. But I also had trouble believing Sam killed him. Anything was possible, but that seemed like a stretch to me. Unfortunately, Sam's acrimonious relationship with Max was not the only factor piqueing everyone's interest. He also had access to a working cannon and everyone knew he envied the gold coins in the Duck museum. Corolla's historical museum didn't have any real gold coins.

Cailey drifted out of my office toward the front door. Tim stepped outside on the boardwalk to take a call from his police radio.

"You look nice, Dae," Chief Michaels said. "I hope you're feeling better soon. Horace was sick with worry about you when he heard what happened. I had to have someone drive him to the hospital. I was afraid he might get in a wreck or get arrested if he drove himself there."

"Thanks. I'm fine." I couldn't have been more surprised that the chief noticed how I looked. And I appreciated the way he had taken care of Gramps. I knew he meant well. We didn't always see eye-to-eye on things, but he was a good man to have in your corner during trouble.

He nodded, cleared his throat and left the office behind Cailey and Tim.

"Well?" Nancy asked when we were alone.

I glanced at the big clock on the wall and my heart started pounding. My palms were sweaty and my face felt hot. "I think it's time for dinner."

She smiled. "I thought you must have a date."

"Yes. Well, not exactly a date, maybe." I bit my lip to stop stammering. "I'm not sure."

"You look great! Go knock him dead, girl!"

* * *

It wasn't a long walk from town hall and the Duck Shoppes to the Blue Whale Inn. My mind went there before my body, flying down the stairs to the parking lot and out past the small commercial area of town.

My body paused outside town hall. Trudy's words about Kevin using me to get over Shayla made my feet a little cold in my new shoes. Maybe I shouldn't try to make him think of me in a romantic way just yet.

Not that I'd really thought through or planned out *exactly* what I was going to do to accomplish that goal. I'd never purposely set out to seduce a man, if that was what I was thinking. Maybe "seduce" wasn't the right word—just make him more aware of me. We might be good together as more than friends. But I'd never set out to do that either.

It wasn't like I was a complete novice. I'd dated through high school and college. I'd even dated occasionally since then. But being in a very small area, where the boys you grew up with became the men you'd already decided against, made it difficult. As Trudy had noted, we don't get many new, single men who want to live in Duck.

My loosely considered plan to go home first, shower, put on my new perfume, redo my hair and find Grandma's pearls would make me late for my six P.M. dinner with Kevin. There was only about twenty minutes left.

Maybe I should call and cancel, with regrets. Did I really feel up to doing something important like this right now? What if Trudy was right and it was only a reaction from almost getting killed?

I walked down the stairs to the parking lot and took out my cell phone, totally losing my nerve. It was one thing to get all dressed up and think about having dinner alone with Kevin and another to really do it.

"Ready?" His voice startled me.

"Uh—"

"I thought I'd save you the walk." He looked at my pretty new shoes. "Good thing, I guess, since those don't look like walking shoes."

"I—"

"Do you need to go home first?"

This actually required an answer. I kind of stood there, staring at him. I swallowed hard and tried to shore up my crumbling backbone. "I was about to call you—"

"Now you don't have to. We can talk in the truck on the way over."

We were drifting into the parking lot toward his pickup. He held the passenger side door open and I climbed inside. *Trudy must be right. This had to be part of my injury. I can't even form whole sentences.*

Kevin got in and slid behind the wheel. That's when I noticed that he was wearing a tie. *A tie!* It was beyond a doubt the most awful tie I'd ever seen, some kind of brown with yellow flecks in it.

I'd never seen him wear a tie or the lightweight brown sport jacket he had on. He'd told me once that he'd thrown his suits away before he left Washington, never to wear them again.

I suddenly realized that he was dressed up for *me*, like I was dressed up for *him*. The implication of that hit me like a storm wave, tumbling my thoughts but making my heart feel much lighter. I wasn't nervous anymore. Having dinner alone with me meant something to him too.

What it meant remained to be seen, but it was a start. "You look nice," I said without putting much thought into it.

"Thanks." He smiled. "You look spectacular!"

"Thanks." My heart was definitely feeling warmer now, along with the rest of me.

"What did you want to tell me?"

I looked at his hair and freshly shaved face. He smelled really good. I was used to seeing him in T-shirts and jeans. Not that he didn't look good in those too. "I don't know."

We both laughed and he started the truck. Maybe he was nervous too.

"Still wearing the gloves, I see."

I glanced at my hands. "The arson investigator gave me a good excuse at the meeting today. Everyone thinks my hands were burned."

"And that's a good thing?"

"For right now it is. I don't have to touch anyone or anything. I don't know what else to do until I understand it better."

He nodded, his eyes focused on the narrow road that led to the Blue Whale. "How did the meeting go today?"

I couldn't think of any reason not to tell him what happened. Nothing earth-shattering or even terribly secret had transpired. "Which makes our top suspect a two-hundred-year-old pirate ghost."

"I was wondering about that. A few of the firemen at the museum talked about this being Rafe's fault. I thought he was a past mayor or something."

"You should've asked. I'm sure they would've been glad to tell you the story. Anyone from Duck loves to tell it."

"But basically, the chief likes this man from the museum in Corolla for what happened."

"I think so." I looked at the three-story Blue Whale Inn, freshly painted—blue, of course, to match its name—after thirty years of being a ramshackle eyesore. I had a T-shirt with paint on it from the job.

The circle drive was clean, and the grass beside it had been recently trimmed. It curled around a fountain with a mermaid in it. The wide verandah had a welcoming look, with white wicker chairs and hanging plants. The old hitching post, where guests had once tied up their rides and sneaked inside to share some bathtub gin with friends, was polished. The Blue Whale had become an asset to the community again.

"We're open Thursday through Sunday now since the tourists have slowed down," Kevin explained as I noticed that there were no other cars in the parking lot.

He parked in front and turned off the truck. "We have a few parties coming up for the holidays, but I think I'll have time now to get some work done on the place. I still haven't really touched the third floor."

"What about your staff?" I knew he'd hired about fifteen people, some full- and some part-time.

"I had to lay a few off for the winter, but I kept most of them." He came around and opened the truck door for me. "But tonight's Wednesday and no one's here except us. I made lasagna for you."

So we would be totally alone in the old place. I got out of the truck. The smell of the ocean was strong here, much stronger than on the Currituck side even though it wasn't that far away. I could hear the waves breaking on the shore. Wind chimes rang out in the constant breeze that kept our trees dwarfed.

As we walked up the stairs, I suddenly felt another attack of nerves. Despite the fact that he was dressed up too, or maybe because of it, I was uncertain. What if this went badly? Was this the time to do something that might lead

to disaster? Kevin and I were friends. Did I want to jeop-
ardize that relationship?

"Something wrong?" he asked as he unlocked the front
door. "You seem a long way off all of a sudden."

"I was thinking that I meant to water my begonias tonight." Okay, it wasn't the best excuse. It was all I could
think of and better than "I have to go home and wash my
hair."

He smiled and held out his hand to me. "Let's eat first.
You're going to love my new dessert. The begonias will
probably survive until you get back. Are you—nervous?"

I licked my lips, torn between being careful and being
honest, always a mayor's dilemma. "Yes," I finally admitted with a husky laugh. "I guess I am. It's been a long
time . . . since I, uh, ate dinner."

"Me too." He laughed. "But they say it comes right
back to you. It's like riding a bike."

"There's one other thing I have to get straight."

"You're procrastinating, Dae."

"Not anymore."

He closed the front door and I leaned against him, kissing him gently on the lips.

"That's what I thought," he whispered as he put his
arms around me and drew me closer.

"What?" I murmured with what felt like a permanent
smile on my face.

"We've wasted a lot of time."

We talked and laughed through salad, lasagna and
a very good wine served in the vintage bar off the huge
dining room. There were candles on the table, and the
French doors stood open a little to catch the scent and
sound of the sea.

"What's the first thing you ever found for anyone?" he asked as he dished up his new dessert, a raspberry version of tiramisu.

"I don't know. My mother always said I walked around finding things when I was a baby. A toddler, I guess. Keys, change, you name it. Gramps lost his pocket watch in the basement once, and I led him right to it even though I'd never been down there."

"You have an amazing gift." He smiled at me as he sat back down. "I'm surprised you never tried to exploit it."

"I did a little in college. I used to take five dollars from my friends to find things for them. That's as close as I ever came to making money that way. My mom and my grandfather drummed it into me that my gift was only supposed to help others. They said it would go away if I did anything bad with it."

"It has to belong to the person," he quoted me, "and it can't be illegal."

"That's right. So I hope your missing wine fits my rules."

"You won't know until you try." He sobered and held both his hands out to me. "Will you try?"

I was a little tipsy from too much wine and too happy to protest. If he needed to find some wine, I wanted to help him. I stripped off the gloves and took his hands.

Immediately I felt the normal (for me) sensations of being in someone else's mind. I shook all over and felt a kind of cold detachment as I searched for the cask of wine he was missing. My fingers tingled holding his hands.

It was a lot like walking through someone's personal attic, looking at everything they found precious and some things they wanted to keep hidden. I'd done it for so long that it was second nature to me.

I opened my eyes when I clearly saw the old wine cask.

"It's in the root cellar around back. The man who delivered it got confused and left it there."

Kevin smiled and didn't let go of my hands. "You've still got it!"

I considered his words. "I do, don't I?" I didn't tell him I already knew my gift was still there.

"Let's go see if we can find it!"

We walked around back, the quiet night well lit by the moon. Kevin brought a flashlight anyway. "Have you been back here before?" I asked as an owl called from the trees.

"A lot while I was working on the floors. They were in really good shape. Some things were built to last forever."

"No bones from previous owners?"

"No. If Bunk Whitley is entombed here, I couldn't find him. Neither could the parade of building inspectors who passed through."

Bunk Whitley was a legendary figure in Duck. He was the original owner of the Blue Whale. His exploits, and sudden disappearance, were all the stuff of lore. People had speculated that he was killed by one of his enemies and hidden in the old inn somewhere. With the place abandoned for so long, it was easy to imagine it was true. Still, if he wasn't here, he had to be somewhere. He might wash up someday.

Kevin opened the doors to the root cellar and walked carefully down the stairs until he was swallowed by the blackness below. I followed him, my feet sliding a little on the moss-covered steps.

"There it is!" He panned the flashlight beam across the area. "You're good, Dae."

"Thanks." I wasn't expecting it when he leaned over and kissed me, but I can't say I didn't welcome it—kissing

Kevin was a lot more fun than looking for a missing cask of wine.

He handed me the flashlight (made at a factory in China where they employed small children), then hoisted the cask on his shoulder before we started back out of the damp cellar.

"You know, this place might not be too bad for storing a few things," he said.

"Maybe. If you don't mind it being flooded occasionally." The place was filled with roly-poly bugs, spiders and probably a snake or two I didn't see. Not exactly the romantic spot I'd expected to be in.

The flashlight beam shone on something stuck against the side wall of the cellar. I reached for it without thinking and the touch exploded in my brain.

Chapter 8

It was a gold coin, a cousin to the one I'd given Chief Michaels. It was from the same chest that had washed up on the beach all those years ago. The one Max claimed to have found and donated to the museum.

But this time I had a clear vision of the man who'd actually found the gold. I saw him as he walked down the beach to retrieve the chest. I knew who he was. I recognized him from the old microfiche versions of the *Duck Gazette* that had been stored at the museum. Gone forever now, except in some of our memories.

"Dae?" Kevin called my name with a fierce concern that brought me back to myself.

"It was Bunk Whitley who found the gold." I realized I was sitting on wet ground that was oozing moss and other things I didn't want to think about. "My dress!"

Kevin pulled me to my feet. He must've left the wine

cask outside already because it occurred to me that he had two free hands. "Are you okay?"

"I'm fine." I brushed the sand and soil from the back of my dress, the dress I wanted to keep forever as a reminder that sometimes you just needed to take a chance.

I showed him the gold coin I'd found in the wall. "It's like the ones at the museum."

"I've been down here a hundred times in the daylight and didn't see it." He examined the coin. "Does it have anything to do with what happened at the museum?"

"Not as far as I can tell. Maybe Bunk Whitley stored the gold here for a while after he found it. I realize now that both times that I handled the coins, he was involved." I explained about Max's tale, the only story the town knew, of when he'd found the treasure on the beach. "Why would Max lie? And how did he get the gold?"

"Maybe he didn't want to be associated with old Bunk. From what you've told me, Bunk was a gangster-type figure around here. Or maybe he took it after Bunk disappeared."

"I'm afraid what I'm seeing when I touch the coin isn't very helpful. The vision ends with Bunk picking up the chest and walking back down the beach."

"Maybe that's all there is from that particular moment in time. Not everything has deeper meaning—at least not that we can see right away," he said. "Let's get out of here and crack open this cask upstairs. I might have something dry you can put on."

I picked up the flashlight again and followed him out of the cellar. I wasn't as convinced as Kevin seemed to be that the visions I was seeing by touching these items held any special significance. Of course, maybe I was just skeptical because I didn't have enough experience with this new ability. I was used to being able to tell people right away where their lost treasures were, like I had with the wine cask. This new ability was completely different.

Just a little depressed about the general, seemingly useless information I'd gathered so far, I walked ahead of Kevin to open the back door for him. The moon had gone behind some clouds, leaving the dark night feeling empty. One thing was for sure—I seemed destined to have one of the gold coins. Kevin had insisted I should keep it, not caring when I told him it could be valuable.

He made a fire in the big stone hearth that was the focal point in the drawing room upstairs. I had to pass on one of the old dresses he'd found while working on the Blue Whale. Even as I reached for it, I worried that it might have too much emotional energy attached to it.

It was possible no one had worn any of the dresses since the inn was closed, unlike clothes I had in Missing Pieces that had been bought and sold many times over. Kevin said he'd had everything dry cleaned, but I doubted even a good cleaning would remove the memories those clothes could hold.

I got the gloves from the dining room table where I'd left them and started putting them back on. Kevin stopped me. "What if this new ability is meant to enhance the one you already have?"

"I don't care. I don't think I want it."

"What if I can help you control it?" The words hung between us like a sail puffed up with wind that had nowhere to go.

"I know you think this is a good thing, Kevin. And I understand about your girlfriend, but—"

"I didn't say Ann was my girlfriend," he countered. "Is that something you picked up from me when you were looking for the wine?"

I shrugged. "Only intuition. I don't see people's memories, at least not right now. Or I guess I should say I didn't see any memories in your head. You talked about her like the two of you were involved."

He sat down on the sofa and poked the fire, the light emphasizing grim lines in his face. "She and I were going to be married."

I would've sat down on the sofa next to him and offered whatever words of comfort I could dredge up, but I was conscious of my dirty dress. "I'm sorry. I didn't mean to remind you of bad memories."

"That's okay." He smiled at me. "You were right. You've got some great intuition too. Maybe you should work for the FBI."

"Thanks. But I don't think so." I sighed and held the gloves, looking at them. "How would I learn to control it?"

"Sit down, Dae," he said, and when I wouldn't, he fetched a towel for me to sit on.

We were close together, facing each other, the firelight throwing shadows across the room. He took my hands in his and told me to focus.

"The only thing we can control about the things that happen to us is our reaction. I learned that at the beginning of my FBI career. In your case, the only thing you can control is your reaction to what you touch. You have to get ready for it mentally, then keep it from affecting you on a deeper level."

"And how do I do that?" It sounded hopeless to me.

"Close your eyes and concentrate. Know that you're going to be affected and be ready for it. Did you ever play softball?"

"A little in school."

"It's like that. You mentally prepare yourself to catch

the ball as it comes toward you. You know it's coming, and your brain gets ready to catch it by working out its trajectory and speed."

"Okay. I think for me that might be more like riding a wave," I explained. "When I used to surf, I'd watch and wait for the right wave, then get ready for it as it came at me."

"That's it exactly! Prepare yourself in that same way for the feeling that's going to come at you from something you touch," he said. "Then when it happens, you won't be so thrown by it."

My eyes popped open. I was feeling a little silly and very vulnerable discussing my inner workings with him. I also couldn't help wondering if this was something he had suggested to Ann to help her. "That's a great idea, Kevin. I'll try it right now with this dress."

"Are you sure?" He picked up the strawberry-colored dress he'd brought out for me. "Maybe you should practice on a few of your own things first."

I looked at the pretty red dress. It was made in a style from the 1940s, maybe even earlier. Wide shoulders, narrow waist, it was satin covered in a delicate lacework. "I think I can do it."

"All right. If you're sure. Think of it like the next wave," he encouraged. "You're prepared for it. You know what's going to happen when you touch it. Create a space between you and the outside emotions."

I was determined to best this new ability. I had prepared mentally my whole life to handle this kind of thing. I never knew for sure what would happen when I went into someone's head to help them find something they'd lost.

I swallowed hard on my fear, tried to think about controlling what I'd feel from the dress, and reached out to touch it.

It would be so simple. Close your eyes and walk into the water. No more pain. I gasped as emotions flooded through me.

The dress was handmade for a woman named Adelaide. Her nickname was Addie. She met here frequently with Bunk Whitley. The two shared a clandestine love affair. Addie was married and had a child. She was happy sometimes, but there was too much heartache.

Her sorrow swallowed me, drowning me in a wave I couldn't swim out of.

"Dae!" Kevin called my name several times with urgency. "Get out of it! Control it!"

One minute I was drowning and the next I was sitting on the floor, gasping for air. "I think she was wearing this dress right before she killed herself. She was standing at the window over there thinking about drowning herself." I tried to breathe and talk at the same time. I ended up coughing. "She killed herself because of Bunk Whitley."

Kevin put his arms around me and held me for a long time, both of us sitting on the floor in front of the fire that crackled and steamed as it burned down. "Never mind. Forget what I said about controlling it." He kissed the top of my head. "Maybe you should just wear the damn gloves. That was too much. I thought I'd lost you."

I leaned my head on his shoulder, recovering from the feelings left in the dress from so many years ago. Glad I hadn't actually put it on. "There was no way to know what would happen. I had to try it. I wonder if anyone knows what happened to Adelaide."

Kevin offered but I decided against any more wine. My head was starting to ache. He drove me home in the moonlight, the back roads without streetlights strangely illuminated. Shadows of the past played in the darkness, refusing to come out where they could be seen and understood. Duck's sometimes strange past would always haunt this place, even if someday people finally forgot Rafe the pirate.

Kevin kissed me good night at the door to the house. "Lunch tomorrow? I can't make breakfast. I have a delivery."

"Sure. I'll call you if anything comes up."

"Be careful, Dae." He touched my face and smiled. "I don't want to lose you."

"You won't," I promised before I went inside. I locked the door and faced Gramps. He was grinning like a Jolly Roger as he played with his white beard.

"So? You're awfully late, young woman. What have you been up to?"

"Like you weren't watching through the peephole!" I hugged him, glad to be home despite the excitement of the evening. "What a night."

"Care to share over some hot cocoa?"

"Not tonight." I smiled and headed up to my room. "It's been a long day and I'm too tired to think. Can we talk in the morning?"

"Sure, honey. Sleep well."

But I didn't sleep, at least not for a while. I crept up to the old widow's walk on the roof and looked out over the sound. From here, above the trees and most of the other houses, I could even glimpse the moonlit ocean.

Widow's walks were designed for ship captains' wives who watched for their husbands to come home. Many times they were already widows who wouldn't know for months, sometimes years, that their husbands had been taken by the sea.

The rooftop walk was a very quiet, kind of moody place that had always enchanted me. I was brought up on tales of shipwrecks and legendary pirate figures that made death at sea almost romantic. Even in the summer when I had to fend off bats who liked the spot as much as I did, I loved to come up here.

I could imagine those poor women waiting for their men. As a child, I always wondered why they didn't go to sea with them. Gramps told me it was because women weren't welcome on ships back then. It seemed to me that I would've found a way. There were female pirates who captained their own vessels. I would've been one of them.

But tonight my rooftop walkway was too full of sorrow and the ghosts from the past. I went back to my room and finally fell asleep dreaming that I was wearing the red lace dress, waiting for Kevin to come home.

The next day was busy at Missing Pieces. Not so much with people buying my stuff as with people stopping in because it had begun to trickle out that I had been hurt when the museum exploded. Everyone wanted to know what had happened, play by play.

I explained what I could, then told them all to come to the meeting that night. I hoped the chief had thought about what he was going to say to the anxious citizens of Duck. I was still working on my piece.

More than a few people asked about the pirate curse. I tried to assure them that Rafe hadn't blown up the museum, despite what they might have heard. I had the feeling most of them didn't believe me. It was almost like a "poor Dae" kind of thing. They smiled and patted me on the head or the arm as they looked at my gloved hands. I could almost hear them talking outside the shop: *"Poor Dae hurt her head and now she doesn't know what's going on."*

Tim stopped in before lunch to ask me to eat with him.

When I told him I already had plans, he shrugged and said, "I have some new information about the museum."

He was obviously dangling a carrot in front of me. I decided to bite. "Okay."

"I thought I could tell you what I found out over lunch. The Rib Shack has a special today."

"Thanks." Why did he always invite me to go to the Rib Shack with him? He knew I didn't like eating there. "I can't today. But I'd love to know what's going on with the investigation."

"It's Kevin, isn't it? Old Man Sweeney said he thought he saw him drive you home late last night. You two have finally hooked up, haven't you? What about us?"

It was bad enough to know Gramps was looking out the peephole when Kevin kissed me good night at the door. It was another thing to know Mr. Sweeney was reporting my movements to Tim. "You recently dated Betsy Marlin, that accountant from Kill Devil Hills. Before that, it was Shayla, and before that it was Trudy. Why can't I date someone?"

His face lightened. "You mean like sowing your wild oats out before we settle down? I didn't think of that!"

"I don't think I have any wild oats." I didn't like the turn of the conversation.

"Just tell me you don't love me, Dae O'Donnell, and I'll go away and never darken your door again. Look me in the eyes and tell me."

I put my hands on my hips, stood close to him and looked him squarely in the eyes. "I know we've known each other all our lives, Tim. But I don't love you, not that way. You're like the brother I never had. Happy now? What else do you know about the museum?"

He frowned. "You don't mean it. You're infatuated with Kevin right now. You'll get over it. I'll be here waiting."

"Great. Museum? Spill it."

He looked over his shoulder. "I shouldn't tell you—"

"Go ahead before someone else comes in."

"Chief Michaels had the cannon at the Corolla Historical Museum picked up this morning for testing. Ballistics is going to take a look at it in Manteo. And they can't find Sam Meacham. They want to question him, but he's disappeared."

"Disappeared? Where?"

"Duh! Now who's the dummy? That's the nature of disappearing, Dae." He goaded me. "No one can find you."

"Thanks for explaining."

"This proves Sam is guilty of killing Max," he went on. "No one runs unless they're guilty."

Despite his logic, I didn't agree. I managed to get him out of the shop, then went to meet Kevin for lunch at Wild Stallions, a little bar and grill tucked into a corner of the boardwalk. I told Kevin what Tim had said, and we talked about it over sandwiches and homemade chips.

"Why are you so sure Sam is innocent?" Kevin asked. "You know they argued earlier that day. A cannon is an unusual choice of weapon for people who aren't historians or museum caretakers. I agree with Chief Michaels on this."

"It might make sense in a computer/law enforcement kind of way." I knew what he was getting at. I'd grown up with Gramps working as the sheriff of Dare County. "But even though Max and Sam argued, they were really good friends. Sam wouldn't get so mad after all these years that he'd drag a cannon down from Corolla to kill Max."

"Sometimes even the best of friends go too far. Maybe Max finding a DNA match to prove his theory about Theodosia Burr was too much. We all have breaking points."

I sipped my water and thought about it. "Even if he

was that mad, Sam would never destroy so much history. I might be convinced that he could do something to Max, I guess, but *never* blow up the museum."

He shrugged. "Only one way to know for sure."

"Find Sam. I know. He's gotta be around here somewhere. Maybe I should drive out there this afternoon. If I can find him, he might talk to me."

"You'll be stepping into the middle of an active police investigation," he reminded me. "Need some help?"

"Sure! Can you spare the time?"

"Let's see, waterproof some windows at the inn or go with one of my favorite people to Corolla on a beautiful, sunny afternoon. Tough choice."

"*One* of your favorites, huh?" I grinned. "When you put it that way—"

He paid the check and got to his feet. "I'm all yours."

Corolla wasn't that far from Duck, but everyone seemed to like the idea of a drive that afternoon. Maybe it was the brilliant blue skies and glimpses of curling surf topped with windblown white caps. The sun was warm, and we all knew less beautiful winter weather was coming. It looked as though a lot of people were putting off things they should have been doing—which left us all bumper to bumper, moving toward Corolla like a parade.

"If the chief is saying Sam has disappeared, he must've checked his house and the museum already." I tried to think of the next most obvious place to look for him. "There's a little diner he liked to hang out at. I went there a few times with Max and Sam. Maybe we should check there first."

"I think we should scout out the obvious places too,"

Kevin said. "You have unique abilities Chief Michaels doesn't have, even with your gloves on."

"You mean I should try to find someone who might think of Sam as being lost? I've never tried that before. I suppose there could be a first time." I looked at my telltale gloved hands. "It would have to be someone close to him who's wondering where he is. Otherwise, maybe I could grab something Sam owns and it would tell me something."

"No!" The command in his voice surprised me. "I don't think I can go through seeing you that way again, Dae. I agree that you aren't ready yet."

That was an unexpected tack. "I thought you said I should practice."

"With safe, familiar objects first. We don't know what's happened to Sam yet. Trying to use your new abilities to find him from something he owns might be a mistake. I meant that you have an unusual way of looking at things and seeing things that other people miss. Just don't touch any of them."

"Maybe," I halfheartedly agreed. "If I saw the chief and could convince him to hold my hand, I could probably pick something up from him. That's not likely to happen."

"Chief Michaels believes in your gift," he said. "He might be willing."

"He might be if he didn't think I was trying to figure out his case for him. The chief is kind of funny about that. And Corolla's police chief is even worse. Gramps said he's got a mind like a steel trap that's permanently closed."

Kevin laughed. "Sounds like a lot of people I used to work with."

I thought about his partner, Ann, but didn't say anything. There might be a time for us to talk about her and their relationship, but this wasn't it. What we had together was too new. It would be like taking someone to meet your parents right after flirting with them for the first time.

Corolla was bigger than Duck, with many more businesses, homes and, of course, the lighthouse. Max always felt cheated that Duck didn't have a historic lighthouse. On the other hand, Duck had a pirate curse, so that kind of made up for it.

The lighthouse sat in the middle of historic Corolla Village. Since 1875, it had warned sailors of dangerous waters. Kevin and I got out of the truck and looked at it. Unfortunately, it didn't warn unwary investigators of possible dangers coming from behind.

The unmistakable sound of a shotgun getting ready to fire was followed by a gruff voice. "Who the hell are you and what do you want?"

Chapter 9

I put up my hands in the air in what might've been a comical fashion had there not been a shotgun pointed at me, and turned to face the man holding the weapon. It was Mr. Artiz, the Corolla lighthouse keeper. "Hi there. Remember me? Dae O'Donnell? I've been here lots of times with Sam and Max."

He squinted one eye and looked me up and down. "So you are." He pointed the gun at Kevin, who *didn't* have his hands held high. "Who's he?"

"Kevin Brickman, sir." He put out his hand toward Mr. Artiz. "I'm here with Dae. We're looking for Sam."

Mr. Artiz put down the gun. He wore a red cap on his grizzled head. "Join the crowd. So's everyone else."

"You mean the police?" I asked, calmer now that a gun wasn't pointed at me.

"I guess. One or two of them said who they were with.

The others didn't. That's why I brought old Betsy out here with me."

"I understand," I said, although I didn't. "Would you mind if we have a look around?"

"You might as well. There can't be much in there that they haven't looked at."

Each lighthouse in the Outer Banks is painted a different color or pattern. The Currituck Beach lighthouse, as it's known, is the only red brick lighthouse on the East Coast. It still flashes at twenty-second intervals to warn of shallow water.

The lighthouse and the keeper's home at its base aren't technically a part of the museum, but both are open to the public. I knew Sam and Mr. Artiz had been friends forever. I wasn't surprised when he followed us into the museum.

"I haven't seen Sam since the day after your museum blew up," the old caretaker told us. "What a terrible thing that was. I hope you find out what happened." He walked us back to Sam's office at the side of the Corolla museum, which was much larger than Duck's had been. "The place looks like a hurricane hit it, I'll tell you that much, Dae."

He was right. There were papers, boxes and photos scattered everywhere from the desk to the dusty file cabinets and the floor. But no sign of Sam.

"Do the police think something like that could happen here?" he asked me. "Is that why they're making such a fuss?"

I glanced at Kevin, who shrugged. I interpreted that to mean I should go for it. "The police think Sam killed Max by blowing him up in the Duck museum," I told him. I couldn't say it any plainer than that.

"That's crazy talk! Sam and Max were like brothers."

"Brothers who argued violently all the time," Kevin reminded him.

"Maybe they argued, but they wouldn't hurt each other. The police are climbing up the wrong mast." He looked around the office. "You think Sam left quick once he heard?"

"I don't know," I admitted. "I guess I was hoping I could figure that out."

"Well, you take your time. I don't know if the police or those other fellas left anything useful behind in this mess. But you're welcome to it if they did. Say hello to Horace for me."

"You don't have any idea who the other *fellas* were?" Kevin asked. "Were they wearing uniforms? Could they have been with the sheriff's department?"

Mr. Artiz shrugged his bony shoulders beneath a blue overall. "I never seen them before. They didn't introduce themselves."

He left us alone in the maelstrom that was Sam's office. I didn't know where to start. Everything was such a mess. How would we ever find something useful that might lead us to Sam?

"What kind of things did Sam do outside the office?" Kevin started sorting through the papers on a chair.

"He liked to fish. I remember hearing him and Gramps talk about that a lot. He chartered Gramps's boat once. Otherwise I don't know. Everything I know about him was through seeing him with Max or Max telling me things about him."

I looked around the room, letting my eyes play on everything without focusing too hard on any of it. I was thinking about the way I'd found the gold coin in Kevin's cellar last night. Maybe there was something here, however remote, that could lead us to Sam.

It occurred to me as I swept the room that everything seemed to be out of place except for one item—a horse statue on one of the old file cabinets. Once I saw it, I couldn't look away. My gaze was constantly drawn back to it.

I wished I could go out and grab the lightkeeper's hands to find out where Sam was, but I suspected the link between them wouldn't be strong enough. A person had to have a strong desire to find something in order for me to see it in their head. That meant there was only one thing left to do.

As I continued looking at the horse figure, I was conscious of Kevin moving around the room, trying to help. I slowly removed one of my gloves and reached for the little statue, ignoring its place of origin and other nonproductive impressions.

Salt air. Waves crashing on the northern Currituck Beach. The sounds of horses. A man shaking hands with Sam.

"I know where he is!" I was pleased that the contact might make some difference. And that I hadn't ended up on the floor.

Kevin looked at the statue in my hand. "Are you all right?"

"I think so. Maybe the impression wasn't as forceful as touching pirate gold that people have died for. This little horse has probably been sold in every gift shop in the Outer Banks, although it wasn't made in China."

He smiled. "Where do you think he is?"

"With the mustangs."

The wild Spanish mustangs were a must-see for every tourist who came to the Outer Banks. Like the lighthouses, they were a legacy of our past that seemed to end-lessly fascinate people.

Unlike the lighthouses, the mustangs didn't stay in one place. For those willing to pay ridiculously high prices, tour companies *guaranteed* that visitors would see the horses, but it didn't necessarily work out that way.

The mustangs were said to be descendants of Spanish horses that had made it to shore following a sixteenth-century shipwreck. They roamed the Outer Banks freely for centuries, providing working partners for the Bankers, until development came and the horses became endan-gered. Now they were managed and taken care of, but never tamed.

"Sam could be anywhere along thirty miles of coast-line," I explained to Kevin.

"We could ask around. See if one of the tour guides took him out."

"He knows the area too well to ask for help."

"Tell me what you saw."

I told him about Sam shaking hands with a man who was close to the horses and the beach. "But that could be anywhere."

"Would he be likely to hike out there?"

"Probably not." I smiled. "He's as physically chal-lenged as Max. Neither one of them ever walked where they could drive. But as far as I know, he doesn't have an SUV or a Jeep. A regular car would have a hard time going in to look for the horses."

"How else could he get there?"

"Maybe he got a ride from someone. Maybe Mr. Artiz knows who that could be."

We went to find him. He was sitting on the lighthouse stairs, cleaning his shotgun. He glanced up and frowned when he saw us coming. "Now what?"

"How would Sam go out to see the horses?" I asked.

"I don't know. How does anyone get out there?"

"Does he know anyone with an SUV or some other four-wheeler?" Kevin asked with a little more authority in his voice.

It didn't matter. "I don't keep tabs on Sam."

"Thanks anyway." Either he didn't know or he didn't want to say.

As Kevin and I began walking away, the lighthouse keeper called out, "Could be one of those mall-cop things, like in the movies."

"Mall-cop thing?" Kevin wondered aloud.

"Segway!" I knew exactly what he meant. "I saw the ads for them on TV. Thanks, Mr. Artiz!"

We got back in Kevin's truck. He was still mystified. I explained. "They're those tall motorized scooters you balance on. I'll show you. There's a place out here that rents them."

We parked at the outfitters place, and I rented two Segways, complete with helmets and maps to the wild horses. The man at the front counter kept trying to sell us a guide until I told him I'd been out plenty of times to see the mustangs. "Have you rented one of these recently to Sam Meacham?"

He glanced at his book of rentals. There weren't many on the page since it was a slow time of the year. "Yeah, sure. He was here a few days ago. He was taking a man out to see the horses, like you, Mayor O'Donnell."

"Do I know you?"

"I recognize your name from your driver's license and credit card. I heard it on the news report about the museum exploding. Hope that doesn't happen here. Do you think it really was the pirate ghost?"

"Of course not!" I told him. "Thanks."

"What did the man with Meacham look like?" Kevin asked the outfitter.

"I don't know." He thought back. "Medium height. Maybe brown hair. He had a two-way radio. Could be a highway worker."

"Thanks."

"If you see them, tell them I need the Segways back. Normally I'd call the police, but it's Sam and everything. But I still need them back."

The Segways were a lot easier to balance on than I'd thought they'd be. In no time, we were both up and going down the hard-packed sand at the edge of the beach.

The air was fresh and cool, drawing large groups of people to the beach. Huge kites were flying across the whitecaps on the water. One man with a large, purple kite was actually having trouble keeping his feet on the sand. The wind picked him up again and again, threatening to take him out to sea. Finally, two more people joined him to help hold the kite. There was a reason Orville and Wilbur Wright came down here from Ohio to fly their airplane.

There were heavy bushes and some squat trees where the path wandered. At times I couldn't see the water. The steady hum of the Segway motors and the whirr of the wide tires ate up the distance down the coast.

We stopped near a small group of mustangs—a mare, a stallion and a colt standing on the beach. A group of tourists were snapping pictures while the horses posed calmly for them.

"I hope there are more horses than these," Kevin remarked. "I don't see Sam here."

"There are a lot of horses out here. I'm hoping we'll run into some of the Wild Horse Preservation Society that manages the herd. One of them might know Sam."

He nodded and we got back on our Segways. From that point on, it was as common to see the horses as it was to see the statues of them that littered the Outer Banks. Large groups of them gathered to munch on the grass between the sand dunes and sea oats. Young stallions bucked and played with one another. A mare nursed her colt. It was inspiring to see them living so free.

I pointed to one of the Wild Horse trailers near the old life station, and we slowed our Segways again. "Not a bad way to travel," Kevin said.

"It's fast anyway." I didn't want to mention that I felt gritty all over from the sand flying up as we moved. "Let's check in with them."

A burly man in a green sweater who was smoking a pipe greeted us at the trailer with a hearty handshake. He introduced himself as Tom Watts, one of the local Wild Horse workers.

"I'm looking for Sam Meacham from the Corolla Historical Museum," I said when I could get my hand back. "Have you seen him?"

"Of course! He was here yesterday. He was taking his friend around to see the horses."

"Medium height, brown hair?" Kevin guessed.

"That's right. I can't recall his name. He was in a hurry. Sometimes people have to be patient. The horses aren't here for our amusement even though it may seem like that to some."

"Any idea which way they went?" I asked him.

"I told them we had a group of people from the mainland down here doing a study on the horses. They're about two miles up from here. Sam went that way with his friend."

"Thanks." I made the mistake of shaking his hand again. As we went back to our Segways, Kevin said he was glad the descriptions of the man with Sam matched. "Is that what you saw when you were holding the horse statue?"

"I really only saw them shaking hands." I shrugged. "The other man was wearing some kind of ring with an unusual design. I couldn't tell you what right now, but I'd know it if I saw it again. I know that's not very helpful."

"It's all we've got right now. You've managed to track Sam this far, which is more than the police could do."

We roamed the trails for another few hours, but it was getting late. We hadn't seen many horses and couldn't find the group Tom had told us about. We were about to turn back when we both noticed a Segway parked in a heavy thicket.

Thrilled that we'd found it, I got off of my scooter quickly, but Kevin held me back. "Let's take it easy here. We don't know what's going on."

It was very quiet at this far end of the island. There was only one Segway and no sign of Sam or his friend. Kevin searched through the thicket and further up along the path, but found nothing.

"It could belong to someone else," I suggested, looking around, probably not as efficiently as him.

"There doesn't seem to be any sign of a struggle or any problem. Just to be on the safe side, let's call in the serial number and see if it matches up to what the outfitter in Corolla has listed for Sam."

It was a good idea, but of course, there was no cell phone signal. We tried his phone and mine. Both spent all their time searching for service.

"It's no use. We can't find out like this." Kevin put his cell phone away.

"There's another way."

"I know what you mean, Dae. I don't know if it's a good idea. There's no way of knowing what you might see."

I took off one glove and approached the scooter. I agreed with Kevin that the Segway might show me something I wouldn't like to see. On the other hand, it might reveal something important. We were too far from Tom Watts's trailer to go back and see if he had some adequate form of communication. And I had to be back in Duck for the town meeting or the chief would get kind of riled.

"This might be the only way to know where Sam is. I think that's important enough to take a chance. If I fall on the ground again, just leave me there. I'll get up eventually."

He came to stand behind me and slid his arms around my waist. "How about if we prepare for that problem and I won't let you fall. Be careful, Dae. If there's something you see that doesn't look right, get out."

"Do you think something has happened to Sam?"

"I don't know. I've had a bad feeling about this since we saw his office at the museum. And finding only one Segway isn't a good sign."

"You could've said something."

"I'm not intuitive." He shrugged. "I'd rather let you lead the way."

"As long as you're my backup, that's fine." I smiled at him and we briefly kissed before I put out my hand and grasped the handle on the scooter.

Running. Lungs burning. Fear, terrible fear. Blackness. Nothing.

I pulled away from it, gasping, but in better control than I had been with Adelaide's dress.

"All right?" Kevin asked, his arms around me. "What did you see?"

"I'm fine." I moved away from him, staring back at the scooter. "Sam was here. Someone was chasing him. He thought his life was in danger. He ran until he couldn't run anymore. That's all I could see. I think something terrible happened to him out here. We have to tell someone."

"All right. We'll have to go back to the trailer and call for help. If the cell phones won't work there, I noticed a ham radio antenna. We could use that."

"That means calling the Corolla police." I grabbed my scooter. "Chief Michaels isn't going to like this."

"Dae O'Donnell." Corolla Police Chief Walt Peabody got off his ATV and walked toward us, removing his sunglasses as he came. He was a lean, hard man whose pale gray uniform matched the frigid gray of his eyes. In the lifetime I had known him, first as an officer (he gave me my first speeding ticket) and then as the chief, I had never seen him smile. "You can't cause enough trouble in Duck. You have to come down here."

Sam and Max weren't the only ones in Duck and Corolla with competition issues. Chief Michaels and Chief Peabody never had a good word for each other. They could be equally as uncivil with residents they felt overstepped their bounds.

"Chief, I'm not here to cause any trouble. I'm sure you know that Sam is missing—"

"Yeah. We've had an APB out on him since we searched his home and office. We're doing so in an effort to assist the Duck police. You didn't have to come up here and check on us."

"I wasn't," I said flatly. "I came up to help find Sam. I think he might be in trouble." I told him what I knew of Sam's disappearance without divulging information I'd gathered from his personal effects. I didn't think Chief Peabody would believe me.

"That's real nice of you, Mayor. But we can take care

of our own. And I'm sure you know that calling us out like this isn't a good idea unless you know something pertinent to finding Sam."

I glanced at Kevin and the answer came to me. "We have reason to suspect that Sam has met with foul play."

Chief Peabody looked at Kevin too. "Is this your lawyer, Mayor? Is he helping you look for Sam?"

"I'm Kevin Brickman." He stepped forward and shook hands with the chief. "I own the Blue Whale Inn."

"I heard about you." The chief squinted at him, the sun in his eyes. "Helping her meddle in police affairs isn't a good idea."

"Mayor O'Donnell does have some pertinent information." Kevin told him about the man with Sam.

"How did you figure out Sam was out here at all?" the chief asked.

"We talked to the outfitter," I answered. "Then we spoke with Mr. Watts here, and he told us the same thing."

The chief turned his cold gray eyes on Tom Watts. "So what do you know about this? And why haven't you reported it to the police?"

"I didn't know the police were interested," Tom said. "News doesn't make it this far out very quickly. I've been here for the last two weeks. I told Dae that I saw Sam with the man she described. That's it. They said they were going to see the horses."

"I think we found Sam's Segway about half a mile from here," I added.

"What makes you think it belongs to Sam?" Chief Peabody questioned.

"I don't know for sure." I shrugged. "But there is an abandoned Segway over there and it might belong to Sam. It shouldn't be hard to check out the identification number and find out. I can call if you want me to."

The chief's face hardened into an even more disapproving expression, if that were possible. "I think we can handle this from here, Mayor. No offense, but it's best for civilians like yourself and Mr. Brickman to mind your own business. We don't need any of your hocus-pocus down here in Corolla to maintain the law. Have a nice day."

Chapter 10

It was getting late, and there was no way to argue with Chief Peabody without telling him about the hocus-pocus that had led me here. He called in some reinforcements and took Tom off to one side, maybe to ask for more details. Maybe not.

"We should be getting back," Kevin said. "I think he has the idea anyway."

"You could've told him you were with the FBI before. Maybe that would've made it sound more convincing."

"Former FBI agents aren't usually best buddies with the police. It's not something I advertise."

I realized my remark was out of line and apologized. "I know. I guess I didn't want to sound like a nut job. You're right, though. At least they're going to look for him. I hope they find him and he's okay."

"But you don't think so, do you?"

I couldn't answer. The visions were too new. The darkness at the end of the fear and the running could mean anything. I was taking it to mean that something bad had happened, but maybe not. I truly hoped not.

We headed back to Corolla on the sand trails and turned in the Segways when we got there. I still needed time to go home and change before the town meeting. I wasn't looking forward to it, especially since I was coming home from Corolla without anything new to share.

"I know I'm not in law enforcement," I said to Kevin as we got back in his pickup. "But Sam's actions don't seem to be those of a man who's running away because he killed someone."

Kevin nodded. "I agree. I wouldn't go get on one of those things and head out into the island. Logic dictates Sam going to the mainland and hiding out. Too many people know him here. That's a bad thing, unless there's someone willing to hide you."

"I know it's not enough to keep him out of jail if the police really believe he blew up the museum and killed Max. But maybe it might make them think about it differently."

"Maybe. If he has a good alibi, that would be a lot better. It's hard to beat a good alibi."

"I guess we won't know unless they find him."

"You've done what you could for now." He smiled at me. "At great personal risk too, I might add. I don't know if I would've touched that scooter not knowing what I might find. You're a brave person."

"And foolish." I laughed. "Don't bother to deny it. I can hear it in your voice."

We'd reached my house, and I hopped out of the truck after it had pulled in the driveway. "Foolish? I don't know. Crazy might be more like it."

"Thanks!" I slammed the truck door. "See you at the meeting."

The house was quiet and dark when I got inside. Gramps had left a note on the kitchen table telling me that he was out doing volunteer fire department drills and that there was a casserole in the oven.

I glanced at the casserole and decided to skip it. I grabbed a granola bar from the cabinet and went up to take a quick shower.

I opened a new bar of soap and went through all the sensations that described where and how it was made. Already it was becoming routine to me. I looked at my hands as I got washed and wondered why the explosion at the museum had triggered this effect in me.

I thought about all those times my hands had tingled when I approached something valuable. It was one of the ways I decided what to buy when I went shopping for treasures. Maybe this new ability had always been there, lying dormant, waiting for some event—the explosion in this case—to set it lose.

Kevin wanted to protect me from making mistakes that might cause me to end up like his FBI partner. But I'd realized this afternoon, when I grabbed the statue and then the scooter, that I couldn't shy away from this new aspect of my abilities. I couldn't protect myself from it any more than I could keep myself from getting wet in a downpour.

It was here. It was part of me. Though it might be uncomfortable right now, I knew I'd master it. I'd learned from the best when my mother had taught me as a child. I appreciated Kevin's guidance, definitely his backup, but with time, these new abilities and I would learn to get along fine together.

After getting out of the shower, I dried off and changed into a plum-colored knit dress that made me look like a sober and dignified mayor—with style. I wasn't ready to be too sober or dignified yet.

I looked at my slightly sunburned face as I applied plum-colored lipstick and brushed my wayward hair. I'd spent all day with Kevin. It had been an enjoyable experience. In many ways, we seemed to fill in small gaps in each other's personalities. It was exciting and nerve-wracking at the same time. What would I say to everyone, especially Shayla? I didn't want Gramps planning our wedding already, but I knew he'd be interested too.

That's one of the problems with small-town life, but it was one of the perks as well. People might be there when I didn't want them to be—but then again, they were always there when I needed them.

I smiled at myself in the mirror. Being with Kevin was different than I'd expected yet everything I'd thought it could be.

I left the house and started walking down Duck Road toward town hall along with several other people headed in the same direction. The Duck Shoppes parking lot was full, always a barometer of how well attended a meeting would be. It looked like people wanted to hear what the chief had to say about the explosion at the museum.

Shayla stopped me as I started up to the boardwalk, demanding to know where I was all afternoon. "I thought we had an appointment to go over your chakra again."

I admired the beautiful black shawl she wore with such flair. Shawls always looked awkward on me, and I was never sure what to do with them. Usually I ended up taking them off. "Sorry. I forgot. There was so much going on."

Her eyes narrowed as she looked me over. "It wouldn't have anything to do with you seeing Kevin, would it? Your chakra is a little fuzzy today but better than yesterday."

Obviously, Old Man Sweeney had been happy to share his knowledge of my whereabouts with the rest of the town. "Shayla—"

"Don't bother explaining, Dae. Kevin doesn't want me anymore. Maybe he wants you. But for how long? The man is fickle."

"I don't know," I admitted, feeling bad for her. "Look, we had dinner at the Inn so I could look for a wine cask he was missing. It wasn't anything serious."

"So you aren't dating now?" Her brown eyes narrowed, gauging my response, until I thought she might be asleep. Except for that terrible frown.

I wanted to lie. Even though I was usually jealous of Shayla and her laid-back, Big Easy attitude, I wanted to reassure her that she wasn't being left out. But how could I after what had happened between Kevin and me? Besides, there was no point in not telling her something she was bound to find out anyway. "We're sort of dating, I guess."

"Ha!" She wrapped her beautiful shawl around her slender body and marched up the stairs.

"What does that mean?" I yelled after her despite the looks from all the people who were on their way to town hall.

"It means if you lie like that, Dae, your nose could grow like the doll in the fairy tale."

I stormed up the stairs to stand beside her. "Puppet," I corrected automatically. "Pinocchio was a puppet."

"Doll. Puppet. Whatever. You *lied* to me. If you wanted Kevin, you should've said so. I asked you. You said you weren't interested."

"You dated him already and broke up with him," I reminded her. "That kind of makes him fair game."

"Fair game?" She pursed her lips. "If you weren't my friend, I'd slap you. He's not fair game. We were taking a break, that's all. We never said we wouldn't get back together again."

"Then I guess you will, *if* we break up."

She stared at me as if wishing I were a voodoo doll she could put pins in—then walked into town hall alone.

I sighed, trying not to think about it, at least not for a while. I needed to be clearheaded about what I'd say at the meeting. Then I could mull it over and decide if being with Kevin would be worth jeopardizing my friendship with Shayla.

Inside, town hall was filled to capacity. People were standing along the side walls and sitting on the floor. Nancy was scurrying around trying to find chairs for as many people as she could. "We're gonna have to find a bigger place," she huffed as she went by.

I took my spot at the head of the council table and looked at my nameplate. I chose the small, wood gavel that bore the name of the town. I was the first person to use the gavel—the first mayor since incorporation. It was an awesome responsibility sometimes. Not all ribbon cuttings and public appearances at the Jaycees'. There were times, like tonight, when a big smile wouldn't suffice.

I knew people wanted words of comfort. I could give them those words, but something about the set of Chief Michaels's mouth told me he'd be more to the point. I guessed we each had our duty to do.

When the room couldn't hold any more and the sound of so many people talking at once made my head feel like it was going to explode, I called the meeting to order. Residents sat down politely and stopped talking. Reverend Lisa gave the invocation, which included words of memorial for Max.

The room got very quiet after that. Because it wasn't a regular meeting of the town council, there were no minutes to read or town business to talk about. I started to speak, but Councilman Wilson cut me off. "We need to

know what's being done about the museum and Max Caudle's death. No fancy words are going to take care of the
problem."

Even for Randal "Mad Dog" Wilson, this was abrupt
and bordering on rude. I'd heard rumors that he planned
to challenge me for mayor in next year's election. I hadn't
expected he'd start so soon. On the other hand, when
would he ever have another audience like this one?

"I don't have any fancy words for what's happened." I
got to my feet and addressed all the people I knew so well.
"This has been a terrible time for Duck and for all of us.
The police are doing everything they can to find out who's
responsible for the explosion."

"If Chief Michaels was really doing his job, this wouldn't
have happened," Councilman Wilson continued. "I checked
today while Mayor O'Donnell was out gallivanting around
with a certain innkeeper and found out that we don't even
have a plan for a terrorist attack. What kind of preparation
is that?"

"I can't speak for Chief Michaels, and I won't defend
how I spent my day. But I would like to remind the councilman that he's been in elected office as long as I have. It
seems odd to me that he only recently realized there were
any problems in Duck."

Councilman Wilson lumbered to his feet. He was a
large man—easily six-four and three hundred pounds. "In
answer to the mayor's challenge—"

"Are we here to talk about what happened at the museum or to listen to politics?" Chief Michaels demanded.
His words were met with applause from residents. "That's
what I thought. I'm here to tell all of you what I know about
the explosion. You may not like what I have to say, but I
promise you it will be the truth."

I felt a little embarrassed, even though I was only defending myself against Councilman Wilson's attacks. I realized then the election wasn't going to be a walk in the park. I was the only one who'd run for mayor in our first municipal election. Now that I'd been mayor for two years, I was going to have to defend all my actions to everyone. Was that something I was prepared to do?

Chief Michaels was explaining what happened at the museum to the rapt audience. "We located what we believe are Mr. Caudle's remains in the building after the explosion. We're currently waiting for DNA reports to come back and confirm what we found."

"What about the pirate curse?" Joe Endy asked, raising his raspy voice to be heard in the room. "Rafe Masterson paid Max a visit, I'll be bound. He took his gold back too. Nothing much you can do about it, Chief."

"And I wouldn't even try, Mr. Endy," Chief Michaels told him. "Folks, I'm here to tell you that no pirate ghost is responsible for what happened to Max. I know all of you, some since you were kids. I like a good yarn as much as the next one, but that's all Rafe Masterson is. A real flesh-and-blood killer is responsible for Max's death and the mayor being injured. That scares me a hell of a lot more than any pirate ghost."

Mr. Endy didn't look too pleased with the chief's statement. People usually humored the ninety-year-old around here. The chief had been a little blunt by Duck standards.

"So if it's a real person responsible," began Cody Baucum, one of the owners of the Wild Stallions bar and grill on the boardwalk, "do we have any leads about who it is?"

"We're checking out every aspect of the situation," Chief Michaels replied.

"In other words, no," August Grandin said. He owned the General Store. "That's police speak for we don't know, right, Chief?"

The room kind of got out of control for a minute. I banged my gavel a few times and people began to settle down. I noticed Agnes Caudle in the back of the room as she slowly got to her feet. Seeing her there, the crowd quieted.

"I'd like to thank Chief Michaels and his officers as well as the members of the Duck Volunteer Fire Department for everything they've done. Max is gone, but he believed in this town. He wouldn't want what happened to tear us apart. We have good people here, and they do the best job they can. Shame on any of you who don't support them. That's all I came to say."

Agnes sat back down, wiping her eyes. She and Max had two daughters, who now sat on either side of their mother. I knew both of them from school. One was a little older than me and the other a little younger. I didn't get along with either one of them.

"Thank you, Agnes," Chief Michaels said, acknowledging her. "That means a lot to me and the rest of the department. We'll find out what happened to the museum, but it's gonna take some time. You all are gonna have to be patient and let the procedures work."

Kevin got to his feet. I hadn't noticed him there. "I believe you're doing what you can, Chief. I'd like to suggest we begin thinking of ways to rebuild the museum. If we really want to do something for Max, it seems like that would be what he'd want."

Everyone seemed to agree with his idea. Kevin offered to let the town use free space he had at the Blue Whale to store donations for the new museum. Vergie Smith, Duck's postmaster, volunteered to collect donations to be used for a new building that would house the artifacts.

We all agreed to hold a memorial for Max at a time and date to be announced. I called the meeting to an end, and people began to leave, slowly since they had plenty to say to their neighbors and wanted to wish Agnes well.

Everyone seemed in better spirits now that there was something concrete and positive to do rather than just waiting to hear what was going on in the investigation. People always feel better when they have a plan of action. I thought the chief had done a good job of dispelling the pirate-ghost theory and I told him so.

"Thanks, ma'am. But you know there'll be somebody who brings it up again. I think it's easier for folks around here to accept that ghosts are responsible than it is for them to accept that a real person could've done this. By the way, I got an interesting call from Chief Peabody out in Corolla today. Seems he thinks you and Brickman were down there snooping around. Were you looking for Sam?"

"Something's happened," I confessed a little. "We didn't find Sam, but we found a scooter he rented to go out and see the wild horses. He had someone with him when he left on the trip, but there was no sign of either of them near where we found the scooter. I asked Chief Peabody to check it out. He didn't seem too happy about it."

"I've told you before, Mayor, no one likes a person messing with their investigation. Sam might be a suspect in our situation, but his disappearance has to be handled by the Corolla police. You and Brickman need to stay out of it before you get in trouble. Walt Peabody isn't as indulgent as I am."

I'd never thought of Chief Michaels as *indulgent*, but I kind of agreed with him about Chief Peabody, especially given Peabody's frosty reception of Kevin and me this afternoon. I glanced around the room, looking for Kevin— he seemed to be gone already. I didn't see Shayla either. Best not to go there.

Instead, I helped Nancy clean up and put away all the extra chairs as people ambled back to their homes and businesses.

"Kevin was good tonight, huh?" Nancy asked. "He made people think about something they could do instead of everything they couldn't do. I'll have to look through my Duck memorabilia and see what I have. I think this is something we could all get behind."

"And maybe the chief will solve the case while we get behind it," I added.

Councilman Wilson coughed as he wandered up behind me. "I hope there are no hard feelings, Dae. You know I think the world of you and your grandfather. But politics is a tough business. You had it easy the first time around. It could get ugly this time. Better think before you take me on."

It was a mystery to me why Mad Dog Wilson would give up his voting privileges on the council to be the mayor. I didn't bother asking. I knew I'd find out at some point. Instead, I smiled at him—my big, mayoral smile. "With all respect, Councilman Wilson, you might want to think again before you take *me* on."

Wilson nodded in an absent manner, wandering away as he always did, examining the chairs and tabletops for dust. Clearly he hadn't expected me to talk back.

Nancy laughed. "You set him back a peg or two."

"The incumbent is hard to beat. At least that's what I've always heard."

"That's the spirit."

"Speaking of spirits, I was wondering if you'd be willing to do some research for me?" I told her what I knew about Adelaide and her death.

"So we'd be looking for someone named Adelaide who drowned on the Atlantic side." She wrote down the name on a scrap piece of paper. "Any other info you can give me?"

"No. That's all I have. I think this would've been in the 1950s. But I'm not sure about that either."

"I'll be happy to research that, sweetie. You know how I love a mystery."

The parking lot and the streets were mostly empty by the time I finished helping Nancy and left town hall. She offered me a ride home, but I wanted to walk. I waved to her as she pulled out on Duck Road.

I wasn't worried about Mad Dog Wilson. I knew Max's death and the destruction of the museum on my watch probably made him think I was vulnerable. He might be right, and he might even win the election. The one thing I had learned as mayor was that you could order more trucks of sand to build up the dunes, but you couldn't save Duck from the people who live here. And people were as unpredictable as the Atlantic.

I walked down to the spot where the museum had been, hoping to find some clue I'd missed that had been left behind by the thorough investigation. Not a single piece of wood, artifact or rock was there. Only the bare concrete pad, blackened by shadows and the fire, remained as mute testimony that the museum had once stood there.

It would've been a good time to contact Max's ghost—I had no doubt it was hovering close by his favorite spot. Maybe he had some idea about what had happened. Maybe he even knew who'd killed him. If wishing could make it happen, one of those shadows chasing the breeze would be him and he would tell me what I needed to know.

But I wasn't Shayla, and even if I were, it wouldn't necessarily mean I could contact him. The dead seemed to like to keep their own secrets, leaving us to discover them as best we could.

I walked back home to find Gramps in his chair with his feet up. He was watching *Dancing with the Stars*—one of his favorite shows. My mother had told me that he and Grandma had loved to dance when they were younger. They had even won several trophies. "Well?" he asked when he saw me.

I filled him in on what happened during the meeting—and after.

He laughed. "I guess Mad Dog thought he could get you to give up early before he had to work too hard."

"Why does everyone call him Mad Dog? He seems pretty tame to me."

"He used to be a stock car driver. He was fearless—until his car caught fire after a wreck. He was in pretty bad shape for a while. Never raced again. Maybe that's why he went into insurance."

"Well, I don't plan to give up. He might beat me, though, if we can't figure out what happened to Max. You know he'll use that against me."

"Ronnie will figure it out," he assured me, eyes on the figures dancing across the TV screen again. "You'll see."

"Thanks." I kissed his cheek. "Good night, Gramps."

"Good night, honey. Sleep tight."

I had just started up the stairs to my room when there was a loud knock on the front door. Being mayor meant my office moved to my home after hours, giving any resident the opportunity to call or drop by. Mostly to complain. "I'll get it."

I opened the front door to find both Chief Michaels and Chief Peabody on my doorstep, their police cars in the drive. Brad Spitzer, the arson investigator, was with them too. "Better put on some coffee, Gramps," I said, turning back into the living room. "It looks like it could be a long night."

Chapter 11

The five of us sat around the kitchen table with mugs of coffee and a platter of stale donuts. It was all I had to offer. I didn't want to run to the grocery store—I was pretty sure they weren't here to eat.

Chief Michaels and Chief Peabody glanced at each other as they came in, sat down and put their caps on the table. I noticed, despite the other differences, that both men took their coffee black—and wisely decided against a donut.

"I'll get straight to the point," Chief Peabody started. "I don't know what you were doing out in Corolla today, Mayor O'Donnell, but we haven't been able to find any trace of Sam Meacham. There's been no record of his credit cards being used after he rented the Segway. No trace of him doing anything since the day after the Duck museum blew up."

"On the other hand," Chief Michaels cut in, "we found

out today that the cannon from the Corolla Historical Museum *is* the weapon used to destroy our museum."

Both men looked at Brad, who had helped himself to a donut and was dunking it into his coffee, which was heavily laced with cream and sugar. "Sorry," he muttered with a full mouth.

He wiped powdered sugar on his napkin. "Yes. The results show that the piece of cannonball we found in the museum here matches the cannonballs used by the Corolla museum. They fire their cannon on holidays and so forth, which gave us a good comparison. The cannon had been fired recently, and the wheel length and size of the carriage match the wheel tracks the police found on the hill overlooking the Duck museum."

"That only means the cannon did it, right?" I asked, looking at the two police chiefs. "Not that Sam did it."

Chief Peabody slurped his coffee. "What do you know about Meacham?" he asked me. "How did you know he rented those scooters? We went over his place real careful. *We* didn't know."

Chief Michaels cleared his throat. "The mayor is gifted."

"What do you mean *gifted*?" Chief Peabody demanded, glaring at us. "What the hell does that mean?"

Gramps poured more coffee. "Dae is psychic. She can see things the rest of us can't."

"Oh well, in that case, we'll step aside and let her figure out the rest of it." Chief Peabody sat back from the table and folded his arms across his chest.

"Gifted?" Brad ruminated over the word between bites of donut. "How does that work?"

"I touch things and get visions from them. I can also find things by touching the people who lost them."

Gramps's eyes narrowed, but he didn't say anything.

"So you touched something that belongs to Sam and saw him in one of these *visions*?" Chief Peabody asked, his voice full of disdain.

"Yes." I described what I'd seen and felt that had led me to the Wild Horse Preservation Society's rescue station and the abandoned scooter.

"Why don't you have her on the payroll, Ron? You could probably solve this thing in a day."

"So you had a vision of where Sam would be?" Brad asked.

"And a man who was with him. He may have done something to Sam. He could be the one who killed Max too. Maybe Sam knew about the cannon and was going to say something."

"That's a lot of maybe." Chief Peabody shook his head. "We don't do police work on visions and maybes. What's this fella look like who was with Sam?"

"I don't know. I never saw his face." There was nothing more to say. I glanced at Gramps. I knew the look on his face. He wanted to know why I hadn't told him about my new ability, but he wouldn't ask until we were alone.

"Is that all you have, Mayor?" Chief Michaels asked me.

"I'm afraid so. It got me to the Segway, but I guess you couldn't find Sam from that."

"I don't know." Brad finished eating and sat back from the table with a smile on his face. "I think that was pretty good considering neither of you could find even that much."

"No one asked you," Chief Peabody snarled. "Go back to Manteo."

Brad laughed a little—apparently not taking him seriously. Chief Michaels stood and put his hat on. "If you see any other visions about this case, you give me a holler."

"I will."

"Maybe you could CC me on that, *Your Honor*," Chief Peabody added sarcastically as he shuffled to his feet and picked up his hat. "That way we'd all be in the loop."

Gramps saw them to the door. I put the coffee cups in the sink and threw away the rest of the donuts. I waited there for him, knowing he'd have plenty to say.

"When did all this happen?" he asked when he returned after locking up.

"Right after the explosion. I can't explain it. Kevin says he's heard of things like this happening from trauma. I don't know much about it beyond that. I'm trying to get some control over it."

He nodded. "Of course, I wish you would've trusted me with the information, but I'm glad you told someone. Kevin seems like he can handle things."

"I planned to tell you. I wanted to understand it first. You've been through so much with me. I didn't want to worry you."

He came across the kitchen and hugged me. "You *always* worry me. And you always will. You feel the same about me. But that doesn't mean we can't tell each other things when they happen. Right?"

"Right." I hugged him back. "Next time I almost get blown up and find I have a new ability, I'll tell you right away."

"Get to bed! I don't know where you got that smart mouth from. You've always been sassy. I guess helping you get to be mayor made it even worse."

"Being your granddaughter is what made it worse," I teased. "Everyone always said you had a smart mouth while you were sheriff."

He sobered and looked me in the eyes. "If you have

any more visions about this case, come to me before you take them to Ronnie or Walt. Let's talk about them first. Okay?"

I agreed without questioning why he'd be so serious about it, but I thought about it for a long time before I went to sleep.

The remnants of Tropical Storm Floyd moved in during the night. I heard the heavy rain and gusty winds settle in a little after midnight. The old house creaked and groaned around us, but we'd seen much worse. Even though I'd sat through hurricanes in this house, I'd never once worried about being safe. Maybe it was naïve, but the house had been here for several lifetimes and hundreds of storms. I trusted it to keep me and Gramps from harm.

I lay awake for a long time listening to the symphony nature made, wondering about all the mysteries in the world that seemed to have more questions than answers. I finally fell back asleep, but rain was still drowning the Outer Banks when I got up the next morning.

Gramps was up too—in his yellow rain pants, jacket and boots. He was making breakfast.

"You're not going out in this weather, are you?" I asked as I sat down to sprinkle brown sugar on my oatmeal.

"The winds mostly died down during the night. You know the fishing will be good today. Besides, I'm chartered and—"

"You never miss a charter." I added milk to my bowl. "I know. Be careful, huh?"

He kissed the top of my head and put on his matching yellow rain hat. "I will. I love you, Dae. Have a good one."

I never thought Gramps could love anything the way

he'd loved being sheriff. I'd been wrong. He loved taking that old boat out at least as much. Maybe more. It didn't matter what the weather was like. He didn't care. Short of a hurricane, he was going out—especially if there was money to be made.

I stirred my oatmeal and wondered where to go from here. I was stumped after talking to the chiefs last night. Sam was nowhere to be found, despite my vision. But where was the connection between Sam and the cannonball that blew up the museum?

I knew Chief Peabody and probably Chief Michaels believed Sam was guilty of killing Max—even though it might've been an accident. Both of them had sounded like they thought Sam had fired on the Duck museum out of spite, possibly not with the intention of killing Max.

I couldn't adequately explain the fear I'd felt when I touched the Segway—maybe the last thing Sam had touched. Even if I could, I doubted they'd understand or appreciate it. To them, Sam was simply trying to escape, which in law enforcement terms meant he was guilty.

I knew I should go to the shop even if there weren't many customers who'd come out in the bad weather. The people who call the Outer Banks home tend not to take after the town's namesake (ducks). We are more like turtles, hiding in our shells until the sun comes out. If nothing else, I should check my merchandise, look for UPS packages and make sure there was no damage from the storm. Maybe while I worked, I'd get an idea as to what my next move should be to help find out who'd caused the explosion that killed Max, and why.

I put on my raincoat and boots—I think everyone who lives here has them—and headed toward the Duck Shoppes. Pieces of bushes, sand and trash covered Duck Road, but there was almost no traffic at all. I made a mental note to ask the council for extra cleanup money for public works. It looked like they could have some overtime coming.

Most retail shops were closed, windows boarded against the wind and rain. It seemed drastic to me, but many of the owners weren't from Duck originally. Sometimes it took a while to learn how to tell the remnants of a storm from the real thing.

Still, that meant no coffee except what I could make at the shop. It was never as good as coffee with steamed milk and some kind of chocolate or hazelnut, but it would have to do.

Nancy was at town hall answering phone calls about the storm. She handed me my messages without missing a beat. There was nothing pressing—unfortunately—but there was a call from Agnes Caudle.

I realized with a strong twinge of guilt that I hadn't gone to see her since Max died. A lot had happened to me, but that was no excuse. In comparison, she was going through so much more.

Nancy was still on the phone when I left, talking to someone about a downed power line. She waved and I did the same, pocketing Agnes's note and heading for Missing Pieces. Once I got everything checked out there, I'd pick up a few things and go to see her. It was the least I could do as a longtime friend and the mayor.

I hoped other people hadn't been as forgetful. I knew it was unlikely. People here stuck together when bad things happened. Her kitchen and dining room were probably littered with cakes and casseroles, while her answering machine would be filled with offers to take her places she needed to go. Of course, there were always flowers and cards.

The Currituck Sound was ragged looking as I followed the gray boardwalk past Curves and Curls, Trudy's shop, and reached Missing Pieces. Nothing seemed to be damaged outside. There were also no UPS packages. I let myself in the shop and turned to close the door, almost shutting it in Kevin's face.

"I thought I might find you here," he said with a smile. "It looks like damage was minimal on this side of Duck. We're a little more beaten up on the Atlantic side. I lost a couple windows when a lawn chair blew into them. On a positive note, the roof didn't leak."

"I'm glad to hear it." I continued into the shop, not quite sure how I should react to him. I didn't ask if he'd left the town meeting with Shayla, but it was hard not to.

"Your house made it through okay?"

"Yeah. It was fine. It's been through a lot worse. Of course, I'm sure the Blue Whale has seen a lot worse too."

"Is something wrong?"

"No. I told you the house is okay. I think the shop is okay too. The storm was only a lot of rain and wind. We're lucky it blew itself out in the ocean before it got here."

"I'm talking about you personally, Dae. Has something else happened?"

I thought about it. "The chief came by last night. Well, actually, both chiefs came by with the arson investigator. I was surprised to see them, but—"

"I'm not talking about that either." He came up close to me. "I'm talking about *you*. Did you encounter another problem with your abilities? You seem remote this morning."

I looked into his ocean-gray eyes. "You left with Shayla last night. Do you have something you want to tell me?"

He seemed a little bewildered. "I didn't leave with Shayla. I didn't even know she was there. I started to wait for you, but you were talking with Councilman Wilson and I didn't want to interrupt."

"Oh." I guess that answered my question.

"You thought Shayla and I—?"

"Yeah. Kind of. But that would be okay if that's how it worked out."

He put his arms around me. "That's a lukewarm attitude. You wouldn't even put up a fight?"

I didn't get to answer because he kissed me and I forgot what I was going to say. It didn't matter anyway. I'd heard what I needed to hear.

"What's your agenda for today?" he asked, his forehead against mine. "I already boarded up my windows, and the glass won't be here to replace them until Monday."

I explained about Agnes. "I can't believe I haven't gone to see her."

"I'm sure I don't understand all the ins and outs of this kind of thing. But I have a feeling being almost blown up yourself probably gets you off the hook. I'm sure trying to stay sane despite being able to see the minute details about everything you touch might qualify you for an exemption too."

"Thanks. I still feel guilty, but I appreciate the sentiment. I'm going to make sure the shop is in one piece, then I have to go and buy some food to take to Agnes."

"Count me in on the plan. I can learn from someone who knows Duck society from the inside out as well as proper Duck etiquette."

"All right." I had to smile. "I'll show you the ropes."

Missing Pieces was in good shape. The shop had managed to escape any problems—this time. I'd had my share of broken windows, leaky roofs and flooding. It was part of life on the Outer Banks.

Kevin looked around at all the pieces in my shop, picking things up and putting them down as he inspected them, just like any other shopper. I was watching him (pretending to work) when the bell on the door rang and Mrs. Euly Stanley came in.

The large green poncho and hood she wore made her look even smaller than her five-foot-nothing fragile frame. Her boots seemed to reach all the way up to her waist. She pushed back her hood, revealing a wealth of curly gray hair. "Dae! There you are! I was afraid I wasn't going to find you today. You have to see what I found in my attic."

Kevin joined us at the front of the store, and we went through the pleasantries of introduction and inquiring about each other's state of well-being.

"What did you find, Mrs. Stanley?" I asked when it was over.

"Just look!" She withdrew a lovely antique gold bracelet from the pocket of her poncho. "It belonged to my great-great grandmother. There's a matching necklace somewhere. I wanted to show it to my granddaughter, Chrissie. Can you help me find it?"

"Of course! Let's sit down over here and take a look." I glanced at Kevin and smiled. He seemed to understand and drew up a chair close to the sofa. Mrs. Stanley took off her wet poncho and sat beside me, waiting expectantly.

I took her hands in mine. They were cool and slightly damp. She closed her eyes and, I could imagine, thought about her ancestor's missing necklace.

At first I couldn't see anything—only a dark, confused muddle of colors and shapes. That was normal for most people. There were only a few who had some kind of clarity when I looked for something they'd lost.

A shape began to form out of the swirling colors. There was something there—dull gold chain leading to a—"It's a locket!" I exclaimed. "A gold locket with a picture inside."

"Yes! That's it!" Mrs. Stanley said. "My great-great grandmother. That's it, Dae! Where is it?"

"It's in the pocket of a skirt—calf length, herringbone tweed. It's hanging in a tall chest filled with other clothes and a lot of hats."

The necklace formed clearly in my mind. I could see the portrait inside of it and the image broke my concentration. "Mrs. Stanley—your great-great grandmother was Theodosia Burr. This is the link Max looked for all of his life. He knew it was here and he was right."

"What are you saying, Dae? My great-great grandmother's name was Mary."

"Max hypothesized that Theo took on a new persona when she found herself shipwrecked here. Or maybe she couldn't remember who she was. We might never know. But I have a miniature portrait that looks just like this—maybe she was a few years older. The face is unmistakable."

"Are you sure? No one in my family has ever mentioned anything about it. Was it possible they didn't know?"

"Maybe there could be some mention of it in your family history. All of your relatives kept such good records. Remember when we found the mention of the first church built in Duck through your relative's Bible?"

Her brows knit together above intelligent brown eyes. "I think there's a diary. I'll have to check with my mother. To think we could be related to Theodosia Burr Alston! It would be wonderful! Those ladies in the Duck Historical Society would be green! But I thought Theodosia died at sea—killed by pirates."

"If you could find that diary and we could compare my picture to the one in the locket, we might know for sure."

"You're right of course! I'll get everyone in the family together, and we'll see what we can find. This is *so* exciting! How I wish Max were here to tell us all what to do. I miss him so."

I took a deep breath. "Could I hold the bracelet, Mrs. Stanley? Just for a moment."

"Of course!" She took it out of her pocket again.

"Dae?" Kevin caught my attention.

"It's fine," I answered. "You're here to catch me, right?" He nodded. "I'm here."

Mrs. Stanley smiled. "How very nice for you, Dae. You have a new beau." She put out her hand, and I took the bracelet from her.

Warmth. Laughter. A sparkling emotion that was love as she watched him put it on her wrist. He kissed her hand as he finished, and she threaded her fingers through his dark hair.

I couldn't see her face, but I knew—I knew that it was Theodosia. I could feel it. There was no doubt that this bracelet and the matching locket belonged to her.

"It was handmade by a traveling jeweler who created one-of-a-kind treasures. He gave it to her for her birthday. She was his wife. They loved each other so deeply." I sighed over the tender emotion without realizing it.

"My goodness." Mrs. Stanley said. "All of that from the bracelet? Your gift is growing, Dae!"

Mrs. Stanley put on her poncho and promised to let me know if any progress was made toward finding the missing locket and diary. She smiled at Kevin and shook his hand before leaving the shop.

"That was a risk," Kevin warned when she was gone. "It could've involved her death or some other calamity hidden in the emotions of the bracelet."

"It could've," I agreed. "But it didn't. It was one of the loveliest feelings I've ever felt. They were so in love."

"I think you're missing the point. You knew what you needed to know from the locket. Why touch the bracelet?"

"I thought there might be something else and there was. I'm fine. You don't need to worry so much. I can handle this."

"It's too new for you to know what you can handle."

I smiled at him and kissed his cheek, still feeling the afterglow of the romantic emotions between Theodosia and her Banker husband. "You need to lighten up. Everything is fine. It's better than fine. It's wonderful."

As if to disprove my words, Kevin's pager went off just as August Grandin burst into the shop. "You have to come and see this! Rafe Masterson has struck again!"

Chapter 12

"That's me." Kevin kissed me quickly before he ran out of the shop. August and I were right behind him. I barely remembered to lock up.

Thick black clouds of smoke filled the sky. It was hard to tell exactly where it was coming from—but following all the emergency vehicles was a good bet.

Already a crowd had gathered at the pink clapboard house on one of the side streets away from Duck Road. Flamingos and plastic dwarfs were trampled as booted feet dragged heavy hoses to put out the fire.

A voice called out what I was thinking. "That's Max Caudle's house! Where's Agnes?"

It was too much like the museum. The smell of smoke and the urgent sense of panic caused a choking sensation in my throat. How could this be happening again so soon? None of us were ready for another disaster.

"It's the pirate curse," Billy Rogers said, making the sign of the cross on his chest. "Rafe has come back again."

"Don't be ridiculous!" Mark Samson, who owned the Rib Shack, looked at him like he'd lost his mind. "That old thing doesn't cause real-life fires."

"Agnes may still be trapped inside," another voice added to the sense of hysteria.

A dog started barking—high-pitched yapping—as Max and Agnes's apricot-colored poodle ran through the yard toward the crowd. Chief Michaels, Tim Mabry and some of the other Duck police officers arrived and began redirecting traffic, giving the firefighters time and space to do their jobs.

Gramps was on pumper duty at the big fire truck. I ran to his side, surprised to see him there. "I thought you had an excursion."

"My fare didn't have the stomach for it."

"Did anyone look inside yet to see if Agnes is in there?"

He glanced around, checking the pressure on the hoses. "I don't know, Dae. Let me ask Cailey. She's up near the house somewhere."

Cailey had been in the house but hadn't seen Agnes. She'd opened the door and let the dog out. "I don't think she's home," she told Gramps. "The fire had to be started with an accelerant. It's burning too hot and too fast."

I saw Kevin suiting up alongside several other men from the community. Some of them I'd gone to high school with—some had been my elementary schoolteachers. Luke Helms, new to the area, was putting on the volunteer firefighter's gear too. It didn't take long before new residents were enlisted. Already dozens of volunteers had arrived and were in the Caudles' front yard.

A window blew out of the top floor, sending shards of glass past the geraniums and the high-peaked black roof.

Someone was up there in the opening. Smoke rolled out of the hole where the window had been.

"Help!" Agnes called out, her voice cracking from the smoke. "Help me, please!"

People all around me started crying and praying as we watched in horror while Agnes waved her arms and tried to get out of the dormer window. She was coughing fitfully as she finally managed to crawl outside on the roof. She swayed as she stood high above the ground. The crowd called out for her to stay put, help was coming.

There was only one truck with a ladder long enough to reach her. It was being used as the pumper. Without it, there wouldn't be enough water to put out the fire. And we all knew there wasn't enough time to disengage the big hoses and get the ladder up to her.

My eyes and throat were burning, but I saw two men in firefighter's gear run toward the house with a long ladder. I didn't know who they were or where they'd found the ladder. The crowd went silent as we watched them try to reach Agnes in time.

Seconds ticked by like hours. Agnes lost her balance and fell to her knees. The angle of the roof was too steep for her to regain her footing. She was toppling forward even as the two brave souls were coming for her.

I could hardly watch. Would they be there in time or would we face a double tragedy? My hands were clenched in tight fists—impotent rage running through me as all the rest of us could do was watch and pray.

The first man reached the roof in time to keep Agnes from falling. She grasped at him like a drowning swimmer. The second man was right behind him. Everyone caught their breath as Agnes's savior lost his footing trying to help her. Luckily, the next man stopped them both from rolling off the roof.

When it seemed as though they would all be safe, a part of the roof collapsed right behind them. Hot flames shot up through the hole fed by the new supply of oxygen. It roared—as angry as any pirate ghost, threatening to take their lives.

I found myself praying that neither of the men up there was Kevin. But who would I wish this fate on? I knew every man and woman in the fire department. I knew most of their families and their friends. I felt guilty wishing only for Kevin's safety. *Please don't let anything happen to any of them.*

Two more firemen moved in with one of the big hoses. They began pushing the fire back into the hole in the roof. The two with Agnes crawled toward the ladder that meant life and safety if they could reach it. A group from the crowd—no training or equipment—ran to hold the base of the ladder and offer whatever assistance they could.

The black smoke almost prevented me from seeing one man guide Agnes's feet to the ladder while the other held her hands and helped her start down. The water that was keeping the fire away from them also made the ladder slippery. Several times on that long journey to the ground they almost fell. Finally, all three were on the flattened green grass.

As the paramedics rushed up, I joined them. I wasn't sure who the two firefighters were—at least they were both safe. Agnes was a dear, old friend. The other two were our new heroes. I felt sure they both had some kind of special town award coming to them when this was over.

The heat from the house was unbearable. Two or three people helped each of the firefighters get away from it. I helped a few others get Agnes out of the area. The paramedics followed along, trying to check Agnes for injuries even as we were running toward the street.

Agnes was crying hysterically. She was covered in black soot—no way to know if she was burned or not. I held her hand while the paramedics tried to put an oxygen mask over her face. She kept pushing it aside even though she was coughing. I tried to calm her down, and she reached out to grab me with both arms.

"I don't want any of it, Dae! It killed Max and almost killed me. It destroyed our home—our lives. Take it! It's cursed!"

Before I could ask what she meant, she pressed something into my hand. It was black from the soot it had accumulated in the fire—but there was no doubt what it was.

Max was desperate. He didn't know what else to do. He opened the box again and looked at its contents. There was more than enough for Agnes's surgery. All he had to do was keep his mouth shut.

Agnes mercifully lost consciousness. The paramedics put her on a stretcher and moved her to the ambulance.

I looked at the black soot from her touch. I was covered in it. I rubbed the coin she'd given me against my shirt until the bright gold beneath it began to gleam. This wasn't pirate gold. This had been made more recently—in Germany. The man who'd given Max this gold to save Agnes's life was a much older man, someone I'd never seen before.

I tucked the gold coin in my pocket, glad that my encounter with it had been mild compared to pirate gold. I looked around in the smoky crowd to locate the two firefighters from the roof. A group of volunteers were helping remove charred gloves and melted boots. As soon as their hoods were removed, I saw that one of them was Luke and the other, Kevin. I'd known it was him even as I hoped it wasn't.

I was close enough to hear Kevin joking with the paramedics as they checked him and Luke for injuries. Luke was quiet and somber, but thankfully, they both seemed fine. I couldn't get any nearer with so many people crowded around for more important reasons than my own—wanting to wail pathetically and throw my arms around Kevin.

"Looks like Sam's surfaced," Chief Michaels said to me. "That fire was arson. I don't have to be with the fire department to know it."

"That doesn't mean it was Sam."

"It doesn't mean it wasn't either. Somebody did these things, Mayor," he responded, provoked. "Sam knows about cannons—his cannon destroyed our museum. Now this. He ran. That makes him our prime suspect until we know better."

I felt stupid and chastened. Of course he was right. I'd been trying to protect Sam. That may have even colored my vision about him. He might have been running away from the police, not someone who wanted to kill him. I didn't know him as well as I knew Max. I was going to have to stop being so protective of people because they *seemed* like they couldn't be guilty. Sam had issues with Max. Maybe it got to be too much.

How that related to the new gold coin in my possession was anyone's guess. Maybe the two incidents weren't related. But I knew I owed the chief an apology. "I'm sorry, Chief Michaels. I hate it, but I know you're right." It took a lot for me to say that.

"Your heart's in the right place," he responded sympathetically. "You don't understand the criminal mind. Sometimes good people turn bad."

The fire was all but contained. People were starting to move away from the smoldering remains of the pink house Max and Agnes had shared for so many years. They were going home to cherish what they still had and mourn the loss to the community.

I noticed the TV crew from the mainland had set up near the police perimeter. I walked close, deciding to use *them* for a change. I told them about our two heroes, and they followed me, armed with cameras and microphones.

I was the cool, smiling mayor who introduced Luke and Kevin to the media, who loved them at once. They were a perfect image for the six P.M. news that night. Handsome heroes with sooty faces that saved a woman from a terrible death.

I looked on as the reporters asked their questions, trying to capture the excitement of the moment. Kevin nodded toward me with a question in his eyes, and I winked at him. This was good for Duck despite the way it came about. It was right for people outside the Outer Banks to see our lives—both good and bad.

Of course, that gave the reporters the run of the restricted area. They took advantage by talking to Cailey and Chief Michaels. Then they were lucky enough to find an old Banker who still believed in the curse of Rafe Masterson. I could imagine their eyes lighting up over that.

"What was that all about?" Kevin asked when we were alone. Luke had gone to talk with Cailey and Gramps.

"It's your fifteen minutes of fame," I explained. "You were a hero today. Why not let them tell your story?"

"You might've asked first."

I looked at his blackened face. He seemed serious. "I'm sorry. I thought you'd enjoy it."

"You thought wrong." He got up and took his gear to the fire truck.

I followed him. We were obviously having our first fight. "I didn't realize. I was proud of you and Luke. I wanted everyone to know what kind of people we have here in Duck."

He didn't say anything—just finished putting his gear away.

"Hey! I said I was sorry. *Really* sorry. Why are you so upset?"

"It reminded me too much of closing a big case for the FBI. They liked to show off too. I'm not a volunteer fire-fighter to show off."

He turned away from me, and I realized this went much deeper than I'd imagined. "Let me buy you a drink. We can talk for a while." I didn't want us to go our separate ways like this.

For an instant, he stared at me as if he didn't know me. I wondered if he was going to give in or if he'd stay mad all night. Finally he nodded. "Okay. But we go someplace quiet and you're buying."

I let out a sigh of relief. As long as he wasn't going to be angry anymore, I could handle the price. "You got it. We can get a dark table at Wild Stallions. I'll even spring for those potato skins you like so much."

He finally smiled—creases of pale skin visible be-tween the cracks in the soot on his face. I wondered if I should tell him and risk breaking the mood. Maybe it would be better for him to go out and deal with the soot later.

"We'll have to swing by the Blue Whale so I can take a shower and change clothes. Hero or not, I'm not going out like this."

"That's fine," I agreed. "Whatever you need."

He draped one arm across my shoulders as we started walking. "You're kind of a pushover for a good glower, aren't you?"

"Only from you." I smiled at him. "The world should be a happy place, don't you think?"

"I think going to mayor school might've warped your sense of reality."

"Funny. I was thinking the same thing about you except with the FBI."

We walked around all the congestion built up because of the fire. The acrid smell of smoke was with us all the way across Duck to the Atlantic side. Kevin let us both in the Blue Whale, then poured himself a glass of good whiskey, which he swallowed in a single quick gulp.

"I thought I was buying you a drink *after* you changed clothes."

"You are. And potato skins. The hot kind, not the wimpy ranch kind."

I washed up while he went to his room behind the big kitchen. Fortunately, there was only a little soot on my hands and face. And my sweater, which I took off. It wasn't that cold.

I looked around at all the wonderful items he'd purchased with the inn. He hadn't realized it would be so full of treasure. I wished I'd been there first.

He was starting to get a good-size collection of items for the new museum too. At least a dozen people had already dropped things off since last night. I hoped the new museum was going to be bigger than the old one or it would never hold the generosity of Duck residents.

"Can you believe the pile already?" Kevin asked, rejoining me in the large lobby.

"That was fast!" I looked at his clean Blue Whale Inn T-shirt, jeans and sneakers. His dark hair was still damp from the shower, and his face was scratched but clean. He smelled like soap and some spicy cologne.

"I didn't want to risk you fudging on your offer to buy me a drink. Otherwise I might start glowering again."

"But now that you're clean, it wouldn't be as effective. It was all that soot that made you look so dramatic."

We left the Blue Whale and walked in silence back toward downtown Duck. The sirens were quiet—nothing but the distant sound of cars on Duck Road and the always-present breeze from the water.

"Agnes gave me something before they took her to the hospital." I brought out the soot-covered gold piece and set it in his hand.

"Is this one of the pirate gold pieces?"

"No. This is new." I told him what Agnes had said before she gave me the gold coin. "Somehow this is connected to what happened to Max."

"I'm sure Chief Michaels can imagine Sam Meacham coming back to finish whatever revenge they think he's capable of."

"I know. But even if Sam is guilty of killing Max— why try to kill Agnes? She doesn't care if Theodosia Burr lived here or not. She never took part in any of their historical arguments."

"I understand," he said as we walked up the stairs to the boardwalk. "But we're talking about another incident suspiciously like the first one. Sam needs to come back and talk to the police so they can hear his side of the story. If this were my case, I'd like him too."

Wild Stallions was quiet and tame for a Friday night, at least when we first got there. We had a couple of drinks and shared some potato skins and onion rings before a group of football coaches came in and the beginning of a crowd decided to join them.

We watched the news on the wide-screen TVs, with Kevin and Luke's unsmiling faces featured prominently during the coverage of the fire. Duck residents cheered their local heroes—as I knew they would. Kevin seemed to hunch over his drink a little more.

"Seriously—you don't like people calling you a hero?"

"No. It doesn't mean anything. We were doing what we were supposed to do. And people have a way of calling you a hero one minute and changing their minds the next."

"I won't ever let anyone call you a hero again," I promised, a little mouthy from the few drinks we'd had. "Not on my watch."

"What's next in the search for Max's killer?" He changed the subject.

I shrugged. "I guess I'll go see Agnes in the morning and ask her what she can tell me about the gold. I've never known her to be superstitious about anything, but she sounded like she blamed the gold for what happened to her and Max."

"Maybe you should ask her how much gold we're talking about. Like you said, the chances are good that these events are connected. The gold might be the key. People do crazy things to get their hands on some gold—even more than they will for cash."

"Good idea. Maybe there's some way to find out if Sam needed the gold. Maybe he needed money and found out about the new gold Max had—however he came to have new gold. We know how he had the pirate gold. But that would be harder to convert to cash. People are a little leery of antique gold unless they deal in that type of thing."

"Chief Michaels has probably already looked into that since the arson investigation revealed that the gold in the museum was gone."

"And again, Sam looks guilty because he'd know where to take pirate gold and exchange it for something easier to use." I took another swallow of my drink and ate the last onion ring. "I guess I might as well face the idea that Sam is guilty of all of this."

"I'm sorry. It's hard when you want it to be someone else that's guilty."

"Did that ever happen to you?"

"Plenty of times. There's always the chance you'll make the mistake of looking with your heart instead of your head. Sometimes the person is a sympathetic figure— like Sam might be when we find out why he needed the gold. It happens to even the most hardened investigator."

I had started to thank him for his insight when two large fishermen came to the table—all smiles and mugs of beer. "Hey man, we want to thank you for what you did today. Let us buy you a round at the bar. We all want to shake your hand."

Kevin went with the guys, but he was glowering again. It didn't bode well for our walk home. I had just decided to cut out early and avoid an ugly scene with him when Officer Scott Randall burst into the bar and grill with major information. "Sam Meacham is dead," he told everyone over the sound of the sporting event on TV and the loud cheers from the bar.

"When did you find out?" I asked.

The young police officer blushed when he saw me. "Sorry, Mayor. I didn't know you were here."

"Now you do. Don't worry, I won't tell anyone. When did they find him?"

"A little while ago. His body washed up near Kitty Hawk. Chief Michaels thinks it might be a suicide."

Chapter 13

Despite our disagreement at the fire and his later, unwanted fame at Wild Stallions, Kevin offered to drive me to the hospital in Kill Devil Hills the next morning. We'd had a cursory discussion about Sam's death the night before, but both of us were too tired and too upset to talk much on the way home.

The sun was shining Saturday morning as we drove down Duck Road. Trudy had offered to keep an eye on the shop for me. Shayla still wasn't speaking to me. Gramps squeezed into Kevin's truck with us to pay his respect to Agnes. I was squished between my two favorite men—a nice place to be.

"If there's no note, can it be suicide?" I asked the two ex-lawmen about Sam's death. "I mean, how do they know he killed himself? Just because he drowned doesn't prove anything, right?"

Gramps shrugged, mindful of the orange mums and

daylilies he'd brought for Agnes. "In most cases unless someone falls out of a boat, a case like this is investigated as a suicide. They'll do an autopsy to be sure, Dae. But Sam Meacham probably couldn't handle what he'd done and decided this was the easiest way to take care of it. It's not that unusual."

"What about the friend he was with in Corolla?" Kevin asked. "Do they know who that was yet?"

"I haven't heard anything about it. But I'm not in the loop like I used to be," he admitted. "Frankly, I don't think they've really pushed that part of the investigation."

"I can understand that." Kevin nodded.

"Why?" I questioned. "Why wouldn't that be important?"

"The way Sam's office looked—Chief Michaels said his home was tossed around the same way—like someone was looking for something. Unfortunately, we may never know who this other person with the Segway was or if he was involved in what happened. He could've been some-one Sam met at the rental place, for all we know." Kevin finished his thoughts on the matter, then looked at Gramps.

"We don't have all the facts yet, Dae," Gramps said. "We may never know everything that happened. But if Sam's death is officially ruled a suicide, it will go a long way toward solving the case."

"So we're supposed to think Sam was running away to kill himself and took the time to rent a Segway before he did it. What happened to the other guy? Was he hanging around taking pictures of the mustangs while Sam walked into the water?"

Neither one of my two favorite men answered. I charged ahead. "Well I don't believe it. Sam planned to blow up the museum and kill his friend with a cannon-ball, went through all the elaborate work it took to accom-plish that and after doing it, he was so overcome by remorse that he killed himself. That doesn't make any sense to me."

"It might sound crazy," Kevin admitted as we picked up speed in a clear area between Duck and Southern Shores. "But believe me, this isn't as crazy as a lot of other things I've heard. People have plotted for years to kill someone in much more elaborate, detailed ways than shooting off a cannonball. When it's over and you realize what you've done, you fall apart. It's different planning to kill someone than it is actually doing it."

Gramps seemed to agree with that line of thought. "I investigated cases like that too. People change when they follow through on something like this. They aren't the same anymore. Some are hardened by it—others crumble like dry seaweed."

"I guess that must be what Chief Michaels is thinking too." I pointed out the entrance to the hospital so Kevin wouldn't pass it. "It still doesn't make any sense to me. I'm glad I'm not a police officer."

Traffic had been light, so we'd made good time getting to Kill Devil Hills. I wondered how Agnes would take the news of Sam's death. Would she be happy he'd killed himself or sorry that he wouldn't go to jail for his crimes? Agnes didn't seem the vindictive type, but as Gramps and Kevin had recently instructed me, you never knew how someone would react until it happened.

When we were in the elevator going up to the second floor, it struck me that Sam's death could prove whether he was responsible for the house fire. It seemed a certainty to everyone else that he blew up the museum. But if it turned out that Sam was already dead when Agnes's house was set on fire, who else would want to hurt her? And wouldn't finding that answer cast some doubt on Sam being the only one who would want to kill Max?

I didn't ask those questions aloud. The elevator chimed as it reached the floor and the doors parted. Both of Agnes's daughters were there. They hugged me and Gramps and grimly shook hands with Kevin.

"I don't understand how anyone could want to hurt Mom or Dad," Celia, the older one, said, her eyes red from crying.

"It's crazy!" Vicky, the younger, protested. "What's happened to Duck that would allow some insane person to hurt my mom and dad? Everyone always loved them when we were growing up."

"I don't have an answer for you, girls." Gramps hugged both of them again. "I hope we'll have some real evidence soon. I know it's hard not understanding."

"Mr. Meacham ate dinner at our house." Celia shuddered. "All the time he was plotting to kill Dad."

"You're letting your imagination go wild," Gramps said. "Wait for the evidence. Until we have everything, we don't know the truth."

"Is she awake?" Not that I wasn't sympathetic to Vicky and Celia's emotional states, but I could feel the pull from the coin in my pocket. I needed to know what Agnes was talking about at the house yesterday.

"Yes," Vicky said. "She's not too bad for someone who almost died in a fire. A few burns and some smoke inhalation—she's tough. I thought we'd never convince her to stay here last night."

"She's a Banker born and bred." Gramps smiled. "May we see her?"

"It's all right with us." Celia bit her lip and glanced at her sister. "She threw us out a few minutes ago. She said we're making too big a fuss. She's never liked anyone taking care of her. Maybe you could talk to her, Sheriff O'Donnell. She might listen to you."

"Lord knows she won't listen to us," Vicky added.

"It's only Horace now, girls," he said. "I'll be glad to have a word with her. And I'll be careful not to fuss."

"That would be wonderful!" Celia said. "Sorry about calling you sheriff. Old habits and everything. You were the sheriff while we were growing up. I guess you'll always be the sheriff to us. Whatever you can do to help with Mom. We'd like to be in there to hear what the doctor has to say when he comes."

"I'll be careful." Gramps hugged them again, and we all turned to go into Agnes's room.

We silently decided to let Gramps go in first since he'd known Agnes the longest. "Aggie?" He knocked gently and leaned his head around the door. "It's me—Horace. Mind if I come in?"

The patient inside stirred on the bed in the shadowed room. "Horace? Is that you? Please come in."

Gramps gave us all a look—*so far so good*. He started into the room, and the rest of us followed, with Celia and Vicky bringing up the rear.

"You brought flowers!" Agnes exclaimed. "How nice. And Dae, you're here too. And that nice man from the Blue Whale. It's wonderful to see all of you."

When we were in the room and the door was closed, I felt a twinge of frustration. This wasn't the way I'd planned it. I wanted to speak to Agnes alone about the gold coin she'd given me.

"How are you feeling?" Gramps made small talk with her.

She frowned at her daughters, who were cowering in one corner. "You brought them back in with you? How could you?"

Neither girl spoke, but Gramps patted Agnes's bandaged hand where it rested on the bed. "Now, you know these girls want what's best for you. I don't know what the feud's about, but this isn't a good time to be fighting over anything."

"Easy for you to say." She sniffed. "You're not a prisoner in this death trap they call a hospital."

"I hear you might be going home," Gramps said. "I think that's some good news. Celia and Vicky were worried about you. You gave us all a fright."

"And I'd be dead if it wasn't for *him*." She pointed at Kevin. "How can I ever repay you for what you did for me? I thought my time was up when I was on the roof."

Kevin shrugged. "No thanks necessary. We were doing our job, Mrs. Caudle."

"Thank heaven!" Celia called out, then put her hands over her mouth. "Sorry, Mom."

Despite this touching family tableau, I was wondering if there was any possibility that all of them would leave so I could get on with talking to Agnes.

I know it was a little cold—my only excuse was the pressure I felt from the information I'd seen when I touched the gold coin. It made me nervous and a little irritable. Not my usual cheerful self. And I realized it was my own fault—if I'd considered the problem sooner, I would've come alone.

Gramps brought Celia and Vicky to Agnes's bedside, where they all hugged. Kevin joined me near the window where I was skulking. "Are you going to ask about the gold?" he whispered.

I glanced around like a nervous cat in a new home. "I can't. Not with everyone here. I need a few minutes alone with her."

"Maybe I can help with that."

I didn't have a chance to ask how before he wandered

close to the bed again. What could he possibly say or do that would make everyone leave?

"Is there anywhere around here to get a good cup of coffee?" he asked Celia. He smiled at her—I can't describe it, but if he'd given *me* that smile and asked me to go out and find a whale for him to ride, I would've tried to do it.

"Sure." Celia giggled a little. "I'd be glad to."

"I went to get the coffee this morning," Vicky reminded her. "I think I could show him better than you."

"For heaven's sake," Agnes intervened, "why don't you both take him to get some coffee—my treat."

I was amazed that both the girls were willing and eager to go with Kevin. He held out an arm to each of them. They giggled again and latched on to him like fish on a hook. Gramps seemed to catch on right away and suggested that he'd like coffee too. It made me feel guilty that I hadn't told him about the gold coin Agnes had given me.

I needed to have a talk with him later about everything that had happened so we were back on an even keel with each other. I didn't like things this way. I enjoyed having Kevin to talk to—but he wasn't Gramps.

Kevin looked at me as he walked out with the girls, his gaze shifting to Agnes. I nodded. I wondered if he could teach me to smile that way. It could certainly come in handy. Did they teach that in the FBI, or was that something he'd learned on his own?

The door closed behind them, and without waiting for me to speak, Agnes said, "Okay, Dae. You can ask me what you need to now. I know why you're here."

"I didn't know if you remembered." I stood beside her bed, and she touched my hand.

"Of course I remember. I was in a fire. I'm not senile!"

She smiled and her eyes welled with tears. "I wish you could hold my hands and tell me where to find everything I lost. Maybe I could get it all back."

I squeezed her unbandaged hand a little. "I wish I could do that too, Agnes. I lie awake at night and wonder if there was something I could've done to stop what happened to Max. I'm so sorry about everything."

"I know you are. You've always been a good friend. Max thought the world of you. Remember that time you helped him find the old compass he'd lost? He was so amazed at what you could do." She studied my face for a few seconds. "That's why I told you about the gold."

"What did you mean about it causing all of your problems?"

She pleated the pale green sheet between her fingers and looked away. "Three years ago—when I had to have that open-heart surgery—do you remember?"

I nodded. "Of course. I helped keep the bakery open while you were in the hospital. Max wouldn't let me help him at the museum, but he said I could sell cookies."

She laughed a little at the memory. "He always took great pride in that little museum. I know you know it was his life. Not that he didn't love me and the girls—but the museum was his heart."

I agreed silently, not trusting myself to speak without crying.

"We didn't have the money for the surgery, Dae. We sure didn't have insurance. I had resigned myself to dying—and I was all right with it. I felt like Max and I had made our choices. It was too late to get all maudlin about it. Max felt differently."

"Then you found this gold?" I laid the coin on the bed beside her.

"Not found." She stared at it. "Max got it from some-

one. There was a whole chest of it. I'm not sure who gave
it to him. He never told me. I thought it was a godsend,
and I agreed to have the surgery. But I was wrong. It was
a curse."

"How so?"

"Max changed. He started going out at odd hours of
the night—no explanation. At first I thought it was another woman. I don't expect you to understand, Dae, but
when a man and woman go through something like one of
them being very ill, it can take a toll on the relationship.
That made sense to me. I decided to follow him and confront him with my knowledge. I wanted to make things
right."

"But it wasn't another woman?"

"No. It was a man." She smiled, tears in her eyes. "Not
that way either! It was a fisherman—ordinary looking,
ratty clothes. Max met him at one of the local bars. He
took Max out on his boat, and they didn't get back until
after two A.M."

"What did he say when you confronted him?"

"I'll never forget the way he looked or how he reacted.
He got real quiet—like he was scared that I knew about it.
He made me promise never to say anything to anyone
unless I wanted him to die. He said we'd be taken care of
as long as he kept quiet."

I was completely mystified by her story. "Are you saying that you think the person who gave Max the gold blew
up the museum?"

"Yes. I couldn't say anything. I was too afraid. I'm
sorry, Dae. I thought he might come after me. I was worried about the girls too. Then I found out yesterday when
he set my house on fire that it didn't matter if I kept quiet.
He wanted me dead too."

I thought about the older man I'd seen in my vision

after touching the coin she gave me. The man I'd seen was too frail to go around blowing up buildings and setting houses on fire. Maybe someone who worked for him had done the dirty work. "You keep referring to a man. Do you know for sure that it's a man?"

"Max always referred to him as a man. I guess that's why I do it. I don't know what happened with Max. I can't believe he'd tell anyone the secret he was keeping. He certainly never told me. He was so terrified of what would happen. The only thing I can think is that he somehow gave it away without realizing it." She stopped and put her bandaged hand to her face. "I don't know what to do now. I'll have to leave Duck. I'd be glad to give back the rest of the gold if he'd leave me alone."

I didn't know what to say. I comforted her as best I could in the situation. She didn't want to tell her daughters for fear one of them might unknowingly give it away. She couldn't tell the police without fear of further reprisal.

What was the secret that Max had died for? What could be that important? And was Sam Meacham somehow involved in all of it? Maybe he'd died for his knowledge of whatever it was.

Later, when the girls came back with Kevin and Gramps, the doctor was right behind, shooing all of us out of the room. He seemed hopeful that Agnes would be released later today, but I wasn't sure that was such a great idea. They could all be on a hit list.

"I'm sure she's upset," Gramps said while we waited in the truck for Kevin to fill the gas tank at a busy station. "But that's not the same as someone trying to kill her, Dae. People get paranoid sometimes when scary things happen. They even make up stories to protect themselves."

"You think Agnes made up all of this?" I took the gold

coin from my pocket. "This is real, Gramps. She got this from someone. Whoever set her house on fire could be ready to do something else if she comes home."

"She can stay with me," Kevin said as he got back in the truck. "She'll be safe that way."

I wasn't sure about that. "What if that person finds out she's at the Blue Whale? And let's face it—the chances are pretty good. You'll all be in danger."

"Possibly." He headed back out into traffic. "But I have two things going for me that she doesn't— an extremely good security system and experience protecting people in trouble. I think I can handle it."

What could I say? It still didn't sound like a good idea to me, but I couldn't say so without casting doubts on his abilities. "What about the man I saw in my vision? He has to be involved. It was his gold. He gave it to Max. Maybe we can find him and rough him up a little until he agrees to leave them alone."

"I like that idea," Kevin said, "but how do we look for him? It sounds like you'd either have to hold hands with every fisherman in the area or touch every fishing boat. Are you up for that?"

"I don't like *that* idea." Gramps frowned at him. "You know interfering in a police investigation can be dangerous—not to mention illegal."

"It's not a police investigation yet," I countered. "Chief Michaels doesn't know about any of it."

"A good reason to tell him as soon as possible. You know I'm right, Kevin. Back me up on this."

"I know." Kevin grinned. "But it's contagious."

"What?" I asked, not liking the look on his face.

"Playing private detective. Maybe I should find out about getting a license." He sobered when he looked at me. "Your grandfather is right, Dae. We should tell the chief about all of this and let him take care of it."

I ignored both of them, annoyed with their verdict. "I guess I don't have much choice. But if Chief Michaels feels like the case is closed with Sam's death, will you help?"

"We'll see," Gramps promised in the same tone he'd always used to put off doing things he didn't want to do.

We got back to Duck finally, and Kevin dropped us both off at the Duck Shoppe's parking lot. I promised to let him know what Chief Michaels said when I could get in touch with him.

"I'd like a promise that you won't try to do any of this without me," he added.

"I'd like snow for Christmas this year," I joked, "but we don't always get what we want."

"Then I'm headed over to the sheriff's office before I go back for that delivery of wineglasses at the Blue Whale."

"No! Okay. I won't do anything even if I happen to touch the right fisherman or boat. I'll call you first."

Fortunately, Gramps had already gone on to meet his friend at the Coffee House so he didn't hear the conversation. I would never have heard the end of it if he had. Kevin took me at my word, and he kissed me before he left.

I went up the stairs to the boardwalk, trying to get back to more mundane things—like wondering if Trudy had made any sales this morning. There was an enclosed area that formed an open-ended walkway between town hall and several other shops. Visitors had to pass through there before reaching the boardwalk that faces the sound and leads to the other stores. It's always a little dark here— even during the day. Sometimes teenagers hang out here at night, and store employees take advantage of the spot to smoke.

I was walking through the area when someone called my name, interrupting my thoughts and making me jump.

Brad Spitzer stepped out of the shadows. "Mayor O'Donnell? I have a few questions for you."

Chapter 14

"Sorry. Did I scare you?" Brad asked when he saw me jump.

"That's okay." I forced a smile. "I wasn't expecting to see anyone. What did you want to ask me?"

"Mind if I walk a little with you?"

"No, of course not—I'm only going to my shop."

"That's fine. It won't take long."

I started walking again, and he fell in step with me as we emerged into the watery sunlight that filtered between the fast moving clouds over the sound.

"Mayor, have you spoken with Agnes Caudle about the fire?"

I felt a little nervous, so my words were carefully chosen. "Yes. I got back from the hospital a few minutes ago. Agnes is doing okay. They might release her today."

"Good news! Does she recall anything about the fire—anything unusual?"

"We didn't get into that. I'm sure she'd be glad to talk to you."

"Maybe. People share things with friends and neighbors—things they won't tell the authorities." He paused and leaned against the railing, looking out over the water. "Mrs. Caudle's house fire could've been a deliberate attempt to kill her. My report will state that a mixture of gas and oil—the same type you might use in a lawn mower or a chainsaw—was used as an accelerant."

I didn't know what to say. It was unusual for someone in Brad's position to give out information like this—unless there was a reason. "At least there was no cannon this time."

I was sorry as soon as I'd said it. It sounded flip and uncaring. I didn't mean for it to, but that's the way it came out.

He straightened up and looked directly into my face. "True. The source isn't as strange. Do you have any idea who might want to hurt both Max and Agnes Caudle?"

"No! Everyone loves both of them. I can't imagine who'd want to do this."

"Sometimes people have a hard time expressing a problem. Mayor O'Donnell, I have to ask—did you have a problem with the Caudles?"

I knew something was up. I hadn't expected him to question me about what happened, but now I understood why he was here. "Are you suggesting I had something to do with either incident?"

Brad shook his head and smiled a little, like he was trying to throw me off. "No, ma'am. But it seems mighty strange to me that you were at the museum when it blew up. You were at the house during the fire. I might even consider it odd that you were at one of the last places Sam Meacham was seen alive."

I lost my mayor's smile and glared at him. "I haven't killed anyone recently, if that's what you're asking."

"You know, we thought everything was tied up with this feud between Max and Sam. But that's off the books now. We know it was someone else."

"Mind telling me why?" The wind blew my hair into my face. I scraped it aside with angry, trembling fingers. Was he *really* thinking I had killed two people?

"Sure. This is still confidential information, mind you. Mr. Meacham was dead long before the house fire, according to the medical examiner's office in Manteo. Even if he was responsible for the first event, he wasn't there for the second."

"I can't deny that I was nearby when the explosion and the house fire occured, or that I found Sam Meacham's Segway," I responded. "But I have no motive for hurting anyone."

"Although you did have opportunity."

I was a little scared and very angry at the same time. I could continue to defend myself to him, but what was the point? If he planned on getting a confession from me, he was going to be disappointed. He would have to continue his investigation to find out anything else. "I won't talk about this with you any further."

"You certainly have that right. Maybe you should consider talking with your grandfather. I understand he was an excellent sheriff. He might be able to give you some guidance. Otherwise, you might need an attorney."

"This is a stupid waste of time and energy, Mr. Spitzer. The real killer is out there somewhere. My only crime might be that I tend to be in the wrong places at the wrong time."

"I've also heard that you like to investigate a little here and there."

"I don't think that makes me a killer."

He took a card out of his wallet. I hoped he didn't notice that my hands were shaking when he handed it to me. "This is my cell number. If you need to talk, I might be able to help you with the DA. Cooperation goes a long way in my book. You help me and I'll help you. Thanks for talking with me, Mayor."

I didn't—couldn't reply. As I walked quickly away from him, my phone started ringing. It was Nancy. She was at town hall and had news about Adelaide, the woman whose dress had floored me when I touched it at the Blue Whale.

"I looked up anyone named Adelaide who'd drowned in recent history," she told me when I got there. "There was a woman in February 1955—Valentine's Day. They found her washed up on the Atlantic side only a few miles down from the Blue Whale."

"What was her whole name?" I took out my notebook.

"Adelaide Reynolds, twenty years old. She was married and had a young daughter."

"Reynolds." I mulled the name over. "Could she be related to Floyd Reynolds, Agnes Caudle's father?"

"I don't know. Want me to check on that?"

"That would be great. Thanks. But not tonight. This is Saturday, remember? I don't think we even pay you to work on Saturday."

"You know I love to come in here. I don't care what day it is." She smiled at me, her eyes searching my face. "Anything I should know about, Dae?"

"I don't know yet. I'm still connecting the dots right now. I appreciate your help, Nancy."

"You know I love to snoop!"

We both laughed, but it was true.

"The Duck Historical Society has planned an emergency meeting," she said. "It's Monday at seven thirty P.M.

They'd like you to be there. I think they may be talking about a fundraiser for the new museum. They probably want you to lead the charge."

"That's fine. I'll put it on my calendar. Now go home. Take up knitting or something." She knew I was joking, at least a little. No telling how much time she really spent up here keeping everything straight for us. If there was a real heart to Duck, it was Nancy.

A new Duck museum. What would that be like without Max? Who would take his place as curator? No one sprang to mind. I knew it had to happen. I knew there would be someone we would all come to accept as our new historian, but it was hard to imagine *who* right now.

I finished my walk to Missing Pieces, slamming the door closed behind me. I was sad and still angry about Max's death. Here I was trying to find out who had done these terrible things and Brad accused me of being the perpetrator. I had to pace back and forth through the shop several times before I started to calm down.

"Dae?" Trudy came up on me with a big smile on her face. "What's wrong?"

"I don't think I can talk about it yet." I stared at her, then started pacing again. "That arson investigator doesn't have any idea what's going on. He accused me—*me*—of having something to do with it. Just because I was at the museum and the house fire and in Corolla before Sam Meacham died. Can you believe it?"

"That's crazy!" She sat down on the burgundy sofa. "But I sold some stuff this morning. That's good news, right?"

"That's very good news. Thanks, Trudy." I sat beside her. "Imagine him thinking I could kill someone! Like I can even run a stop sign without worrying that I'll get a ticket and Gramps will never let me forget it. And now there's Kevin—another person who used to be in law enforcement. What's wrong with me? How can anyone think I could kill someone?"

She shrugged. "Maybe you should ask Shayla. She could do a tarot reading and tell you all about it. Come on. You two have to make up sometime, and you were the one who stole her boyfriend."

I wanted to explain that Kevin and Shayla weren't together anymore before I started seeing him, but I decided to let it go. In the wake of everything that had happened, it seemed paltry. I had to call Gramps and Kevin and let them know about Brad's accusation.

Kevin's cell phone went to voice mail, and there was no answer at the Blue Whale. I tried to call Gramps, then remembered he was out with his friends. His phone went to voice mail too.

"Calm down," Trudy advised. "Things can't be *that* bad."

"I suppose that depends on your definition of bad."

"Well you know you didn't kill anyone or set anything on fire, right? They can't touch you, Dae. All that guy has are suspicions. So he saw you at the fire. So what? Half the town was there, and at the museum right after it exploded."

"You're right." Of course she was right. Brad had to be rattling my cage—trying to find out if I knew anything he didn't know. It was classic investigative technique.

Shayla opened the shop door but wouldn't come inside. "Trudy, can you come out here, please?"

Trudy rolled her eyes. "No. I won't come out there. You're not a vampire—you can walk in without permission. Get in here! We need you."

"I'd rather not. Dae and I are no longer friends. And if I were a vampire, you would've just invited me inside so I could kill you."

"Don't be silly. Dae would've had to ask you to come in for it to work if you were a vampire." Trudy shook her head as if everyone should know these vampire facts. "You two have to hash this out. One of you has to give in and say you're sorry." She took turns glaring at both of us.

"I'm not doing that," Shayla said. "Dae stole my boyfriend. She has to apologize."

Trudy nudged me with her elbow. "Well?"

"I'm not apologizing! Shayla and Kevin had broken up before I started dating him. I didn't steal anything."

"Do you disagree with that?" Trudy asked.

Shayla leaned against the door frame. "Maybe. But she could've told me the truth instead of making me guess."

"Okay." Trudy held out her hands. "Why don't you *both* apologize? Dae, you say you're sorry for how this business with Kevin was handled. Shayla, you say you're sorry for dragging this out when you *knew* you and Kevin were over anyway."

I glanced at Shayla. Trudy was right. This had gone on too long. "Sorry."

"I guess I'm sorry too."

"Good! Now get in here and let's have a hug," Trudy said.

Shayla and I moved toward each other reluctantly but ended up hugging and talking.

"I came by to tell Trudy to warn you that I saw something strange in a tarot I did today." Shayla smiled. "I guess I can tell you personally."

"Strange how?" I closed the door to the shop as we all walked back and sat down on the sofa.

"It was a man of authority crossing you. He has power given to him by the establishment. He'll cause you trouble, Dae. You have to watch out for him."

"Sounds like Brad Spitzer." I explained to her about my conversation with him.

"I saw Kevin in there too," Shayla continued. "He'll help you get through this. There was another man—an older man who has great power and wealth. He has something you need. It could be information or something practical. I couldn't tell for sure. Death surrounds him. Be careful of your dealings with him."

Shayla was phenomenal. She'd described my problem with Brad and had seen part of my vision of the older man who'd given Max the gold. I broke down and told Shayla and Trudy about my new abilities and the visions I'd had.

"Dae, that's powerful!" Shayla exclaimed. "Your abilities are growing. They might rival my own one day. That must be why your chakra looked so weird—that and love will do it every time."

I smiled. "Thanks. Kevin was afraid I couldn't control the visions, but I'm learning to handle them just fine. The terrible part is not understanding what I see. The Segway thing with Sam and the old man with the gold—I don't know what they mean."

"You'll figure it out," Trudy said. "Something will happen and things will click into place. Always do. You'll see."

I made some coffee, and we sat around talking. We didn't bring up the mess with Kevin and Shayla again. I hoped that was water under the bridge now. Shayla went through men pretty fast. It probably wouldn't be long before she found someone else.

It was getting close to three P.M., and only a handful of potential customers were walking up and down the boardwalk. Most of them were locals—which was good for Shayla and Trudy, who had their weekly regulars. Missing Pieces mostly depended on the tourist crowd. Business picked up a little around the holidays, but winter was a long, slow time for me.

I straightened up the shop again after Trudy and Shayla left. I picked up a few items to explore their origins. I was getting better at controlling this new ability, more able to learn from it.

I found that some of the items I thought were treasures were fakes. I hated that, but it was bound to happen once in a while. Some other pieces I thought were mostly junk turned out to be great stuff—I raised their prices.

Feeling confident of what I could do, I picked up my carved African hand mirror that I loved so much. I always kept it behind the counter so customers would know it wasn't for sale. I had a basic idea of where it had come from—the old man at the market in Charleston had told me it once belonged to an African princess. But what I saw today wasn't what I'd expected.

Beyond pain. Beyond fear. Longing for death that wouldn't come. No way out. Trapped and caged.

I looked at my arms and legs—they were covered with open sores, broken and swollen. The pain of hunger and thirst were not as bad as knowing that death was the only escape. I looked in the mirror and saw the ravaged face of a black slave gazing back at me. She would never make the trip to the market alive.

An African princess, the man in Charleston had told me. Had he known she was a dying slave?

I was on the floor, vomiting and crying, my whole body shaking violently. When I could get up, I sat behind the counter for a long time, glad that no one had come into the store. It was hard to get back into myself without the terrible shadow of the woman in the mirror gnawing at my soul.

So much for confidence. So much for not being scared

to touch anything. Kevin had been right about losing myself in this new ability. He hadn't been here to catch me this time—no one had. The terrible stench of death and decay—the fear and hopelessness—were still with me.

When I could stand again, I cleaned up the mess behind the counter and washed my face. I put on gloves to move the mirror to the storage area in the back of the shop. I could never use it or appreciate its beauty again. But I couldn't sell it right away either. Maybe not ever.

I mechanically turned off the lights, closed up and locked the door behind me. I sat on the boardwalk for a long time, looking at the sound. There were things in life much more terrible than being accused of a crime I knew I didn't commit. The hand mirror had shown me that.

It was dark and getting colder—my knee was aching with it. I felt in my pocket and realized I'd left my cell phone in the shop. There were a dozen missed calls from various people. Exhausted and emotionally drained, I ignored them and headed home.

Kevin waylaid me in the parking lot. "Sorry I couldn't get to my phone when you called earlier. I called you back six times. Are you ignoring me or is this punishment for not answering your call?"

I looked at him and wanted to explain but couldn't. "I'm not feeling very well. It's been a bad day. I think I should go home."

"Dae?" He stopped me. "Can I help? At least let me give you a ride."

I agreed—it was easier than arguing. We sat silently in the truck as he drove the short distance to my house. I couldn't talk about anything without blubbering all over. As much as I'd wanted to tell him about Brad's accusations, I couldn't without telling him about my beautiful hand mirror. I wasn't ready for that yet.

"Thanks." I got out of the truck and headed up to the house.

He got out too and walked me to the door. "Whatever it is, I wish you'd tell me. Even if I can't help, at least I can listen."

"Not tonight. I can't. I'll talk to you tomorrow." I went inside, told Gramps I was going upstairs. I heard him talking to Kevin downstairs less than five minutes later. I pulled the covers up over me—shoes and all—my head too. Why couldn't they leave me alone to sort this out?

There was a knock on the bedroom door. "Dae?" It was Gramps.

"Go away. Please."

"I want to talk to you."

"Is Kevin out there too?"

"No." A pause while he decided if he should lie to me. "He's downstairs. We're both worried about you."

"Don't be. I'm fine. I'm going to take a nap. I'll eat something later."

"Dae—"

"*Please*, Gramps." I was already sniffly. "I'll come down when I can talk about this. When it's all sorted out in my head. Okay?"

"All right. I'm here if you need me."

"Thanks."

I cried—a good, long, hard cry. But this one was cleansing. I must've fallen asleep afterward because I woke up and looked at the clock. It was almost midnight. I felt better. I was out of tears and the terrible sorrow had passed. It left me hungry and ready to raid the fridge. *Bad news if my new abilities made me hungry all the time and I gained a lot of weight.*

I put on my Duck pajamas, dark blue with the sandaled Duck mascot on the back. Gramps was still up, watching an old Doris Day movie on cable. He turned it off when he saw me. "I know what you need. Scrambled eggs and toast."

"Add some hot tea and you've got a deal. Thanks, Gramps."

We talked about generalities while he made the eggs and toast. I made a big mug of tea and put too much sugar in it, but it was good.

"Kevin was here until about an hour ago. He's not much of a pinochle player." He laughed to himself.

I smiled at the idea of Gramps teaching Kevin to play pinochle. "Maybe not but I think he's a good person. A little broody maybe."

"I think so too. You make a good couple. Broody and all."

"Thanks."

"You know we never had that talk you promised me the other night. I've been willing to overlook it until now. Maybe now would be a good time for it." Gramps put the eggs and toast on a plate in front of me and took a seat. "Or we could sharpen up your pinochle skills."

"All right! No torture. I'll tell you what I know."

Chapter 15

"As far as I know, your grandmother never experienced anything like this." Gramps was pacing by the time I finished talking. "Is it safe? Is this something you should be doing?"

"It's not like anyone asked my permission. It started before I left the hospital." I told him about what happened to Kevin's FBI partner.

"That doesn't reassure me, Dae." His brow was furrowed with concern. "If Kevin's partner couldn't handle this ramped-up power, what makes you think you can?"

"Because I've been dealing with this all my life. Maybe she hadn't. Because I come from good Banker stock and Mom taught me everything she knew about how Grandma took care of it."

"That didn't seem to have helped you much when you got home."

"I know. But that was exceptional, Gramps. I wasn't ready for it. I won't forget to be ready next time. I won't let it take me by surprise again."

He took a deep breath. "I guess there's not much choice anyway. But I wish you'd told me sooner."

"Why? So you could worry longer?" I finished my eggs and toast. "I'm sorry. I wanted to understand it better."

"And do you?"

"Sort of." I put my plate and cup in the sink. "I'm going over to Kevin's so I can explain to him. He's probably worried too."

"All right. But take the golf cart."

"Why?"

"I don't know—just do it or no going out this late. Duck isn't the same town you grew up in thirty years ago, honey. Take some precautions. I'm going to call that Brad Spitzer first thing in the morning and let him have a piece of my mind."

"Don't do that. I can take care of myself. Besides, like you said, he was only fishing. He was hoping he'd catch something he could use because his best suspect is inconveniently dead."

"Maybe I said that, but I didn't mean it for *me*. Go on to Kevin's. Call me when you get there."

I hugged him and made him promise he wouldn't call Brad in the morning. That's all I needed to get around the mayor has her grandpa calling to complain about how she was treated. He'd done that once in school, supposedly because I didn't have a father. Mom and I made him swear he'd never do it again. It had shadowed me all the way to high school.

I didn't take the golf cart when I went out. It wasn't like the cart could help me get away from anyone. I could run faster than it could move. I started to call Kevin but decided against it. I wanted to walk. If his lights weren't on when I got there, I'd go back home.

Night shadows haunted the wind-tortured bushes and shrubs, investing every old house and narrow street with ghosts that flickered between lights. It could be easy to mistake the mournful cry of a dove or the sleepy call of a lonely seabird as the sighs of a restless spirit.

Sometimes I thought that's all the haunts were in this place—light and shadow mixed with odd noises. The wind never ceased, and the ocean always pounded at the shore. What must it have been like before streetlights and other modern conveniences? How easy was it to believe in pirate ghosts and curses back then?

I'd wanted to believe in ghosts since my mother died, but as the years rolled on with no sign of her, I began to feel like I'd never see her or talk to her again. The father I had never known wasn't so much a loss. I didn't seem to need him because I had my mom and Gramps.

My ghosts seemed to be made more of loss and anger than grave and spirit. Wouldn't my mother come to me if she knew how important it was? Unless ghosts really didn't exist.

I wasn't ready to give up yet, but I wondered sometimes. Duck wasn't like other places where people didn't seem to believe in the spirit world. I'd found that out when I went off to college. People there didn't talk about their dead relatives or wonder if a candle flickering was a spirit moving through the room.

Here, most people had seen ghosts, even talked to them. They never told their children ghosts didn't exist. Our ancestors' spirits were as much a part of our lives as our living relatives.

I got to the Blue Whale without seeing any ghosts or assailants ready to jump out at me. There was a spotlight on the mermaid fountain in the middle of the circle drive. It was always left on—like the porch light—so I couldn't tell from that whether Kevin was still awake or not. But there was a light on in the kitchen area attached to the bar. I decided to take my chances and knock at the door.

If he wasn't awake he might not hear me. But the door opened right away, and he smiled when he saw me. "Dae!" He held me close for a long time before he finally kissed me. "I'm so glad you came over."

"Thanks." His welcome made me feel warm and cozy inside. "I wasn't sure about the time. I know it's late. I should've called."

"You never have to call. Come by whenever you like."

I felt a little guilty about not talking to him earlier. He seemed genuinely worried, and I knew I could've relieved that if I'd been able to tell him everything that had happened. Maybe having this extra ability also meant being extra emotional.

We walked into the lobby, where I immediately stopped short. The collection of historic items had more than doubled since I'd last been here. "We have too much history." I shook my head over the amount of old furniture, clothes, tools, boat parts and other paraphernalia. I couldn't even see most of it because it was in boxes. "Where are we going to put everything?"

"I don't know. I hear they're having a meeting about it Monday night. Carter Hatley told me that Vergie Smith told him someone was donating a house for the new museum."

"A house? That would be wonderful if it's true."

"Do you want something to drink? I have wine, coffee, tea and soda. If you're hungry, I still have some gnocchi left over from dinner."

"No thanks. I came to talk to you about what happened today—yesterday. When you picked me up, I knew I wouldn't be able to talk about it without crying. I know it sounds silly, but it affected me very deeply."

"Let's sit down," he said.

"Good night, Kevin." Celia seemed to come out of no-where as she started up the stairs. "Thanks again for letting us stay here."

She blew him a kiss. I tried not to look as surprised as I felt. "You have Celia, Vicky *and* Agnes staying here?"

"How could I take one and not the other two? They might all be in danger. And it's not like there isn't enough room."

"You are truly a pillar of the Duck community."

"Thanks." He sat beside me on the sofa, one arm behind me. "You were saying?"

I told him about Brad and the African hand mirror. The tale was getting shorter with the telling. I didn't want to linger too much on the details of the hand mirror incident. But when I'd finished, he looked a lot like Gramps had.

"You have to be better prepared—especially with something so out of the ordinary. It wasn't a new yo-yo from China, Dae. What were you thinking?"

I sighed. Two overprotective men in my life might be too much. "I'm fine now. I won't take that chance again, especially with an antique."

"I'll give Brad Spitzer a call in the morning. I can't imagine what he was thinking coming to you like that."

"I'd rather concentrate on how we can find that fisherman who took Max out to meet the man with the gold." I hoped that would change the subject.

"I take that to mean you aren't going to tell Chief Michaels about this latest vision?"

"I'd like to tell him," I reasoned. "But Brad made me realize that they don't have any idea what's going on. I don't believe he talked to me without kicking the idea around with the chief either. Anything I say to them, especially if I'm right, could be evidence that I'm guilty, at least in their minds."

"I don't think so. To begin with, just because they're working together doesn't mean the chief and Spitzer discussed this at all. That's kind of the way it works. Everybody wants to look good by coming up with the right answers for themselves. Spitzer doesn't know you—the chief does. I'm betting he'd listen to what you have to say."

"You're right on that part. I never saw Brad before the museum fire. Just because we all live on the Outer Banks doesn't mean we all know each other."

"I still think you should tell the chief and give him a chance to have some input."

"And I still don't want to tell him."

"What did your grandfather say about it when you told him you weren't going to share this new information with Chief Michaels?"

"I didn't exactly tell him that part," I said. "I thought it might be better not to tell him I wanted to investigate it myself."

"I see." He didn't look happy about it.

"If you're uncomfortable—"

"I am. You should be too. I know you've uncovered information through unorthodox means, but the chief seems like he's willing to work with that. Why not take a chance on him?"

I was disappointed with his response. He was a lot like Gramps—a little too on the side of law enforcement to be able to see outside the box. I realized I might have to go this one alone.

"Dae?"

"Sorry. I was thinking it over. Maybe if I can find one more physical clue I could turn it over to him. If I had the fisherman Max went out with, it might be different."

"I don't know how you'll find him. Holding hands with every fisherman in Duck shouldn't be an option. And if I understand how it works, you'd only be able to help him find any lost items he was looking for."

"Or I could touch every boat." I wished his point weren't so valid. "But how will the chief find him? There are hundreds of fishermen who go in and out of here all the time. He might not even be from Duck."

"That's true," Kevin agreed. "Is that all Agnes knew about him?"

"She knew what bar they'd met at, but that was five years ago. He might not frequent that place anymore. I don't think she'd recognize him."

"The chief could check to see if any gold was stolen about the time Max got the windfall. It would make sense that a thief might give him a small amount to keep him quiet."

I got up from the sofa to stand in front of the massive fireplace. "Why not just kill him right away? Why give him a bunch of gold for his wife's surgery, then threaten him for years? It doesn't make any sense."

"I know you have questions about why your friend died," Kevin said. "I know you want to do this by yourself. I understand that urge, and I know I've been a bad influence helping you. I should've just asked you out to begin with."

He got up and stood close to me, his gray-blue eyes very intent on mine. "But this could be dangerous, Dae, as well as illegal. I don't know how else to say it to keep you out of the situation."

I wanted to argue with him, but I could see it was a losing battle. I wanted to find Max's killer. I wanted to understand why these awful events had happened. I wasn't afraid of any consequences from the police, even though I was already on Brad's radar.

I hated to do it—I had no choice but to lie to Kevin. I wouldn't be able to live with myself if I didn't do all I could to help. "Okay. You win. I'll tell Chief Michaels in the morning. Happy?"

"Only if you tell him everything, not the abbreviated version you told your grandfather. I'll go with you if you want me to."

"I'll be fine, thanks. I hope this is the right thing to do." *And by that I mean lying to you and leaving you out of what needs to be done.*

"It will be." He paused. "Are you up for a walk on the beach?"

"That sounds perfect. We should have a good view of the lighthouse lamps tonight."

"Good. You can point them out."

I really meant to do something about talking to Chief Michaels by Monday morning. Sunday came and went with no opportunity presenting itself. Maybe I didn't try hard enough because my heart wasn't in it. I wasn't sure what I was going to say to him anyway that would make Kevin feel better while still advancing my cause.

So Monday morning I went out early and left my cell phone at home. I had a feeling Kevin might try to call me and ask how my meeting with the chief went. What would I say?

It gave me a very small window to prove my theory before I'd have to either tell Kevin the truth—that I'd lied to him—or tell the chief about the man who may have killed Max.

Not wanting to do either of those things, I left Gramps a note saying that I was busy at the shop for the day. I didn't really have any idea what I should do, but I set out for the docks.

It was a foggy morning, which meant the fishermen would be hanging around waiting for the weather to clear. I had no idea how I was going to tell one fisherman from another or which of them knew Max. I thought if I hung around I might get lucky.

If the fisherman was the same man who went out on the Segway with Sam, he might be wearing the odd ring I'd seen in my vision. I was betting those things went together. It wasn't a coincidence that Sam was dead too. Whatever Max was into had doomed Sam as well.

The docks had once been an infamous place where pirates and other nefarious gentlemen spent time with women of ill repute. Residents foolish enough to venture here might end up serving a captain of a pirate vessel or find themselves doing a gallows jig.

Now the docks were more a tourist area. At one time they had provided the people of Duck with a livelihood from fishing. Now it was more dinner cruises and charter boats. But fishermen still went out, and their catch went to hotels and restaurants whose patrons demanded fresh fish.

The boats were all moored along the piers waiting for the sun to burn away the fog. Their captains and crews sat at the quayside drinking coffee from thermoses or hanging out at the few remaining bars. These places still served rum and beer, but they also made a pretty good breakfast and were known for their steaks and seafood. The tourist trade kept everything clean and open. There was money to be made by providing what visitors needed.

I looked carefully at the boats, especially the ones that

seemed seaworthy enough to go a little further from shore. I knew there were islands off the coast of the Outer Banks where few tourists ever roamed. Most of these were owned by wealthy individuals or the government. It seemed likely to me that one of these would have been Max's destination where he met his wealthy benefactor.

I put out my hand to touch the first one and brought it back before it got close enough to the bow. I'd lost my courage after Saturday's incident. Maybe I *could* tell something from the boats, but I couldn't work myself up to it. I wasn't back to wearing gloves, but I needed to be cautious. I wouldn't do Max any good if I couldn't control what happened to me when I saw something.

I sat down on one of the benches next to a group of boats. It was cool in the ghostly fog. Icy crystals lodged themselves on windows and the flat surfaces of hulls. The names of the boats were colorful—*White Wave*, *Jezebel*, *Ocean Sprite* and *Better Luck Next Time*.

I saw Gramps's boat—the *Eleanore*—named for my grandmother. She was a sleek, twenty-two-foot charter boat with a few berths in the stern and a sturdy hull that had seen her through many storms over the years. She could raise sail or slice quickly through the water using her powerful built-in engine.

I had many happy memories of being onboard the *Eleanore*. We'd had birthday parties with dolphins swimming nearby and beautiful sunsets for the Fourth of July. I hadn't been out on the boat for a long time. Gramps frequently asked me to go out with him, but it never seemed like there was enough time.

Realizing Gramps could be here somewhere hanging out with his friends and waiting to take a charter out made me doubly cautious. He'd be a lot harder to explain to than Kevin. If he'd been with Kevin and me at the inn last night, he would have seen right through my sudden willingness to share information with Chief Michaels. I might be able to keep information from him, but I could never lie to him.

I resolved to touch every boat at the docks, if necessary, until I could find the right one. Obviously I couldn't spend time in the bars and risk seeing Gramps, so this seemed like the only way.

I had just steeled myself for the first touch, choosing the *Jezebel* as my first victim, when a swirl of fog moved away from another boat further down the pier. It was named *Golden Day*. How could I resist? The name was like a sign from the heavens that this was the right boat.

I looked around a little first. It was a few feet longer than Gramps's boat and definitely in better condition. It was probably a lot more expensive too.

I didn't see anyone. I decided to take my chances and stepped onboard. I laid my hand down flat on the deck, but before any image could form, a strong hand pushed me from behind and I tumbled down the stairs into the living quarters. Before I could get back on my feet, the door from above was closed. I heard the sound of a dead bolt scraping into place.

"Hey! Let me out!" I pounded on the door, but there was no response.

Before I could draw another breath to scream for help, the boat's powerful engine started, blocking out any sound I could make. Within the next two minutes, the boat was leaving the docks and heading out to sea.

Chapter 16

I paced the confined space inside the boat. It was luxuriously appointed with carpet on the floor and expensive fixtures, including brass-rimmed portals. Everything anyone could want was available in a tiny format. Except for the one thing I wanted—something I could use as a weapon.

I found radio equipment, but it was all turned off, with no way to power it up from here. Maybe kidnapping people was a normal activity for the boat. Of course, I'd left my cell phone at home. Who knew whether it would have had a signal, but I didn't even have the opportunity to find out. Guess that's what happens when you try to shirk your responsibilities. It wasn't like Kevin hadn't warned me.

It seemed that I'd found the right boat on my first try, but now I wished I'd been wrong. Of all the boats to choose from, I had to choose the murderous, kidnapping boat. Sometimes I'm lucky that way.

I sat down on one of the silk-bedspread-covered bunks and listened to the throbbing sound of the engine while I watched the shore slip farther away. Investigating was dangerous. Kevin was right. Gramps too. It was best left to the professionals—well-armed professionals.

What am I going to do now? No psychic ability will get me out of here in one piece. Maybe I could pretend I don't know anything. It's all a mistake.

I tried to clear my mind—to think about a plan that could help me be ready when the pilot finally opened the door to let me out. It would probably be the only opportunity I'd have to surprise him and get away. I had to be ready for it.

My gaze fell on the fire extinguisher. That was a possibility. I could use it to shoot foam at him and then hit him in the head. Even if he was blocking the stairs, I could run out over the top of him. I took the extinguisher down from the wall, ignoring the vision of it being filled, packed and shipped.

I also found several steak knives in the galley—they looked like weapons to me. I'd have to be pretty close to use one since knife throwing wasn't one of my talents. The knives echoed with good times people had enjoyed onboard the *Golden Day*—laughing and eating dinner with friends.

In fact, everything I touched on the boat had the same happy feelings. There had been parties here, good times fishing and people jumping off the sides of the boat to go swimming. Probably the same things I'd feel from the *Eleanore* if I touched her. It would have all my memories of the past.

But, I reminded myself before I got lost in those pleasant visions, that didn't mean the man who owned the boat hadn't killed Max.

Stay focused. Be ready for the door to open. You have to be sharp if you want to stay alive. This may seem like a pleasure cruise, but you're a prisoner.

I tried to imagine all the things Kevin would do in my position. Did FBI agents go to strategy sessions for coping with various scenarios? They were probably trained to use everything as a weapon. But try as I might, I couldn't think of any way to use a pillow, a coffee mug or a box of paper towels as weapons. Would a pillow block a bullet if the pilot had a gun?

There was no one to ask.

I stood at the door for a long time, ready to fight my way out. After about thirty minutes of the door not opening, I gave up and sat down. But I kept the fire extinguisher and knives close at hand. I also confiscated a box of candles and a lighter that I thought might be useful. There were a few sandwiches and some pickles in the mini-fridge, but I wasn't hungry.

The pleasant, happy, vacation feelings of the boat surrounded me, almost cocooning me from the reality of my situation. Like the terrible feelings I'd experienced while holding the African hand mirror, these were just as overwhelming. The only difference was being on the boat was like spending a warm summer day on the sound.

It would be easy to imagine Gramps being at the helm while we headed out to explore the shoreline going toward Kitty Hawk. We'd done it all the time when I was a kid. He'd tell me all the old pirate stories and show me the places where treasure was supposed to be buried. He knew all the legends and tall tales the Bankers could tell.

In the midst of thinking back on my childhood, part of my mind noticed that the engine had stopped. That tiny fraction of sanity kept pushing at the edges of my memories until all of me was duly alerted. I jumped up with my extinguisher in hand—knives in my pockets.

It occurred to me, as I waited nervously for my assailant to arrive, that I had never stabbed, shot or hit someone in the head with a metal cylinder in my life. I urged myself to be tough, remember what was at stake. There wasn't anyone else here to fight for me. Either I'd get myself out of this spot or possibly end my days washing up on the shore like Sam Meacham.

I heard the pilot's footsteps as he left the helm. I hadn't heard the anchor splash into the water so I had to assume we were about to be tied up at a pier. There could be others waiting on shore. But first I had to get past the man who'd thrown me in here.

The dead bolt slid away from the door. My muscles tensed, and I felt a little like throwing up. What if I couldn't hit him hard enough? What if I got away from him but someone else shot me as I ran off the boat?

The door began to open. I broke the seal on the extinguisher. I might not be a trained assassin, but Gramps had showed me how to use one of these when I was a child. *Would I ever see him again?*

As the door swung open, I waited impatiently for the man to appear. I had to wait for just the right moment to spray him or he'd just back away from the foam. I went over and over it in my mind—shoot the foam in his eyes, hit him with the metal cylinder, get off the boat.

He helped me, actually, by leaning his head in the doorway before he walked down the stairs. "You okay down here, girlie? I ain't heard a peep—"

I didn't wait to hear any more. I held the nozzle out and pressed the lever, releasing a cloud of heavy white foam into his face. He put up his hands to try and shield his eyes, and I saw the strange green-blue stone—the same one I'd seen in the vision with Sam. I realized then that I really was fighting for my life.

As he moved to protect himself, I hit him with the cylinder. He yelled and fell down the stairs to land at my feet. With a cry of victory, I jumped on top of him and ran up into the sunlight.

I was thrilled to be free and that my plan had worked so well. Maybe I was better at this than I'd thought. Still, I had the presence of mind to close the doors and lock them before I went up on deck.

It occurred to me that getting off the boat might not be the smartest thing to do. I took a quick look around, assessing the dock where the boat was tied.

There were several young men on the dock next to the boat. None of them seemed to be paying much attention to what was going on. I kept my head down so they wouldn't notice me. Obviously, I would be hard-pressed to get the boat started without one of them realizing there was a problem and jumping onboard.

On the other hand, I had no chance of getting past them to some sort of freedom—a place with a phone. Again, the men were bound to stop me.

The pilot I'd closed in downstairs wasn't as quiet as he'd found me to be. He was already yelling and pounding on the door. It wouldn't be long before they'd hear him. How was I going to get myself out of this situation?

There was only one answer. I had to swim away from the boat before anyone heard my captive or realized that I was here. I knew the water was cold, and I had no idea how far I'd have to go to find safety. I glanced at the horizon and saw nothing but ocean. It appeared I'd been right about the boat going to one of the outer islands. Not a great time to be right.

I grabbed a snorkel and mask from the equipment

locker near the helm. I also took a wrist compass to keep track of where I was going. I had to stay close to shore and look for help. Swimming out into the Atlantic with no land or boat in sight could be suicide. I didn't plan to help them kill me.

Taking a deep breath, I kicked off my shoes and jumped away from the boat. An instant before I hit the water, I heard a smashing sound and knew the pilot had found a way out of his prison that I hadn't thought of. Lucky thing I was gone.

I was right about the water. It was freezing. Not that I hadn't gone swimming in the sound many times when it was that cold. But I was a kid then—adult bodies are more sensitive. The cold water closed over me and almost took my breath away. Only years of swimming and my training as a lifeguard kept me focused on breathing through the snorkel and kicking my feet to get away from the boat.

I expected to hear bullets whiz by me (whatever that sounded like in the water—another experience I'd never had), but that didn't happen. I took a good look at my compass location and kept swimming close to the shoreline. Even if this was a private island, which seemed likely, there had to be a spot I could get out of the water and not be noticed.

I had no idea what I was going to do after that. At that moment, getting out of the freezing water was the only thing on my mind.

I swam for a long time before I surfaced and looked around. I was still close to the island. My bearings were good on that. The boat was nowhere to be seen. Still terrified of what would happen if they found me, I wondered, *Did I do it? Did I manage to get away?*

I was glad that I'd seen the pilot's hand. I might not be able to explain my vision, but I knew that the pilot was the last person to see Sam alive. When I got back to Duck, I'd bring the police here with me and have the satisfaction of seeing him prosecuted for kidnapping me and killing Sam. He might have some questions to answer about Max's death and burning down Agnes's house too.

But first I had to get out of this freezing water.

I could see one large house and several smaller houses circling around it. I wanted to be as far away from that area as I could. Despite my chattering teeth, I put my head back in the water and kept swimming along the coastline. The water wasn't so cold that the exercise didn't make it bearable. I wanted to get out where I'd have a good chance of not running into anyone.

Another opportunity presented itself a little farther down. No boats. No piers. No houses. At least from my vantage point in the water, all I could see was pine trees. A little experience on these very outer edges of land told me that there could be other people living out here—many times without power or any other necessity. Gramps had a friend who'd lived like that for years. Tourists sometimes stopped off at these spots, never knowing that the island was private property.

Between these hopes and the fear still churning in my belly lay a whole world of possibilities, some not as good as others. I couldn't stay in the water much longer, and I hadn't been lucky enough to spot a Coast Guard vessel. At this point, that would be the only group with a boat I'd trust.

There were only trees, rocks and sand as far as I could see. My numb limbs told me I had to take my chances. I paddled carefully toward the shore, mindful of anyone spotting me. It was quiet when I reached the rocky beach and crept up, shivering. Water ran from my clothes in noisy fountains. Not wanting the sound to alert my cap-

tors, I sat down between some trees to dry off while I
formulated my next move.

So far, so good. Getting away from the man on the boat
had been the hard part. I might be cold, but at least I was
alive.

In the distance, I could hear people shouting and the
sound of several boat engines starting up at the same time.
They were bound to conclude that I had stayed close to
shore. Only a fool would swim out to sea with no source
of rescue close by.

I forced myself to my feet and moved further into the
young stand of pine trees. They were barely taller than
me but better than no cover at all. I figured if they didn't
see me from the boats, they might give up and believe I'd
drowned. That was my best hope.

I didn't want to think about how worried Gramps was
going to be. I'd given up on this being a short-term adventure. It might be days before I got back to Duck. In the
meantime, Chief Michaels and others would be looking
for me. With any luck, they'd be able to track me to the
docks. Maybe they'd send the Coast Guard out to look for
me. But I wasn't sure how long that would take.

I had to force myself to stop thinking that way. I tried
to focus on what my plan for survival should be. My first
concern was obviously dry clothes (if possible) and shelter. Then I needed to think about food and how I'd get
back home.

I waited in the trees, surrounded by the piney aroma,
letting the sun warm and dry me. At long last, I couldn't
hear anyone shouting and the sound of engines had faded
into the distance.

I had no idea what time it was—I couldn't recall how
to tell time by the position of the sun. I'd learned one year

in Girl Scouts, but that was a long time ago. *It's not important anyway. Time to move to phase two of the plan.*

Phase two meant getting up and moving my poor frozen body. Every part of me rebelled at the idea. Most of my clothes had dried, but I was still chilled to the bone. All my joints popped when I finally gritted my teeth and pushed to my feet. I really needed a latte and a nice almond biscotti. And a warm fire. I urged myself forward, farther into the pines. And a warm fuzzy robe.

I thought about all these things, promised myself those and more if I kept moving. Somewhere out here there was warmth, food, and a telephone. I could call Gramps and he'd come and get me. He'd be angry but relieved to hear from me. Kevin would say I told you so. My adventure, which was turning out to be a nightmare, would be over and I'd be home again.

"If I get home, I'm never investigating anything again," I swore out loud for good measure. "I'm never leaving my room again except to go to the shop."

I trudged through the pine trees, which seemed to stretch on forever. The sun was almost directly overhead. Even I knew that meant it was around noon. My stomach gurgled accordingly, letting me know that the rest of my body knew what time it was too.

My dried clothes were itchy and full of sand—my feet hurt from walking over pinecones and rocks. I was as miserable as I could ever recall being. But at least I was free.

The trees finally thinned and ended, leaving me in a huge open space with newly cut grass and a large fountain. In the center of the fountain was a large horse standing on its back legs, like the ones at the entrance to Brookgreen Gardens near Myrtle Beach. I wasn't sure how clean the water was, but I was really thirsty. I reached in and took a handful. It was cool and clear—easing the ache in my throat.

"Ha! A water thief! I knew it would come to this!" An old man in a motorized wheelchair came at me full tilt with a pearl-headed cane. "Get your own water!"

I knew him at once. He was the man from the vision about the gold. I had managed to escape the boats and the men at the docks only to find myself in the garden with Max's benefactor. He didn't seem like much of a threat.

"What do you want?" he yelled again. "How did you get here?"

"Take it easy." I tried to reassure him as I glanced around. No one else seemed to be with him. "I was thirsty. I'm lost."

"You're on my property," he proclaimed. "Head that way." He pointed with his cane. "Keep walking until you reach the ocean."

"Thanks." I swallowed another gulp of water and prepared to disappear back into the pines. I knew he could be the person behind Max's death, but I'd run out of courage and options to continue. I just wanted to go home.

"Wait!" he called out. "If you're really lost, you can come back to the house with me and I'll have someone take you home."

"No thanks. One of your men is the reason I'm lost. He kidnapped me and brought me here. I don't need your help."

"Nonsense. There's no reason one of my men would bring anyone here—unless you were snooping. Is that the case? Where are you from?"

"I'm from Duck. And I wasn't snooping—exactly. I was looking for a boat."

"Duck! My dear young woman, I insist that you stay!

What's your name? I probably know someone in your family. Stay and have lunch with me. I'm sure we can find you a change of clothes. We'll sort out this kidnapping thing. You'll see."

I'd already been here too long. I could see people coming out of the big house on the hill. They were still too far away to do anything, but I wasn't about to wait around until they reached us.

"Wait!" he called out again as I started back into the pines. "I'd love to talk with you. If you grew up in Duck, you probably know my name. I used to be somewhat of a celebrity. Probably before you were born. I'm Bunk Whitley. I once owned the Blue Whale Inn."

Chapter 17

Nothing on earth—except that statement—could have made me stay there. I thought about the pictures I'd seen on microfiche from the old *Duck Gazette*. Old Bunk Whitley. Man about town. A real ladies' man who caused two sisters in town to feud their whole lives. A mystery man who'd vanished years ago, his past strange and shadowy. It was hard to see the legend in this wrinkled old man.

Of course, just because he was a legend in Duck didn't mean I could trust him. But I was fascinated that here he sat before me, in the flesh. "Everyone thinks you're dead," I said, not immune to the lure of mystery.

"I'm supposed to be dead. But it's hard to keep a good man down. I'm sure I know you." His eyes narrowed. "You're related to Eleanore O'Donnell, aren't you? Too young to be her daughter. You must be her granddaughter. I never forget a pretty woman."

The men from the house were running now. I had to make a choice. I wanted to stay and hear all the stories he had to tell. I could only imagine that Max would have risked anything to talk to old Bunk Whitley.

Then it hit me. "You killed Max because he knew you were living out here. You couldn't risk everyone knowing you were alive. There's a warrant out for your arrest. You killed Wild Johnny Simpson at the Blue Whale Inn, then left town."

He laughed. "Don't be absurd! I've never killed anyone in my life. I'm a lover, not a fighter. I find money gets more done than guns. But, my young O'Donnell, tell me about your family. Tell me how old Sheriff Horace is doing. I hate that the *Gazette* closed down. No news anymore except what my men can glean for me."

I knew he couldn't be trusted no matter how affable he seemed. I turned to run, but there was a man in my way—and no fire extinguisher to remove him. Too late.

Bunk laughed again. "Come on. You'll be glad you didn't run off by yourself. There's nothing out there, you know. We'll have lunch and get things straightened out. What did you say your name was again?"

"Dae O'Donnell." The man in front of me smiled. He wasn't holding a visible weapon, but I felt pretty sure he wouldn't let me get past him.

"Mayor Dae O'Donnell? Amazing! I haven't had lunch with a mayor for years. Nash, make sure our guest is treated well. Have Lacey find her some clean clothes and bring her down for lunch in the sunroom."

"Yes, sir."

"Don't let her leave yet, Nash. I'm afraid she'd hurt herself out there. Eleanore O'Donnell's granddaughter deserves better."

It seemed I was a prisoner again—this time because of

my own crazy love of Duck lore. Had Max and Sam died for the same reason?

I lost count of the number of rooms as I was shown to a guest suite. From what I saw in the mansion, everything was expensive and larger than life. I didn't have much chance to linger over anything as Nash kept me moving. The door was locked behind me, reminding me that I was a guest in name only.

I looked out of the panoramic windows, a colorful patio beneath me. It was too far to jump. I was eyeing the elaborate brass four-poster, thinking about using the pink sheets for a rope, when a young woman came into the room.

"Hi. I'm Lacey. Mr. Whitley says you're staying for lunch and you need clothes." Her big brown eyes were friendly but probably not unaware of my position.

"Is there a phone? I need to call my grandfather and let him know where I am."

"I'm sorry. There aren't any phones up here. Maybe Mr. Whitley will let you use the satellite phone downstairs."

She walked to the side of the room where a double mirror opened into a closet with a touch of her finger. "There are clothes in different sizes in here. You should be able to find something to wear."

"Thanks."

"Don't worry. Mr. Whitley has many guests who stay here. You'll be well cared for. I'm sure he'll send you home before too long." She smiled at me. She was very young— maybe under twenty. I wondered how she'd managed to find work here. "If you'd like to take a bath or shower, it's in here." She pointed to the other side of the room. "Mr.

Whitley eats at one, but he said to take your time. He'll wait for you."

I thanked her again and she left. I heard the door lock behind her. What now?

I always hate in books and movies when the woman being held captive gets all dressed up for her captor. On the other hand, my clothes were painfully awful. But what difference did it make if he was only going to kill me anyway?

I considered going down for lunch the way I was—damn the consequences. I decided against it. If nothing else, my last hour I'd be clean and well dressed. Maybe that's why all the captive females agreed to change.

I took a quick shower, forcing myself to ignore a pink marble tub large enough to swim in. It even had a Jacuzzi. The pink marble floors were heated and felt good to my poor abused feet. The bathroom was a thing of beauty that I wished I could take with me to replace our old claw-foot tub and ancient appointments that needed to be replaced years ago.

I found a pair of jeans—even new underwear with the tags still on them, wrapped in tissue paper. The closest thing I could find to a T-shirt was an apricot-colored button-down shirt. I wondered who the guests were who had worn these extra clothes and whether they'd made it home alive.

I rummaged through the bedroom, which included a sitting room with fireplace. The carpet was so soft, I hated to put on the shoes I'd found.

Bunk Whitley had certainly come up in the world from owning the Blue Whale Inn. No wonder he had gold to spare for Max, even if it had come with a price.

I knocked on the inside of the door to let Nash know I was ready. He opened it wide. He didn't say anything, just kept his distance, and led me back through the house to the sunroom. This time I noticed what were probably real Picassos and Renoirs on the walls. Everything was beautifully decorated and elegantly laid out.

"There you are!" Bunk greeted me in the sunroom, which was almost the size of our whole house. "I hope you're feeling more comfortable now, and I hope you're hungry. It's too cold for a swim this time of year, but I bet it gave you an appetite. Roger tells me you were on the *Golden Day* when he came back from getting supplies. I apologize for his rude behavior toward you. Sometimes my men get suspicious with strangers. You understand that being from Duck, I'm sure."

I sat down at the large glass table, the room full of plants and water features. There was fruit, wine and cheese out already with a white-jacketed waiter standing nearby. "Apology accepted. May I go home now?"

"But my dear mayor, I'm so looking forward to having lunch with you. And there are some—discrepancies we should discuss before you go running back to get Chief Michaels out here."

"What discrepancies?"

"Please, have some fruit. Pablo, my chef, is making us a wonderful quiche with fresh-baked bread. The wine is made from muscadines. I'm sure you'll enjoy it."

"I'm not really hungry."

He stopped pandering and sighed. "You drive a hard bargain, Ms. O'Donnell. You're just like your grandmother. Eleanore was a force to be reckoned with. I mourned her passing. She was so young. Is your mother like her?"

"My mother died a long time ago. I guess the women in my family don't live long."

"What a pity!" He shook his grizzled head. "As to those discrepancies, I'm not responsible for Max Caudle's death. I can't even imagine someone firing a cannon in this day and age. What an odd way to kill someone."

"And Sam Meacham?"

"I'm afraid I had something to do with that, but not what you're thinking. It happened with the best of intentions. I sent Roger to offer Sam someplace to hide until Max's killer was found. He knew Roger since he'd been on the island with Max. Unfortunately, he took it the wrong way and jumped off the boat I'd sent for him. He had this odd notion that I wanted to kill him."

He took a sip of the red wine in his glass. "My men tried to bring him back, but he swam away and they lost him. I heard his body washed up. Terrible thing. I truly meant him no harm."

"Mr. Whitley, doesn't it strike you as odd that your men meant no harm, but they kidnapped me? And they *accidentally* lost Sam at sea? I think there may be more going on than you think. Maybe you didn't fire that cannon, but maybe one of your men did."

"I don't believe that's true. But I'll tell you what I know and we'll see what comes of it—if you'll have lunch with me and share Duck news. There's a price to be paid for everything. This one isn't too steep, I think."

I agreed to lunch. What choice did I have? Maybe something he said would make sense and I'd be able to take it back to Chief Michaels. I grabbed a peach and cut a slice off with my knife. "All right. I'd like to meet the man who lost Sam at sea."

"Of course." He nodded at the waiter. "Roger has worked for me for years. He'd never kill anyone—unless it was an absolute necessity. And then never without my permission."

Roger was summoned to our table, where he repeated the story—almost word for word—that Bunk had told me about Sam's death being an accident. Both men looked at me, and Bunk asked me if I had any other questions. Only a fool wouldn't know when they were caught between a cutlass and a dagger. I wasn't going to get anything useful from them.

"A lot of bad things happen around you, Mr. Whitley. Like Wild Johnny's death."

"Please call me Bunk." He stared off for a few seconds and smiled. "Wild Johnny Simpson. I haven't thought of him in a *very* long time. I left him at the Blue Whale that night, completely alive, I assure you. He was going to take care of the property for me since the FBI had convinced me to leave town."

"The FBI?"

"No. Not another question until I ask one of mine— what is Kevin Brickman like? I know a little about him. I would, of course, since I sold him the Blue Whale. But that was through my agent. Does he seem like the type to run an inn? I can't imagine an ex–FBI agent cooking and cleaning."

I told him about Kevin and all the work he'd done on the Blue Whale. "He's even taking in all the historical items for the new museum. I think he makes a good innkeeper. You should try his lasagna sometime."

"That's right. The little museum blew up. Remind me before you leave to give you a handful of coins for the collection. I never got rid of the rest of the gold I found when I was young. There's not much market for pirate gold, you know."

"So the FBI asked you to leave Duck," I said, reminding him where we were.

"Yes. They offered me a new name and a place to live for information I gave them about a gang of smugglers working in the area. I was small potatoes compared to them. I took them up on it for a while, but I could never live under the radar that way. I traveled to Europe and around the world a few times. I finally came back here. I want to die close to home, you see. I knew I couldn't actually live in Duck again—no one would leave me in peace. Being here is very much like being at home."

"And you gave Max more recent gold for his wife's surgery a few years back."

"It's my turn." He smiled at me like a kid waiting for ice cream. "How's Millie doing? I hated when I heard Lizzie was killed. Is Millie still the 'it' girl she always was? That woman knew how to get under my skin."

"I'm not sure about the 'it' part, but she's doing fine. I thought you were in love with Miss Elizabeth, not Miss Mildred."

He laughed and I could see something of the ladies' man he had been all his life. "I loved them both. Never could choose between them."

"And the gold for Agnes's surgery?"

"You have it all wrong, Mayor. I gave Max gold for my *daughter's* open-heart surgery. Max was a good man. He took good care of Agnes—better than I did. I wouldn't have harmed a hair on his head."

Now that was a story I'd never heard before. "Agnes Caudle is your daughter?"

Pablo served the cheese quiche and fragrant, home-made bread with little flower-shaped pats of butter. Bunk thanked him, then smiled as he buttered some bread and handed it to me. "Wait until you try this. You won't believe how good it is."

I waited impatiently for his answer to my question. The quiche set before me smelled almost as good as the bread.

"Agnes is my biological daughter. She doesn't know it. When I heard she and Max were having trouble finding the money for her surgery, I brought him out here and gave him the gold. I wasn't there for her when she was growing up. Not entirely my fault, but I wanted to do this thing for her."

"How can she not know you're her father?" I knew Floyd Reynolds, Agnes's father. Did he know Agnes wasn't his daughter?

"Agnes's mother was Adelaide. Beautiful Adelaide. She was my soul mate. She and I were very much in love, but she was married. Back then divorce was a big deal, and Adelaide cared for Floyd and wouldn't hurt him by leaving. She was a wonderfully kind woman. Could never even stand to kill a spider. She never told her husband that Agnes was my daughter. I trusted Max with that secret. He was the only one besides Adelaide and me who knew."

"If Adelaide was married to Floyd, how did she know you were Agnes's father?"

"There was a genetic marker. Nothing big. We could've done a paternity test, but it didn't matter. We knew Agnes was my little girl. But Adelaide didn't trust me to be the kind of father she knew Floyd would be."

"And then Adelaide killed herself because of you."

He sat up straighter in his wheelchair, shock and disbelief in his lined face. "What are you saying? Adelaide drowned. It was an accident. She didn't kill herself."

"I'm sorry." I played with my linen napkin. I hadn't realized it was a secret. "I guess you didn't know. She took her own life."

"How do you know?" His voice was gruff and demanding, the southern gentleman falling away and revealing the darker side of him. "I've seen the sheriff's report. Adelaide had a little too much wine. There was no mention of suicide."

I realized I'd said too much. I wasn't willing to talk to

him about my abilities. All this terrific reminiscing about the past and the lives of people I'd only heard about had caused me to let down my guard. Talking about what had happened was one thing—admitting how I knew about Adelaide was another. How did I know what he'd do with that knowledge?

"Wait!" He laughed. "Of course! You're Eleanore's granddaughter. You inherited her gift, didn't you? You can see things the rest of us can't. But what brought you to this discovery? If I recall correctly, Eleanore had to be in direct physical contact with a person to learn things about them."

That was the first time I'd ever heard it put that way. Had my grandmother been able to do more with her gift than simply help people locate their lost items? I realized this wasn't the best time or person to ask.

There really were no secrets in Duck, or apparently outside of Duck, if you'd ever lived there. I gave him a brief idea of how it happened that I tried on one of Adelaide's old dresses. "She wasn't out for a swim, drunk or not. She walked out into the ocean, not planning on coming out again. You know that's what the medical examiner is going to rule about Sam's death. Everyone thinks that he killed Max and then took his own life out of guilt. We have to let his family know that it isn't true."

"Yes. That's terribly wrong. Nothing could be further from the truth. I believe Sam was trying to save his life."

"You have to tell Chief Michaels or the sheriff what happened."

He seemed suddenly out of it, still trapped in the past thinking about Adelaide. "Things never work out exactly the way you plan, Mayor. I wish I could take so much back and change so many things that happened. I can't, you know."

"Maybe not—but you can make this thing right, Bunk. What about Max? You said you keep an eye on things. You knew Agnes needed surgery. Why was Max killed and the museum blown up? Who set the fire that almost killed your daughter?"

"I don't know."

"But you have some theories since you thought Sam was next. What made you think that?"

He stared off through the big windows that made a panoramic portrait of his little kingdom. "I do have an idea about why this happened."

"And?"

His gaze came suddenly back to mine with great clarity. "Sam came out here to talk to me once. He came with Max. It was a mistake. There were some things going on at the time. Suffice it to say, it was a matter of being in the wrong place at a very bad time."

"Are you saying someone wanted to murder Sam and Max to get back at you?"

"Not exactly. His target was never Sam or Max. They were collateral damage."

"I don't understand. Can you make that plainer?" My mind was buzzing with all kinds of possibilities.

Bunk moved back from the table with a touch of the controls on his wheelchair. "I'm saying I think that it's time you should go back home. It was very pleasant talking with you, Mayor—may I call you Dae? But for the grace of Horace getting there first, this could be a very different conversation. I held your grandmother in very high regard."

That threw me off balance. I realized that it was meant to. I was being dismissed as rapidly as I'd been brought here. I hadn't even finished my quiche. "Now what?" I tried to stay focused despite the *eww* factor in thinking of

Bunk being my grandfather. Although I *would* have had a very nice bathroom.

"Now I think I need to speak with Chief Michaels. Do you think you could get him to come back out here with you?"

I nodded, completely amazed in his turnaround. "Definitely." I wondered, though, if it would be the sheriff who would need to handle all of this. No matter what, Chief Michaels would be a good start.

Then that was it. Game over. I was whisked out of the mansion with Nash and Roger faster than an eel can slip out of a net. Bunk was as good as his word, however, and met me at the dock with a red box full of old gold coins like the ones that had been in the museum.

"It seems a lifetime ago that I found these on the beach. I built the Blue Whale with them."

I looked at the gold, then at him. "You know, Max always said *he* found these."

He shrugged. "It never mattered."

"Thanks for telling me about all those other things. I feel like I know more about Duck history than I did when I got here."

"You had a right to know. Thank you for sharing that information about your remarkable abilities. Use them wisely." He nodded then added, "How's your father, by the way? Is he still working his boat or has he moved on?"

If learning that Agnes was Bunk's daughter jolted me, a question about my father was like a lightning strike. "My father died before I was born."

Bunk grinned. "Did he? It seems we have other history to talk about when you come back, Dae. There are some other things you need to know."

Chapter 18

"My father is alive?" I yelled at him as his wheel-chair began to glide away. The boat I stood on was slipping back from the dock. "Who is he?"

"All in good time," he shouted as he waved. "I enjoyed our lunch too much not to give you another reason to come back. Bring Horace with you too!"

My father? He was more a mythological figure than old Bunk Whitley. My mother had always told me that he died before I was born. Theirs was a brief, passionate meeting that had taken place out of the blue—resulting in me. My father died before he even knew I'd been conceived in their one night together. It was a scandal at the time as my mother's pregnancy began to show and there was no father. Because they were never married, I carried my mother's name.

My family weathered the scandal. My mother was very quiet about my father, never mentioning him unless I asked. I didn't do so very often because I could see the pain it caused her. I never needed him. I had my mother and my grandfather. We were always enough.

But now, realizing I could have a secret of my own as large as Bunk Whitley being Agnes's father, I urged the *Golden Day* faster toward Duck. Only Gramps would know the answer to my questions. I couldn't imagine any reason for wily old Bunk to lie. He wouldn't gain anything by saying my father was alive.

My brain was lit up like a Christmas tree. It was stuffed so full of information, I felt ready to explode. I looked at Roger, who stood at the helm, and wondered what really happened to Sam. Bunk seemed to believe what Roger had told us. But I saw the green-blue ring on his finger and felt again the fear Sam had left on the Segway. I knew I'd have to tell Chief Michaels about everything—not just my meeting with Bunk. There were a lot of questions to be answered.

I thought about Bunk's insinuation that knowing he was alive had killed Sam and Max, but not by his hand. He didn't ask me to keep it quiet that he was out here on the island. Maybe it wouldn't matter anymore after he talked to the chief.

One of Duck's greatest mysteries—what became of old Bunk Whitley—was about to be solved. But it appeared that Bunk was bringing a whole new set of mysteries with him.

Roger and Nash dropped me off at the Duck docks with the coordinates to find Bunk's island for the return trip. There was no pleasant chitchat between us while I was on the boat or as they left me. Just as well since I didn't trust either of them.

Did I trust Bunk? Probably not, although he had a quality about him that made him believable. I had no doubt that
Agnes was his daughter and that he hadn't killed Max. I
wasn't so sure about Sam. Maybe Bunk hadn't done the
deed personally, but he might be responsible anyway.

It was only three thirty when we got back. The skies
were still heavily overcast, which made it look and feel
much later. I couldn't wait to share all of my information
with someone. Too bad my cell phone was still at home. I
wouldn't leave it behind again. Next time I didn't want to
talk to someone, I just wouldn't answer the phone.

I felt like Professor Challenger coming back from the
Lost World. I wasn't sure where to start. The issue resolved
itself when I spotted Tim Mabry as I reached Duck Road. I
waved to him, and he did a sharp U-turn right in the middle
of the road while flipping on his siren and lights.

That answered my question about whether or not anyone had missed me.

"Dae!" He jumped out of the police car and hugged
me. "Are you hurt? Where have you been? We've been
looking everywhere for you. Your grandfather was frantic.
The chief couldn't officially tell us to start searching for
you because you haven't been gone long enough, but
we've all been searching anyway."

"I'm fine. I feel kind of stupid that I left my cell phone
at home, but otherwise, I'm okay. Where's the chief now,
Tim?"

"I think he's at town hall talking to Nancy. Your grandfather and Brickman are probably there too. You know
how everyone likes to make town hall their command
center."

"Great. Let's go there."

"Is there anything you want to tell me? Do you need to
go to the hospital first?"

"I'm really okay, Tim. And I don't want to tell this story more than once, at least not right now. Maybe you could radio ahead and tell them we're on our way." That seemed ridiculous given the short distance we had to go, but it made him happy.

After Tim sent word ahead, he kept trying to weasel the information out of me. "You know you can tell me anything, right? We were almost married before Brickman came into the picture. And don't bother denying that the two of you are a couple now. I live here too. Everyone knows."

"We were never almost married. We've been friends for a long time. I didn't plan on denying that Kevin and I are together. You still have to wait."

He was content with that—probably because it took only another two minutes to reach the Duck Shoppes and town hall. Any longer than that and he would probably have had another go at it. Considering his line of work, Tim liked to talk a little too much.

Gramps and Kevin were already in the parking lot waiting for me. Chief Michaels was on his way down the stairs from the boardwalk. Nancy was still upstairs, but she was waving and sniffling. There were going to be a lot of explanations necessary on too many different levels.

"Dae!" Gramps got to me first (Kevin hung back and let him take the lead). "Where have you been? I've been worried sick. We all have. You'd better have a good explanation for this, young lady! Not only going off without telling anyone but leaving your cell phone at home. What were you thinking?"

He hugged me a little tighter than usual, and I hugged him back tearfully. I couldn't help but notice all the interested eyes watching us. The parking lot wasn't the best place for our reunion. "I'm sorry. I don't know what I was thinking. But I have some really important information and some questions for you."

"I hope some of that important information is worth my men's time. They've all been out looking for you half the day, Mayor." Chief Michaels glared at me as he reached the side of the police car where I was still half in and half out.

"I think you'll find it is," I told him. "I'm sorry you were worried about me."

"I found her by the docks on Duck Road." Tim cut in, adding his part of the story as though it had great significance. "I offered to take her to the hospital in case she needed female help." He cleared his throat and nodded to convey his concerns.

The parking lot was starting to fill up around us and not with shoppers. "Can we take this inside?" I got all the way out of the car and closed the door. "Someone will call the TV station if we keep standing out here."

Tim laughed. "Not that they'd come without another explosion and murder."

The chief gave him a stern look of disapproval. "That's disrespectful, Officer Mabry."

"Sorry, Chief. I wasn't thinking." Tim hung his head.

"Doesn't surprise me, boy."

I shivered in the cold fog—Gramps, Tim and Kevin scrambled to offer me their jackets. While I was impressed at their chivalry, I took Gramps's jacket with a smile at Kevin. He didn't smile back. Yet another fence to mend.

We all walked upstairs together, me in the middle like some captured fugitive they were worried would disappear again. Nancy hugged me and offered me what I really needed—a cup of hot coffee. She came into my office, notebook in hand. There were already chairs set up to accommodate everyone.

I set the red box full of pirate gold on my big desk and sat down. No one had noticed or asked me about it. I decided not to mention it because it was part of another story for a later time.

With all my personal items around me, I felt better than I had since I left Duck that morning. This place, like Missing Pieces and my home, had become a safe haven for me. Yet another reason to run a good campaign against Mad Dog Wilson for my job as mayor.

Chief Michaels cleared his throat in an exaggerated manner. He approached me and leaned in close. "You don't need any *female* help, do you, Mayor?"

I assumed this was his way of asking me if I'd been molested. I guessed he and Tim found it hard to say the word "rape." "I'm fine, Chief," I assured him. "Please sit down and let me tell you what happened."

I took a deep breath and started from the beginning— the explosion at the museum. The chief needed to know the background to understand how I'd ended up where I was—and where I'd been—today. No one interrupted as I told my story, with an emphasis on Roger and the ring I'd seen on his finger.

I left out the part about my father. I felt that was between me and Gramps right now. It wasn't really pertinent to everything else.

Chief Michaels was the first person to react. He got to his feet and stared out the window behind me at the Currituck Sound. "I knew some of that. The part about the FBI getting Bunk out of here. I didn't know he'd come back. I sure didn't know Agnes was his daughter."

"But you can understand why Bunk gave the gold to Max for her. He wanted to save her life," I explained.

He snorted as he turned around. "Yeah. If you can believe a word out of his mouth. He's done everything wrong

a person can do—smuggling, theft, fraud, illegal bootleg—
I don't know why we'd think he couldn't murder someone."

"He wants to talk to you. I think he knows what happened to Max. He might be protecting someone."

"You mean like his missing son or something?" Tim
added with a loud guffaw.

The chief glared at him. "Bunk's coming here?"

"No," I answered. "He wants you to come out there
with me."

"I don't know." Chief Michaels sat back down. "He
probably has something up his sleeve besides the truth. I
think he's hoodwinked you, Mayor."

"Then why did he let me leave? He could've dumped
me out in the ocean and no one would have known until I
washed up like Sam."

"Well, there's no way to go out there today. The sheriff
needs to be in on this. Maybe the FBI too, for that matter.
I need to talk with them, and we'll see what turns up."

"As far as I can tell," Tim added, "Bunk Whitley confessed to killing Sam Meacham. Walt Peabody needs to be
in on this too, don't you think, Chief?"

"You might be right. Give him a call. Maybe he'd like
to come along on this wild goose chase too." Chief Michaels nodded to me. "Glad you got back safely, Mayor.
Next time you want to investigate one of my cases, let me
know and I'll deputize you."

We both knew he was kidding. You couldn't tell it from
looking at his face, but he was quite a wit sometimes.
He'd homed right in on Bunk being responsible for everything despite what I'd told him about Roger. I thought that
was a mistake.

He and Tim left my office. Nancy followed them, probably figuring the public part of my adventure was over.

She was right. There was still a lot to tackle, but the rest didn't need to be in the town's records.

Gramps glanced at his watch and pushed himself out of his chair. "Look at the time! I've got poker night and don't have a chip or cookie in the house. I'll see you at home later, Dae. See you, Kevin."

I had a few fences to mend with Kevin, though I would've rather talked to Gramps about my father right now. But the secret had been there for all of my life, if what Bunk said was true. I supposed it could wait a little longer.

When we were alone in my closed office, I glanced at Kevin. He'd been very quiet through my tale and its ensuing discussion. "So what do you think?"

"I think you lied to me last night, then needlessly endangered yourself by leaving your cell phone at home so you wouldn't have to talk to me. Not to mention going down to the docks to try and prove your theory without thinking about the consequences."

"Oh. I guess that about sums it up." My words were bright and aided by my larger-than-life mayor's smile, but I felt kind of bad for doing all the things he'd just listed. Or maybe getting caught doing them. "Are you angry?"

"At you?" He shook his head. "At me, yes. I can't believe you blindsided me. After all those years learning to tell the difference between someone lying and telling the truth, you'd think I'd know better."

"So you're *really* angry."

"I would be if I wasn't so damn relieved that you aren't dead. I guess I'll learn from this experience. Your grandfather told me you gave in too easily last night when I asked you to step back. Next time I'll know better."

I wasn't sure whether or not to be glad that he wasn't

mad. All of that sounded pretty ominous. "I didn't want to lie to you, Kevin."

"I know. I've been there. I guess when I envision scenarios like amateurs getting caught snooping around and tossed into boats, the outcome I picture is usually not as good as this one."

"I'm glad you understand." I hoped that's what he was saying anyway. If not, this might be a good time to change the subject. "I haven't really eaten all day. Would you like to grab something at Wild Stallions?"

"I have to go back to the hotel for a delivery. After that, I'm free. Unless you want to eat there."

I thought about the gold in the red box on my desk. "That might be a good idea actually. There's one thing I left out of my tale to the chief." I handed him the red box. "It's Bunk Whitley's gift to the new museum. I think the Blue Whale is a fitting place for it."

He opened up the red box and stared at the gold for a minute. "This was a big part to leave out of the story, Dae. The chief might have to take this in as evidence."

"Well, not today anyway. Can't we put it in your safe for tonight and I'll ask him about it tomorrow?"

He smiled and closed the box. "Yes we can, and *I'll* ask him about it tomorrow."

We walked out of my office and said good-bye to Nancy. "I guess that means you're never going to trust me again, huh?"

He put his arm around my shoulder. "Not for a while."

"That doesn't sound like a good way to have a relationship."

"I guess that all depends. It might be the only way to have a relationship with *you*. Otherwise, you might not be here to have a relationship with. How does minestrone sound? I have a pot simmering on the stove."

"It sounds good enough to forgive you for nicely calling me a liar. Let's go."

It was a strange feeling sitting across from Agnes and eating soup. Celia and Vicky talked about going shopping for new winter boots and asked how long it would be before the insurance money came through for their mother's house.

I didn't know if it was my responsibility to tell them about their heritage. I couldn't prove that what Bunk had claimed was true. I didn't even mention him or what had happened to me today. I listened to the women chatter, looking up to find Kevin's gaze on me.

"What?" I put down my soup and reached for a cheese cube.

"How's the soup?" he asked.

"Good. Very good."

"Not quiche, though, huh?"

I glanced at Agnes and her daughters, who'd stopped their conversation to listen to ours. "I'm not much of a quiche eater. These cheese cubes are good too. Who made them?"

Celia laughed. "Happy cows in California via Harris Teeter, I think. I cut them."

"You did a wonderful job," I commended.

Agnes said, "I'm on my way to the historical society meeting. We're talking about a place to put all the donations. I think Mildred Mason is donating her sister's house to be the new museum. It would be called the Elizabeth Simpson Historical Museum."

"That would be great," I answered. "Max always hoped that would happen."

"I'm sorry it had to take his death to bring it about."

She pushed aside the rest of her soup. "Still, I know you're right. He'd be thrilled. I know the board will accept it without any problem. All we'll have to do is fund-raise for the money to pay the taxes and upkeep. It's a good deal."

It was all I could do not to tell her about Bunk. But how would I explain it, and why would she believe it? Later, after the others were gone and Kevin and I were cleaning up, I mentioned my reluctance to share Bunk's claims. "I think it was best not to mention it," I said.

"I agree," Kevin replied, reassuring me. "It's terrible timing for Agnes, and there's no proof. There may never be any proof, Dae. You might have to live with that secret."

"I know."

He took me home a short while later. I still wasn't done thinking about everything I'd learned on the island. "There must be someway to prove Bunk is Agnes's father."

"Paternity tests," he said. "If both of them were willing. But that opens a whole new can of worms. It wouldn't really benefit Agnes to know that the man who raised her wasn't her father. I don't think that's something you'd want to know either."

"I suppose that's true." I thought about the questions screaming in my brain about my own father.

"Like knowing that her mother committed suicide because she and Bunk couldn't be together, some information doesn't serve the general good. In this case, it might be best to let the past stay buried."

"I know you're right."

"But you want to clear Bunk of Max's murder."

"Yes, but only so we can find the real killer. You saw the way the chief went after Sam as a suspect. Now that he knows about Bunk, we may never know the truth."

"You mean once he can prove that Bunk did anything. Confessing to you is one thing, Dae. Telling Chief Michaels is another. What's going on here? Is there a party you forgot to tell me about?"

He'd started to pull into my driveway, but it was full of cars—police cars. One other car and a van were parked on the street.

"I don't know. I know that's the chief's car, and I think that one belongs to Walt Peabody. I don't know about the other ones."

"I think you'll find that black Ford belongs to the SBI. Probably Brooks Walker since he's our local agent." Kevin parked on the street.

"What do they want?" I wondered out loud.

He grinned as he took my hand. "They want to talk to you. I'm sure they all want reassurances about spending the time and money to go out to the island."

"Great!"

"There might be an FBI agent too. Bunk was supposed to be in their federal program. They might want to know what happened. They might even want to pull him in for not going along with the plan."

I wasn't looking forward to talking with a group of law enforcement people tonight. I wanted to ask Gramps about my father, but not with an audience. Bad timing.

"That looks like the arson investigator's van." Kevin nodded at the white van with the Dare County seal on it. "I think I'll go in with you."

"I'm not worried about Brad, if that's what you're thinking. What's he going to do? Arrest me in front of all these people?"

"He can't arrest you at all, Dae. He can only investigate and give his findings to the chief. That's one reason why it was inappropriate for him to talk to you about the case the way he did. I'm sure his superiors had something to say about it after your grandfather and I pointed it out to them."

"Gramps said he was only fishing."

"Yeah. Without much bait either. Come on. Let's see what's happening."

We went inside together. The house smelled like coffee and conflicting aftershaves. The men were sitting around the kitchen table—until they saw me. They all got to their feet at that point.

"Mayor," they said in unison.

Brad nodded but didn't speak. I supposed he wasn't happy that this new turn of events had messed up his theory about me killing Max and Sam. Gramps brought out another chair for Kevin. The doorbell rang and I went to answer it. It was Cailey Fargo on the doorstep. She hugged me. "I'm so glad you're safe, Dae. Everyone was worried about you."

"Thanks. Come on in. The party is this way."

"I knew Brad was all wrong when he told me he considered you a suspect," she confided in a low voice. "I think he's a little desperate to find someone to blame. It's his first investigation, you know. I'm sure he's worried about doing a good job. People get that way sometimes. He's kind of wound real tight anyway, if you know what I mean."

"I appreciate you telling me that. It means a lot."

Gramps asked us both if we wanted coffee. I turned it down—Cailey took a cup. I sat between her and Kevin, with Brad brooding on the other side of the table. Once everyone was seated, filling our little kitchen, the discussion began.

"I want to say upfront that this whole thing is a waste of taxpayer money." Brad fired the first salvo right across my bow. "I think we all know this is nothing but a ploy to take the heat off of someone right here in town who's responsible for everything."

Chapter 19

"We all have a stake in this," Brad continued. "We need to find out the truth—not a convenient lie to cover up what really happened."

He was glaring at me the whole time he spoke. He was accusing me without actually using my name. I didn't care. He'd find out how wrong he was when we went out to the island.

Kevin had been wrong about the FBI. They were nowhere to be seen. Agent Brooks Walker with the SBI wanted to be part of the group going out to the island. In fact, he wanted the local police to stay out of it entirely. "This should be our case," he said.

"The man's been living out there for years and no one knew," Walt reminded him. "You can't come in here and take over our case."

"He's a suspect in our murder cases." Chief Michaels piled on the logical reasons he should be allowed to continue with the case. "You can't claim any jurisdiction here, Agent."

"All right. It's against my better judgment, but I guess you're already involved," Walker grumbled. "We'll head out there first thing in the morning. Who has the coordinates for the island?"

They all looked at me. "Bunk's men gave them to me when we got back to Duck. Whose boat are we going out on?"

"I don't see any reason you should go out at all," Walker told me. "You're neither law enforcement nor an involved party. Give me the coordinates and we'll take it from here."

"I'm afraid not. I'm supposed to be bringing *you* out there. I don't think Bunk will like it if you show up without me."

There was some major griping, but I didn't care. I was the one who found Bunk, and I was going back out there tomorrow. It probably wasn't so much that I wanted to be part of the operation as I wanted to know whatever he could tell me about my father. If my grandfather had kept the knowledge that my dad was alive for all these years, I wasn't sure I'd get any real answers from him. In case Bunk was dragged off to some federal prison, I wanted a chance to talk with him first.

When they finally accepted that they weren't going without me, despite all their complaints and protests, Walker, Peabody and Chief Michaels handled it without further discussion.

"We'll use a Coast Guard vessel," Walker told everyone.

"We'll be taking police boats," Chief Michaels stated.

"We'll be going out on the *Eleanore*," Gramps said.

"That's not a police boat, Horace," Chief Michaels replied. "It has to be some law enforcement vessel. I'd go with the Coast Guard before taking a private boat out there."

"You all go out on your boats, if you want." Gramps stared steely-eyed at them. "Dae, and the location of the island, are going with me on the *Eleanore*. I don't trust any of you to keep her safe."

He gave Kevin a half smile. Kevin nodded in return. I assumed that meant he'd be going too. That was fine with me. I wasn't looking forward to being the only civilian with the masses of law enforcement headed out there.

I kind of felt sorry for Bunk in all this. No doubt he'd brought all of it on himself. But I believed his story about what happened to Max. I believed he was Agnes's father and wanted to help her, whatever else he'd done.

It was agreed that we'd all meet at the docks at six A.M. Gramps and Kevin could be there, Walker said, but couldn't bring a weapon. Same thing for me.

"That's it. I've had a big day." I got to my feet. They might be there talking and planning all night. "I'll see you all in the morning."

Most of them stood and "Mayor-ed" me again—except for Brad, who nodded. Kevin smiled and stood up to kiss my cheek and say good night. Gramps walked me to the stairs.

"Good night, honey," he said, hugging me. "Don't worry about this. It'll be okay."

"Gramps, there's something I have to ask you."

"Yes?"

I noticed the sudden silence from the kitchen and knew I couldn't say what was on my mind. It was better to wait until we could talk without a room full of people listening in. "It'll keep. Good night."

* * *

I was awake long before my alarm went off at five thirty the next morning. I tried to imagine what the day would bring. Would Bunk deny what he'd told me when he was faced with it? Would he be arrested? It seemed there was so much that could go wrong.

I'd been right about everyone downstairs. I'd heard the group break up at around two A.M. I remembered the planning sessions Gramps held with his deputies from when I was a kid. Many of them took place around that same table. They planned and replanned—trying to account for every possible scenario. I wondered if they were ever surprised by what happened. Would they be surprised today?

I finally got tired of thinking about it, dressed in warm clothes and went downstairs. Gramps was already awake, drinking coffee and storing extra bullets for his gun in a jacket pocket.

"I thought they said no guns." I made myself some tea and set bread to toast.

"Yeah, well, I'm not going in there with old Bunk Whitley's hired guns and no weapon. I'm sure you'll find Kevin will be carrying a little something too."

I sat at the kitchen table and looked at the man who'd been everything to me my whole life. His features were creased with age, skin leathered by the hot sun and sea. I recalled how proud I was when he'd come to school to pick me up in the sheriff's car. I'd never forget the things he'd said to keep me going after Mom died—even though he'd been hurting too.

But now I needed answers from him. Would he give them to me? "Gramps, Bunk told me a few other things about people in Duck."

"I wouldn't necessarily put a lot of stock into everything Bunk said, honey. He might be right about Agnes, but it strikes me that it's something he knew you couldn't ask her about without causing a fuss. He probably banked on that."

"He told me my father was still alive."

He didn't stop cleaning his pistol. "And?"

"I want to know if it's true."

He glanced up at me. "What do you think?"

"I think I'd like a straight answer. Is he alive or not?"

He put the pistol into a shoulder holster that would be hidden by his jacket. "Do you believe I'd do anything that would hurt you in any way?"

"Gramps! Please! If you were a suspect in a murder case, I'd believe you were guilty by now."

"Dae—" The phone rang and he went to answer it.

I felt like there were pins and needles sticking into every part of my body. I knew it wouldn't be easy for Gramps to answer me. Clearly, it wasn't. But his response so far made me think Bunk knew what he was talking about. Why would Gramps hide something like this from me?

When he came back, he said, "We have to go, Dae. There's a problem with the Coast Guard boat. We're going to have to pick up Walker and his men."

"You haven't answered my question." I wouldn't be put aside for Walker or anyone else.

"I know I haven't, honey. I wish your mom was alive to answer this question for you. It's not really my place."

"You're my only living relative—as far as I know. Can't you answer this question?"

"I can." He nodded. "But you aren't going to like it."

I braced myself. "It can't be worse than not knowing."

"All right." He pulled on his red plaid jacket. "We'll talk in the truck on the way to the docks."

"With Kevin?" Gramps didn't own a truck and rarely drove anything but a golf cart. He had to mean that Kevin was coming for us. I knew he wouldn't discuss this with him there. "No!"

"Dae, can't we talk about this later? There's a lot going on right now, in case you hadn't noticed."

"I don't know. I guess I'll wait here until you get back."

He let out a heavy sigh. "You know everyone would just end up back here waiting for you."

"Exactly. Maybe we could discuss this with all of them too."

I saw a look on his face that I hadn't seen since high school when I came home from the prom at one A.M. "You're a stubborn woman, Dae O'Donnell."

I didn't disagree. "Did I get that from my mother—or my father?"

"Dae—your father *is* alive. At least he was last year when I saw him at the Coral Reef bar in Kill Devil Hills."

I'd wanted to know—had demanded to know. But knowing floored me. "He's alive? All these years I had a father? He didn't die before I was born?"

His cell phone rang. "We have to go. I'll tell you the rest later. I'm sorry for this. I guess I hoped it wouldn't come up. I know you're surprised."

"Surprised doesn't really cover it. All this time—why did you lie to me?"

"It was your mother's story to tell, not mine. She planned to explain one day when you were old enough to understand. She would've too, if she'd lived. After she died, I didn't know how to say it. Believe me, I would've told you when you were a child. But your mom felt different about it."

His cell phone rang again, and there was an insistent knock on the front door.

"We have to go," he said again. "This will have to wait.

Don't forget, this isn't just about you. You represent Duck too. These people are counting on you."

I needed some time—a long soak in a hot bath, maybe some donuts, definitely some ice cream. I needed to know the world hadn't just turned upside down, that the people I'd always depended on hadn't really kept this truth from me. But there wasn't time since I needed to do my "duty."

"Like I was counting on you to tell me the truth about my life, Gramps?" I yelled at him. "Who is he? I need a name. I'm not leaving here until I get a name."

"Dae—"

"You owe me that much."

His mouth became a grim line. "Danny Evans. His name is Danny Evans."

"Thanks." I picked up my jacket and walked outside.

"Everything okay?" Kevin asked when I walked past him.

"Just fine."

Danny Evans. I have a father. He isn't dead, and his name is Danny Evans.

As the *Eleanore* made her way to the coordinates I'd given Gramps—the only thing I'd said to him since we'd left the house—the police boats followed like an armed escort through the dark Atlantic.

We'd picked up Walker and five of his men from the Coast Guard boat that had broken down right offshore. I could feel Walker's embarrassment at having to be rescued from the dead vessel by a civilian.

There was no extra room on the *Eleanore* after that. I sat beside Kevin in the stern as the dark began to fade and dawn arrived, rosy and golden, on the horizon.

"You and your grandfather have a fight?" Kevin guessed as he shared coffee from his thermos with me.

"You could say that." The clear light of morning picked out the men's weary faces around us.

"Was it about going out to the island?"

"No. I don't want to talk about it."

"All right." He put his arm around me, and I felt the hard metal edge of a gun under his blue winter vest.

"You brought a gun too." I nodded. "Just like Gramps."

"Old habits." He shrugged. "We don't know what we're going into out here. That's why your grandfather didn't want you to come out alone."

"Only you and he would consider being with a group of SBI agents followed by a dozen police officers as being alone."

"Is there a problem between you and your grandfather?"

"Maybe. I don't know." I turned to him. "Could I move in with you?"

He choked on his coffee, then recovered. "This is a little sudden."

"I know. But it's not what you think. I need some time to myself. I could rent a room from you. You wouldn't even know I was there."

"That wouldn't happen." He kissed me lightly, then smiled. "You might as well tell me what's going on."

I told him the briefest details even though all of it wanted to burst out of me. I hoped the men around us couldn't hear my tearful whispers. Kevin held me and didn't speak until I was finished.

"I don't know why this happened," he finally said. "But I know your grandfather loves you. There must've been an important reason to keep this from you."

"I've thought that a million times. But what possible reason could there be to lie to me about my father?"

"I don't know."

"And my mother. I thought we were so close because it was always the two of us. What am I supposed to think now?"

"I wish I had the answers."

"One thing's for sure—I have to find him."

"Maybe that's why your grandfather didn't tell you about him."

"I've thought of that."

"But you don't care."

"Would *you*?"

"Probably not."

We were getting close to the island. I could make out the shape of the big house on the hill. The sun was up, warming the cold winds made icier by the speed of the boat.

All the men onboard checked their guns, adjusted vests, hats and gloves, then stood facing the upcoming landmass. It was still early—barely eight A.M. Walker talked to each man, giving out instructions. I imagined Chiefs Peabody and Michaels were doing the same on the other boats.

It looked and felt like a raid, not the peaceful conversation and negotiation I'd been expecting. Knowing what I did about Bunk, I believed he'd know what to expect.

But as we came closer to the coastline, there was an air of stillness about the place. Was it because it was early morning? No, it felt like something else. I didn't know what—until I saw the first man lying at the edge of the dock. There was another man facedown in the water near him.

Gramps stopped the *Eleanore*. He radioed the police

boats behind us, and Walker spoke with Chief Michaels and Walt Peabody for a few minutes. Evidently, this wasn't a scenario they'd considered either.

"You should go below deck," Walker said to me when he was done talking on the radio.

"He's right, Dae," Gramps agreed. "This looks bad."

"I'm staying where I am, thanks. I think I can handle it if you can."

Walker shrugged and turned away, mumbling loudly about civilians being involved with law enforcement activities. Gramps went back to the helm. The three boats progressed more cautiously toward the narrow strip of land. Everyone's eyes were alert, scanning the coastline for any sign of activity.

Nothing moved. As we got closer, I could see there were three other bodies on the dock. There was blood splattered everywhere. Boats rocked at their moorings, and I could see that some of them had bullet holes in them. Another, the one that had brought me home yesterday, looked as though it had been set on fire and was barely above water.

"What happened?" I stared out at the devastation that had taken place in the last twenty-four hours.

"Maybe a rival," Kevin said. "A man like Bunk Whitley is bound to have some enemies. Are you sure you want to see this?"

Not really, I thought, but I said I did. I didn't want to see it, but I didn't want to hide from it either.

They brought the police boats up to the docks first, and several officers, guns drawn, spilled out to anchor the boats. Gramps nudged the *Eleanore* up to the mooring, and I jumped out to secure her as I always did when I was onboard. I didn't think about it until I looked up and saw Kevin there beside me. Behind him were several angry-looking SBI agents. Apparently, I'd done their job for them.

The first group from the police boats was already disappearing toward the house, radioing back that the area seemed to be deserted. We followed in their wake. The only people still left on the island seemed to be the dead security men at the dock. There was no one else between the water and the house. Chief Michaels called back to everyone else to let them know the house appeared to be empty too.

I tried not to look too closely at the dead bodies, but I couldn't help myself. I saw Nash among the dead but not Roger. Maybe he'd been killed somewhere else, but the carnage seemed confined to the docks. I was determined to mention my suspicions about Roger to Chief Michaels. Roger could certainly be the killer Bunk was trying to protect.

The devastation at the house was haphazard and wasteful, like something a child would do during a temper tantrum. Paintings were slashed and burned. The fountain was broken and thrown out of a window. Clothes were strewn everywhere along with cooking utensils and food. Not a single pane of glass was left unbroken in the sunroom where I'd had lunch with Bunk.

"What do you think?" Chiefs Michaels asked as he joined Peabody and Walker in the foyer.

"Beats me." Peabody shook his head. "Safe's been emptied. Can't find a thing of worth not ripped apart or burned."

"Looks like some kind of revenge," Walker added. "Sometimes that's the way these things play out."

But Kevin, who'd stuck with me like a shadow, disagreed. "The timing is too perfect. For the first time in years, your group knew Bunk was out here. But before you could get out here to question him, he's gone? Except for the dead men at the dock, there's no real lasting damage here. Someone could come back, clean up and live here again next week."

Walker and the two police chiefs nodded. But Gramps said, "I don't believe Bunk would kill a few of his own men out front for a show. He's too old school, too much the country gentleman the way Dae described him. I think someone attacked him out here and he left the island. Probably won't see him again anytime soon either."

I could read in his bitter tone that he wished Bunk had never come back. Without Bunk's interference, I wouldn't know about my father and Gramps and I wouldn't be on the outs. I supposed I'd wish that too if I were him. Maybe I did a little anyway. I didn't like us arguing. But I couldn't let this lie about my father go unchallenged.

So the chiefs argued with Walker, and I walked around the grounds thinking what a change a day can make. Kevin kept pace with me, but he was quiet as I looked around for some clue about what had happened.

I picked up a few things and held them, but they revealed only garbled images that made no sense. I believed Bunk would leave something for me. Call it intuition, but he knew about my gift. I thought he might find a way to use it to his advantage.

Kevin and I walked through the gardens. The SBI and police departments had given this area only a cursory glance since they were more interested in the house and the dead security men. We were near the fountain where Bunk and I had first met when I spotted his walking stick. I never saw him use it but he'd had it with him the whole time I was here. It was out of place and drew me to it. It seemed exactly the kind of thing he might use to contact me.

"Wait!" Kevin stopped me as I crouched down to pick it up. "You don't know what you might be taking on if you touch that!"

Chapter 20

"Be careful," Kevin warned.

I nodded before I reached for it, as prepared as I could be for whatever I might pick up from the walking stick. Images exploded in my head when I touched it. It was made in Thailand, especially for Bunk, but it was one of dozens exactly like it. He was never without one.

The problem with that was there were no memories, no strong emotions for me to feel. It was like picking up something new, something with no background to share.

I was disappointed. I'd hoped the stick had a message for me. Kevin examined the stick and pried off the top piece, glancing toward the house. "People like to hide things in these."

Kevin wasn't psychic, but he'd guessed well. Inside was a small, rolled-up piece of paper. I could feel Bunk's amusement on hiding it for me before he left the island.

Mayor Dae O'Do nnell,

I'm sorry to have to leave so abruptly without see-
ing you, but my nemesis got wind of our arrangement
and decided it wouldn't do. I fear I can't tell you more
without endangering your life. And that, my dear,
won't do either.

Until we meet again.
Yours faithfully,
Bunk Whitley

"Well it proves he was here." I frowned and rolled up
the paper again.

"The FBI probably already knew he was here," Kevin
said. "Just because they didn't tell anyone else doesn't
mean they didn't know."

"Whoever this guy is, Bunk is really afraid of him."
With good reason, I thought, considering the dead security
guards.

"You can only hire so many people to protect you. The
fact that whoever did this got so close despite Bunk's crew
of trained professionals—it must've really scared him."

"I suppose so." Bunk was gone with all the answers.
And he'd left us still trying to find the right questions.
"Why would someone want to kill him?"

"Who knows?" Kevin shrugged. "A wily old devil like
him probably has a hundred people waiting in line to do
the job."

"But this one he couldn't strike out at." I told Kevin that
I hadn't seen Roger among the dead. "I think Roger may
be the one Bunk couldn't kill because he cares about him."

"And why would that be, Mayor O'Donnell?" Agent
Walker asked, catching up with us.

"I don't know exactly. I think whoever did this is related to Bunk. Family, you know?" I thought about what Bunk had said in the sunroom about Max not being the target. "Maybe Agnes was always the target, not Max or Sam. She was at the museum before it exploded too. Maybe Max and Sam got in the way, like Bunk said."

"You mean the woman he told you was his daughter?"

"Yes. Max knew the truth and he was killed. Bunk said he was worried about Sam. Maybe Sam knew the secret Bunk was trying to hide, even though it was by accident. Someone tried to burn down Agnes's house with her inside. Maybe it's all about the gold and who gets it when Bunk dies."

Walker seemed to think it over but then dismissed the idea. "I don't buy it. Sorry. Organizations don't work that way. The spoils go to whoever takes over."

"I don't know if you could classify Bunk Whitley as an organization," I said.

Walker nodded at the cane Kevin still held. "Did that belong to him? We'll have to take it in as evidence."

I didn't volunteer the note. I wasn't sure it would really make any difference to Walker or the case. But it meant something to me.

Walker told us we'd have to leave the island. They were locking it down for a special SBI forensics team that was coming in to go over everything more thoroughly. I was ready to go anyway. I guessed I'd found what I came for in part, if not everything. Bunk's quick departure (probably by helicopter—Kevin pointed out the tracks in the sand) left me wanting to know more but with no one to ask.

Since Walker and his men stayed on the island, that left me, Gramps and Kevin going back on the *Eleanore* together. Kevin conveniently left me and Gramps alone at the helm, probably thinking we should talk about our problem. I decided I was ready if Gramps was.

"It was a long time ago, Dae. I guess I never expected it to come up. Or at least I hoped it wouldn't. I can't even figure out how Bunk knew about it. We kept it a secret between us, your mom, your grandmother and me."

"I think Bunk makes it his business to find out useful secrets. Maybe he thought he could use it against you. You *were* the Dare County sheriff at the time."

"Maybe. He probably got it from your father. He's that kind of man."

"What kind?"

"The troublemaking kind. He's been in and out of jail his whole life. I begged your mother to stop seeing him, but she kept sneaking out. Then it was too late. She found out she was pregnant. She couldn't wait to tell him. She really thought he'd want to settle down with her and the baby."

"But he didn't?"

He laughed in a terrible, sad way. "No. He took off for parts unknown. He told your mother to call him when she took care of the problem. She was so far gone over that boy that she almost did it too. Your grandmother found her at an abortion clinic in Elizabeth City and dragged her home by the ear."

The thump-thump-thump of the engine kept time with my heart. I'd asked for the truth not knowing how awful it might be. My father didn't want me, and my mother almost got rid of me. My eyes stung with tears that I forced myself to hold back so Gramps would continue the story.

"Then she decided she wanted me?" I asked hopefully.

He glanced up as though to say he was sorry, but there was more. "I'm afraid not, honey. She left to go and find him, to make him change his mind. She was gone when your grandmother suffered a heart attack and passed on. Eleanore died of a broken heart—I don't care what the doctors said."

How had they kept all of this from me? I remembered my mother talking about my grandmother so many times yet she never mentioned it. "That's terrible."

"Your grandmother was in the ground before your mother came back with you. She'd thought seeing you would change your father. It didn't. He threw both of you out on the street. Your mother had to beg for bus fare to get back home. When she got back, the two of you were starving—thin as rails and sickly too. You cried all the time. I hated to tell her that her mother was dead, but I had no choice. For a while, I thought it might kill her too. I was scared to death of trying to raise a little girl on my own."

"Gramps—"

"Never mind, Dae. You didn't know. But that's why we never spoke of it. Your mother got better a little at a time, and we went on raising you the best we could. But that's it in a clamshell. I asked your mother many times when she was going to tell you about your daddy. She always said she was waiting for the right time. Guess it never came."

Apparently, all the women in my family died abruptly leaving guilt-ridden children behind. Why hadn't my mother told me? I wasn't a kid anymore when she'd died. Was she that afraid my father would corrupt me too? Or was it too embarrassing to admit what she'd done?

I scrubbed my eyes with my hands. "I'm sorry, Gramps. You were right. It wasn't your story to tell. I wish Mom would've told me."

"Me too, honey." He moved his hand over his face,

then looked up to stare out over the Atlantic. "Maybe I should've told you sooner. I don't know. I hate that you had to find out this way. I just didn't know how to say all that without hurting you. I guess Bunk helped us out with that, huh?"

Things were quiet for a few days after we got back from the island. I organized and reorganized Missing Pieces. I had a few customers too.

I hated to do it, but I sold my African hand mirror to a woman who admired it. Much as I loved it, I knew I would never use it again. Looking at it was a constant reminder of the terrible sorrow I'd felt from it. I couldn't bring myself to destroy it, and I figured the woman who bought it would never know the mirror's past. The shop seemed emptier without it, but I knew it was for the best.

After so much excitement, I felt a little disappointed, even bored, getting back to my normal life. There were no late-night visits from Chief Michaels, no puzzles to solve. I even missed the unhappy frowns from Agent Walker. I could only imagine all of them being very busy dissecting the information they'd found on the island.

They were lucky to have that information. When the museum burned, it destroyed the only copies of the old *Duck Gazette*. A lot of history was lost forever. I wished we'd put it in more than one place. But it was too late for second thoughts, no matter how well intentioned. Everything I ever knew about Bunk Whitley had been in the museum's microfiche collection. After meeting him, I wished I knew more.

I went out with Shayla and Trudy for what was supposed to be a girls' night out. It ended up being a chance for Shayla to show off her new boyfriend. He was a navy

SEAL with perfect abs and an attitude to match. I was glad she'd moved on after the thing with Kevin. It made me feel less guilty even though Trudy kept assuring me that there was nothing for me to feel guilty about.

Trudy drove me home after the night out. I really wanted to tell her about my newfound father. But the words wouldn't come. I'd known her all of my life. I really wanted someone else to talk to about it, but I couldn't tell her.

So I bottled it up inside and glanced through the Outer Banks' phone listings starting with Duck and working my way around the island. There was no Danny Evans listed.

Maybe it was just as well. Did I really want to contact him after all these years? What would he say? Would he be sorry he kicked me and my mother out when I was a baby?

Somehow I doubted it. He might not even remember me or my mother. Obviously he'd never come to see what happened to us during the last thirty-plus years. I had to assume it was because he didn't care. We still lived in the same place where he'd met her. How hard would it be to drive by?

I didn't want to make a fool of myself over the whole thing anyway. I was curious, of course. Who wouldn't be? But I wasn't rushing out to hire a private detective either. If Danny Evans wasn't interested in who his daughter was, she wasn't interested in him either. At least that's what I told myself at night before I went to sleep.

The Duck Historical Society met and accepted the gift of Mrs. Elizabeth Simpson's house as a new museum. The elegant old house on the ocean side had a historical background of its own besides being a great place for a museum. Max would've been so proud.

It was also right next door to the Blue Whale Inn, which would make transporting the hundreds of artifacts that were cluttering Kevin's lobby even easier. I volunteered to help with the move on that Saturday. It was cold and rainy—the icy, driving rain that comes from the ocean and leaves everyone shivering in their homes.

No one stayed home that day, though. Everyone showed up to help. People from Duck knew how to put on a rain poncho and boots better than most.

Gramps was busy in the morning but planned to come by the museum later in the day. I walked over by myself thinking I might open Missing Pieces later if the sun came out for a while. There wouldn't be many customers looking for treasures in this weather, but I needed every sale I could get.

I held my head down against the rain and wind. I looked up when I noticed a car moving slowly along beside me. Someone was offering me a ride. I wished it were Kevin, though I knew he was busy preparing a huge luncheon for all the volunteers. But any ride in the rain would be welcome, so I stepped up to the car.

Brad Spitzer pushed open the door for me. "Hey! Can I offer you a ride, Mayor?"

I hesitated. I didn't know him very well, though I'd accepted rides from other people I knew even less about. What I *did* know about him I didn't like. And what if we got into another discussion about how he thought I killed Max?

On the other hand, it was cold and wet. I felt like icicles were hanging from my poncho. How well did I need to know him to drive the short distance to the Blue Whale? He was a public official, after all.

I climbed in the car and apologized for getting the seat wet. "Thanks for stopping. I'm on my way to the new history museum. Not far."

"Not a problem." He started forward, no traffic on either side of Duck Road. "I admit to having an ulterior motive for offering you a lift, Mayor."

I squeezed closer to the door. He was going pretty slow. I figured I could always jump out. "Oh?"

"I wanted to apologize for the things I said to you about Max Caudle's death. I'm sorry I insinuated that you might have something to do with it. I don't know what I was thinking." He glanced at me and smiled. "I was frustrated, I guess. My first big case since becoming the head arson investigator and I was blowing it."

"That's okay." I smiled back. "People make mistakes."

"Thanks for understanding."

"Sure. Thanks for not thinking I killed anyone."

He laughed a little. "I didn't have a chance to tell you the other night, but what you did out on the island was really brave. A notorious racketeer like Bunk Whitley had to be hard to face down."

I didn't think any of my actions had been particularly courageous. "It wasn't so bad. And it was almost unbelievable to meet old Bunk Whitley. He's a legend in Duck."

"Yeah. I'm not from Duck and I've heard of him."

"Yeah." I didn't know what else to say. If he was hoping to hear interesting exploits from the adventure, he was doomed to disappointment.

"I'm curious about what exactly Bunk said to you. You didn't go into details at the meeting. You had lunch with him. He must've talked. Did he give you any clues to his past crimes?"

I wasn't sure how to answer that. I didn't want to tell him about my father. "Not really. We mostly talked about general stuff." I decided lying was my best course. Like I said, I didn't know him very well. I wasn't going to discuss Agnes, her mother's suicide or any other sensitive subjects.

"Really." He glanced at me as though trying to verify that I was telling the truth. Probably one of those law enforcement techniques they teach. "As I understand it, Bunk discussed Max Caudle and Sam Meacham's death with you. Old Bunk even took responsibility for Meacham's death. Is that right?"

"Sort of." By this time we were parked in the Blue Whale's driveway. It would've been easy to step out of the car with a fast good-bye and make for the shelter of Kevin's inn. But Brad had given me a ride here. I didn't want to be rude.

"That's fine if you'd rather not talk about it," he conceded to my great relief. "But I have another question for you."

"Oh?" My skin prickled, and I glanced out the window through the cold rain to the bright blue building in front of us.

"The chief says you have a gift, Mayor. That you're psychic. He says you can help people find things they've lost by holding their hands. Is that true?"

He seemed sincere—his eyes were worried and his voice wavered slightly, as though this really meant something to him. It wasn't a secret that I could find lost things. Maybe I'd prejudged him because we'd gotten off on the wrong foot. "Yes. Sometimes that's true."

"Could you—would you be willing to help me? I've been looking for something for a long time. It belonged to my father. He and I are strangers. It's the only thing I have of his. I'd take it as a personal favor if you could help me find it again."

Going through my own struggle with an unknown father, how could I say no? I wanted to help him if I could. "I'd be glad to. We just need a quiet place to sit for a few minutes."

I could see Kevin (I thought it was Kevin, hard to tell

in a poncho and boots) walking out of the Blue Whale and headed our way. This wouldn't be a good time or place. "I'm going to be here for the rest of the day, but maybe later tonight or tomorrow would work out."

"That would be great! Whenever you can do it, Mayor. I've waited a long time. I can wait a little longer." He scribbled down his cell phone number and handed it to me.

"Call me Dae, please, everyone does. I'll give you a call and we can meet somewhere."

"Thank you, Dae." He smiled—it was like the sun coming out after the rain. Proof, I guessed, of how much this meant to him. "I've never believed in anything like this, you understand. But I want to. I really want to believe this can be the answer for me."

By this time, the hooded figure had reached us and it was Kevin. He rapped on the passenger-side window, peeking out at me from under the hood of his brown raincoat. I rolled down my window.

"Dae? Are you okay?" He gave Brad a significant stare.

"Sorry!" Brad smiled at him. "I didn't mean to keep her so long, Brickman."

"That's okay," Kevin said, though he didn't seem to mean it.

"Thanks again," Brad said to me before I got out of the car. "I'll talk to you later."

"Okay. See you." I closed the car door and ran up to the Blue Whale with Kevin.

"What was that all about?" he asked. "I thought the last time you talked with him he accused you of killing Max."

"Anyone can make a mistake." I sniffed the air, avoiding several anonymous people in ponchos, their arms filled with Duck history. "Lunch smells great! I guess I'd better get started if I'm going to earn my seat at the table."

* * *

It was hard to believe a town as small as Duck could have so much history to share. There were dozens of old dresses, suits and kids' outfits worn by Duck residents from the 1800s through the 1950s. There were antique writing desks and chairs that had graced sea captains' quarters. Not to mention hundreds of boat parts, from lanterns to anchors.

Many people said they'd been waiting, holding these items until Duck got another, larger, museum. Of course, no one had dreamed it would happen this way. There was an air of regret that it had taken so long to move the museum out of the tiny building Max had overseen for so many years.

The members of the Duck Historical Society made a special announcement during the luncheon of orange salad, fresh-baked bread and twice-stuffed ravioli I'd watched Kevin prepare. They told us that a bronze plaque was being made to honor Max and his contributions to the community. It was supposed to be ready midmonth, in time for the ribbon cutting on the new museum. His memorial would also be held at the same time.

There was a spontaneous burst of applause. Agnes, Celia and Vicky were there, crying as they listened to the appreciative remarks about Max. Agnes said a few words about her husband's love of history, which were followed by another round of applause.

The Duck Historical Society members thanked Kevin profusely for his wonderful lunch. The dining room in the Blue Whale was completely filled with volunteers. I was amazed to see how many people were willing to give their time for the move.

I could imagine how the dining room had looked in

Bunk Whitley's day. Probably not that different. Kevin had added some modern lighting and decoration, but the crystal, sterling and china were older, reflecting a more elegant, graceful time.

By midafternoon everything that had been stored at the Blue Whale was in the Simpson house. It wasn't in any order. Portraits of old Bunk and Banker relatives were pushed against chamber pots, old photos of fishing boats and jewelry from the early 1800s made from shells.

My back, arms and legs were killing me, but I'd been careful and wore gloves so as not to have any incidents with these objects. There were a few things I knew I was glad not to touch—a noose left over from the last man hanged in Duck, a blunderbuss and some knives that were of questionable origin. I didn't think those were only rust stains I saw on them.

"Nice to have your lobby back?" I asked Kevin after everything had been moved.

"Sure, but business is slow right now anyway. It was a good time to do it even if the circumstances weren't anything anyone wanted."

"What will happen now about Max and Sam?" I asked him, sitting down on the old high-backed circle chair in the center of the lobby.

He shrugged. "I guess it will depend on what they find on the island. Maybe Bunk Whitley killed Sam and Max. Case closed."

"Old Bunk Whitley kill someone?" Mrs. Pearl Dabbs, one of the town's wealthiest and oldest citizens, not to mention a charter member of the historical society, caught the last of our conversation. "I'm sure he never killed anyone in his life. He was a lover, not a killer."

Chapter 21

Kevin and I exchanged looks. Neither one of us wanted to get into that discussion, but it seemed as though we had no choice.

"I let Bunk escort me a few places after my husband died," Mrs. Dabbs explained. "He was always courteous, polite and the perfect gentleman. Of course, that was after his wife's tragic death in Europe that summer. I can't remember what killed her, but I know it was something terrible like an avalanche or something."

"Bunk was married?" I asked as she sat beside me. She was tall and thin, always wore carefully creased slacks. She reminded me of Katharine Hepburn.

"Yes, he was. They had a child together. His wife wasn't from Duck, you see. He brought her home, from Paris I think, but I'm not sure about that. She did have some kind of accent. She was very beautiful, as you can imagine. I can't think that Bunk would court anyone who wasn't. He always had to have the best of the best."

"How long ago was that, Mrs. Dabbs?" Kevin joined in. It was like trying to look away from a bad car wreck. Discussing Bunk Whitley might not get us anywhere, but he was fascinating.

She smiled and squeezed his hand. "Probably in the late sixties or early seventies. You know, Bunk would be so happy you finally reopened this old place, Kevin. If he were alive, he'd probably come here every night with a different woman on his arm. I can tell you I'd be proud to be one of them."

"Thanks."

"Did Bunk have a son or a daughter?" I had to ask.

She frowned as she tried to recall the answer. "A son, I think. But I'm not sure. The child was sickly, you see, and he didn't stay here long. Bunk sent him to a boarding school after his wife passed. Or at least that's what I heard. Of course, if it involved Bunk, there were always plenty of rumors."

I followed Kevin to the huge kitchen as a few other members of the Duck Historical Society came to claim Mrs. Dabbs's attention. "So Bunk has a son we didn't know about and a daughter we know about."

"A daughter that doesn't know she's his daughter."

"Well now if we find Bunk's son, we could use his DNA to check Agnes's DNA and we'd know for sure if she was related to Bunk."

"Which doesn't really make any difference." He changed his dirty apron for a clean white one. "Although it might advance your theory about Bunk protecting the person who killed Max and the possibility that the murderer was really trying to get to Agnes because he doesn't want to share his father's money."

I sat on a tall stool at the stainless steel countertop as Kevin began chopping some scallions and dicing some eggplant. He had another dinner booked for tomorrow night—a party of thirty people coming in from the mainland. "I don't know. Agent Walker said whatever money Bunk has wouldn't just pass to his heirs. Even if he has a son, that blows my theory."

"Agent Walker could be wrong," he said as he chopped. "Or this whole thing is about the gold. I told you people do crazy things for gold. Maybe all of Bunk's assets are in gold of one form or another."

"It wouldn't travel well."

"True. Which advances *my* theory that Bunk will be back. The gold has to be on the island somewhere."

"Except for whatever amount he gave Agnes. Not that we know how much that was."

"She must've hidden it somewhere if it's a substantial amount. I helped her move in here and I didn't see anything like that."

I tapped my fingernails on the metal surface, and he immediately handed me a cutting board and a knife. "Sorry." I smiled. "What's this?"

"Portobello mushrooms. Chop."

"Which would mean Bunk could be running from his own son who killed the security guards at the island. I'm sure now that it's Roger. He probably killed Max too. He might be the one who torched Agnes's house. Maybe he was looking for the gold as well as trying to get her out of the way."

"It's possible. He might've used the promise of the gold to hire some people to do the job. Unless Bunk's son is a mercenary, it's unlikely he could go in and take out that many trained guards."

"Maybe he *is* a mercenary. He was working as Bunk's trained thug. Who knows where he learned how to do that."

He put the eggplant in a bowl and added some marinade as he changed the subject. "Have you tried to contact your father yet?"

"No. Not exactly." I chopped the mushrooms a little harder. "I looked him up in the phone book. No such listing."

"Step two?"

"I don't know yet. I'm not in any hurry to find him. He certainly hasn't wanted to see me."

Kevin didn't dispute that idea. "I could probably find him for you, if you want. If he has a record, he's in a computer file somewhere."

"I know. I thought about asking you. I'd be uncomfortable asking Gramps to look him up. I'm not sure yet. But I appreciate the offer."

"Okay. Done with those mushrooms?"

When Kevin was finished in the kitchen, we sat in the bar area for a long time drinking a good red muscadine wine. He told me about a few of his FBI cases, and I told him stories about Duck's history. Maybe not exactly a fair trade, but he seemed to enjoy the stories. I thought he probably played down some of his FBI stories and accused him of hiding the good parts. He laughed and said people had romanticized ideas about FBI and CIA agents.

It was dark and cold, but the rain had stopped by the time I was ready to go home. I was glad I'd accepted his offer of a ride anyway. The wind was still blowing fiercely across the island. Not a fit night for anyone to be out.

"I hope you don't mind that I need to stop at the ABC store for brandy. I thought I got some with my shipment this week, but I guess they forgot it." He opened the doors on the truck, then got behind the steering wheel. "It's hard to make peaches with brandy sauce without the brandy."

"Sure. I think I can wait that long to get home."

"I'm glad you and Horace have made up. I know it was hard."

"A little. What's harder is imagining him not saying anything about my father all these years. He can hardly stand not telling me what he got me for Christmas. I guess you never know."

"He was motivated." He pulled the truck around the circle drive and into the street. "People can be surprising when they have something to hide."

"How can you know so much bad stuff about people in general and still want to hang around them?" It seemed to me like it would be easier to go out on an island like Bunk's and never see anyone again. "When you've seen people at their worst, like you and Gramps have, what makes you able to see the good in them?"

"We probably don't really see any good. We just aren't surprised by the bad anymore."

"Really? So all you see when you look at me is the bad things I've done and that I'm about to do."

He laughed. "Not exactly. I think most people in law enforcement are realists—they know people can be liars, thieves and killers. They don't care anymore. It happens and you deal with it."

"I guess that's why I'd never be involved in law enforcement. I don't think that attitude would suit me."

We went to the ABC store in Duck at Wee Winks Square, but they were sold out of the kind of brandy Kevin was looking for. We got back in the truck to drive down to Kitty Hawk in search of brandy for peaches.

The road was empty. People were probably inside their warm houses watching something on TV instead of braving the dark night. I probably would've been home in my pajamas, wrapped in a blanket, watching some romantic movie. But it was more fun being with Kevin. The truck was warm, and all I had to do was get in and out. The evening would be over soon enough.

On our way out of Duck, we drove down the street where Max and Agnes's house had been. An old streetlight still stood at the bottom of the driveway. It served only to point out that the house was gone, eerily illuminating the burned-out remains.

But there was also a light coming from the rubble.

"Did you see that?" I asked Kevin as we passed it.

"What?"

"A light of some kind at Max and Agnes's house. It looked like it was moving around the pile of debris left from the fire."

He glanced at his rearview mirror. "Could be junk collectors."

"Or someone else who knows Agnes has gold hidden in the house. Like you said, she didn't bring it to the Blue Whale with her. Where else would it be?"

He slowed down and made a U-turn to go back to the house. "Maybe you should call 911."

"Why bother them when we could scare them off?"

"You mean we could catch whoever killed Max and burned the house because they came back for the gold, right?"

"No! I'm not thinking about that at all," I said adamently, although what he said was true.

"That's what I was talking about." He parked on the side of the road. "Everyone lies."

"Like you don't care anything about finding out who killed Max."

"I'm curious," he agreed. "But I left my gun at home, and my karate is a little rusty."

"Don't worry. I'll handle it." I laughed. "If a big smile and running fast will make a difference."

There was a car pulled behind the big pile of wood, bricks and furniture. "That's Agnes's car," Kevin said. "I guess she changed her mind about wanting the gold."

"Or she's here for some other reason. It's her place. Maybe she's trying to find something she can salvage."

"Yeah. In the middle of the night. I told you, gold makes people crazy."

We didn't exactly sneak up, but Agnes shrieked when she saw us, and Celia and Vicky both took threatening stances with their shovels.

"Oh! It's only you." Agnes put her hand to her heart. Both girls lowered their shovels. "What are you doing out here?"

"We could ask you the same thing," I said. "We saw the lights and thought someone was trying to steal what was left."

"That's not the case," Celia said sharply. "So you can leave now."

"You might need some help if you're trying to get the rest of the gold out of there." Kevin didn't bother mincing his words.

"Gold?" All three women started laughing in a terrible fake way. "We're not looking for gold. What gives you that idea?"

"Look," I told them, "Agnes already told me there was gold left in the house the day it burned down. She said I could have all of it because she didn't want it anymore. I think she said it was cursed."

Both daughters turned on their mother. "What were you talking about, Mom? Why did you say that to Dae? You know there's no gold out here."

Vicky laughed again. "She was talking out of her head. We're looking for family heirlooms that may have survived the fire. We were embarrassed to do it during the day when everyone could see us."

While the other two women agreed with her and started that awful laughing again, Kevin cut them off by saying, "Did you keep it in a fireproof safe? Was it upstairs or in the basement? You can make this go a lot faster if you'll be honest about it."

Vicky, Agnes and Celia blinked their eyes like three owls caught in the woods.

"Really, I don't want the gold," I added to convince them. "Let's just get it out of here. I'm freezing."

Finally convinced that we didn't want to steal the gold, Agnes told us the safe had been upstairs in the bedroom. She showed Kevin about where the bedroom had been before the fire. He walked around with a flashlight while we watched him.

"Mom really didn't want the gold anymore, if it makes you feel any better," Celia whispered. "She really thought it killed Dad and caused the house to catch on fire."

"Has anyone said what caused the fire yet?" I asked her.

Agnes answered, "That nice arson investigator from Manteo told me someone dumped kerosene in the bottom of the house. He said they'd be investigating. That's the last I heard. That's why I decided to get the gold out."

"It's not like anyone would blame you for wanting to keep the gold," I told her. "It's legally yours. You should keep it."

"That's the problem," Agnes admitted. "That's why

we're out here at night. I'm not exactly sure it *is* legal, Dae. I'd appreciate it if you wouldn't say anything to anyone."

"You've had it for years, Mom," Celia said. "I'm sure there's some statute about possession of something even if it's illegal."

"Nope." Kevin returned and added, "If you got this gold illegally, even if you've had it a few years, it's still illegal. But I think I found the safe. Bring those shovels over here."

They gave up all pretense at not eagerly anticipating finding the gold. We hurried with the shovels and flashlights to the area Kevin said we'd find the safe.

I began to realize as we stood around talking that Celia and Vicky hadn't known there was any gold until Agnes mentioned it after the fire. She and Max had kept it a secret from them. Now the two girls wanted their share.

I wondered, as Kevin had said, about the gold and if it was illegal. Had Bunk obtained it through illegal means or through investing over the years? I didn't know much about investing, having never been able to invest much. But I knew a little something about the laws of salvage, courtesy of my Banker heritage.

If Bunk had originally started his fortune by finding the pirate gold on the beach, the gold that had been in the museum, that was legal. Agnes was entitled to the gold she had if Bunk obtained it legally.

The beams from the flashlights illuminated the terrible devastation left behind by the fire. Some portions of walls were still standing like ghostly reminders of what had been. Otherwise everything from the structure of the house to its contents had crumbled into one giant heap of debris. I wasn't sure how Kevin had managed to locate anything in this mess.

"It should be right here," he said as he pushed aside a

large part of what looked to be charred flooring. He kept moving through pieces of plasterboard, chunks of wood and furniture remnants that had dropped to the bottom of the house. I recognized what was left of an old cabinet, now smashed and singed, that Max had purchased one sunny Saturday at a nearby antique show. I'd been there with him, looking for things for Missing Pieces.

Both Agnes and the girls were eager to assist Kevin as they pushed aside lumps of unknown materials with their hands and shovels. It took a while, but eventually I could tell we were standing in the basement area (one of the few basements in Duck). The washer and dryer were filthy but not melted, at least as far as I could see.

The acrid smell of burned house began to envelop us. Everyone was coughing, but we continued moving toward our destination.

"How much farther?" Celia finally whined as Agnes took Vicky's shovel so she could have a break.

"These things are designed so that the weight drops them through the burning floor," Kevin explained. "From the location of the safe, this is where it should have fallen."

Every once in a while as we worked, we'd hear a crunch or crash as the debris resettled in response to our work with the shovels. When Vicky had been gone awhile, Kevin took Celia's place so she could go and look for her sister. Both girls finally came back, Celia muttering that Vicky's new boyfriend always called at bad times.

Kevin's shovel finally hit something hard and solid, the *chink* of metal against metal resounding in the still night. Everyone paused while he dug out some of the ash-covered material around it. In the small flashlight beam, a dull silver face with numbers appeared out of the debris.

"There it is!" Agnes declared moving closer to Kevin. "We found it!"

"I hope you remember the combination," Celia said to
her.

"Of course she does." Vicky nudged her hard with her
elbow.

They cleared away some pieces of wet, dirty fabric that
may have once been drapes. The safe seemed fairly large
to me. Not the size of a bank vault, but much larger than
the bread-box-size safe I had at home for important papers. This was more like a refrigerator. Was there *that*
much gold?

Agnes got down on her hands and knees in front of the
safe and blew on her cold fingers for warmth. The wind
suddenly picked up, whistling around us like Rafe Masterson's pirate ghost riding the night wind, watching us
dig for gold.

Two turns to the left. I couldn't see the numbers, though
I imagined Kevin could since he held the flashlight for
Agnes. Two turns to the right and the safe door opened. I
could see a small amount of gold gleaming from inside.
Cold and exhaustion made me hope there wasn't more in
there than what I could see with my flashlight.

"Well, thanks for your help." Celia began at once trying to push me and Kevin away from the find. "I think we
can handle it from here. If we need you again, we'll call."

"If that thing is filled with gold, I think you might need
some help transporting it," Kevin said. "Chances are your
car isn't going to hold that kind of weight."

We all looked at the small Toyota hybrid Agnes had
driven there. He was probably right. They'd been lucky
to fit all three of them in the car. If there was enough gold
to get excited about, it wasn't going anywhere in that
vehicle.

"You mean you'll take it back in your truck?" Agnes
asked Kevin.

"What's the fee?" Vicky demanded in a shrill voice. "No one does anything for nothing."

Agnes hushed her daughter. "Quiet, both of you. You're talking to the man who has been letting us live rent free in his home since the fire. Both of you get down here and start walking this gold over to the truck. I want to hear apologies and thank-yous from both of you while you're doing it."

Kevin brought his truck up to what was left of the house. It took each girl a few minutes to get a good look inside the safe (obviously there was enough gold to get excited about) and gather up a couple handfuls to take back to the truck. At this rate, we'd be here all night.

I was already surprised that the police hadn't shown up. They check doors at all local businesses to make sure they're locked after hours. Something like this should have caught their attention by now. I might need to bring this up at the next town council meeting. Maybe they were all too busy looking for Bunk Whitley. Duck only had a small police force.

Eventually it was my turn to stick my hands into the pile of gold. I wasn't wearing gloves, but I had already experienced the touch of this gold when Agnes had given me the coin after the fire. This time, I recognized Bunk as he gave Max the money to save his daughter's life. Bunk's concern for Agnes—that was the true emotion that lingered in this shining mass.

The coins slipped and slithered through my fingers. I had no way of calculating what all of this was worth. It had to be a small fortune. No wonder Celia and Vicky had pushed their mother into getting it back.

Kevin and Agnes found a few flowerpots. After dumping the plants out, we used the pots as small pails to transport the gold. In the gleam from the overhead light, the back of Kevin's truck began to fill with the fortune.

It was past two A.M. before the last of the coins and some small gold bars were in the truck. Kevin pulled a tarp over the gold.

"I'm a little worried about that falling out of there," Agnes confessed.

"With all the weight of those bricks, you don't have to worry about it," Kevin assured her. "It's not going anywhere."

Agnes may have developed a sense of insecurity despite her words to the girls because she insisted on us going first and them following. Maybe she planned to pick up any gold that might fall out. Kevin and I got into the pickup and started back down Duck Road toward the Blue Whale.

"Now's the time if you've ever wanted to live on an island outside the U.S. jurisdiction," I joked.

"That might not even be necessary since at this point, ownership of the gold could be questionable. Were you thinking Caribbean or Pacific?" He smiled at me as the gold slid around in the back of the truck.

I was thinking about where they would keep all this gold once they got it to the Blue Whale when I heard a loud crash behind us.

Kevin looked in the rearview mirror and frowned as he stopped the truck. "Looks like we're not the only ones out this late after all. Someone just back-ended Agnes."

Chapter 22

The dark vehicle—an SUV of some kind—didn't come to a stop as I had expected the driver to do. Instead, it used its momentum to spin around in the empty road and race back toward Agnes's car.

"Stay on the other side of the truck," Kevin yelled at me as he ran toward Agnes's car. "Call 911."

Agnes screamed as she struggled to get out of the car. I couldn't tell what was wrong. But I knew if she didn't move quickly, the driver in the SUV would hit her again.

It didn't look like she was going to make it. I could see her frightened, smudged face in the glare of the headlights. Celia and Vicky were yelling at her, but they didn't move from the side of the road where they'd run after escaping from the crumpled hybrid.

Kevin grabbed Agnes and yanked her bodily from the car. The two of them tumbled down into the cold, wet ditch. The SUV hit the hybrid again, pushing it on its side, before speeding away down Duck Road toward Corolla.

The 911 operator answered as I watched the SUV go by. It was too dark for me to make out any of the license plate—if there was one. The Dare County dispatcher said she would send help, but the incident seemed to be over.

I ran back to make sure everyone was all right. It was only a few seconds before Tim Mabry and Scott Randall showed up in a Duck police car. Agnes and the girls were crying too hard to give them any information about what happened. Kevin and I filled in the blanks with a basic description of the vehicle and how viciously it had attacked Agnes's car.

"It wasn't an ordinary hit-and-run," I told them. "This person hit Agnes, then turned around and hit her again."

"We'll take care of it, Dae," Tim said. "Are you sure you're okay?"

"I wasn't involved," I reminded him. "And you're losing time you could use looking for that crazy driver."

He and Scott left at that point, just as the paramedics were arriving. No one was hurt, and all three women declined a ride to the hospital. Ben Moore came out with his tow truck, remarking on the amount of damage done to Agnes's car. "These mainland drivers get scarier every day," he said as he winched the car upright to pull it back to his body shop. "You all are lucky to be alive."

I agreed with him. But this was more than some drunk or impatient driver, possibly Roger's handiwork. Kevin agreed as he urged all of us to get in the pickup and off the road. It took a few minutes to convince Agnes to leave her car, but eventually she complied.

The pickup had only one passenger seat. I couldn't see Agnes riding in the back (she was hysterical and soaking wet), so I gave up my place in front to ride with Celia, Vicky and the gold in back.

The gold coins were better to look at than sit on. They were hard and cold and slithered around every time the truck moved. It was a chilly trip, too, going down the road with no protection from the wind.

"Why would anyone do something like that?" Vicky demanded, still crying.

Celia was silent, playing with her cell phone, calling someone over and over and, from what I could tell, getting no response.

Vicky finally grabbed the phone from her and threw it over the side of the truck into the darkness, probably never to be found again. "Stop messing with that thing! We were almost killed out here and all you can do is call that stupid loser boyfriend of yours."

"Shut up! You don't know anything!" Celia shouted back at her. "You'll see and then you'll be sorry."

I didn't know what she meant, but I was sitting between them, already uncomfortable and wishing the short ride back to the Blue Whale was over. We were probably all in shock, definitely cold and filthy. It almost seemed funny that we were sitting on a fortune in gold that couldn't help us.

Kevin was one step ahead of me when we finally got back to the Blue Whale. I'd been ignoring the arguing, weeping sisters by thinking about what we could do to hide all this gold. I didn't think he had a safe like Agnes did, but I figured one of the empty rooms on the third floor would be a secure place to store it. The only problem was getting it up there. After moving it once, I knew it was too heavy and unmanageable to take upstairs or in the old iron-cage elevator.

I thought Agnes and the girls would want to be right on hand for whatever happened to the gold, but I was wrong. They had worked themselves into such a state that all they could do was go up to their rooms. The incident on the road and our response to it must have eased Vicky and Celia's suspicions about our intentions toward the gold.

"So I have an idea about storing the gold," Kevin said after the three women had retired to their bedrooms on the second floor.

"Me too! I had to have something to think about to keep from killing Celia. Anyway, could we wait to do whatever it is until after I have a shower and change clothes?"

"I don't see why not. I'm going to pull the truck around back to the delivery area. The gold should be safe there until we can move it."

"Do you have some clothes I could put on that aren't full of emotional turmoil?"

"I think we can work that out too. Follow me."

He loaned me some of his clothes—an old pair of jeans that must've shrunk in the wash and a long-sleeved shirt that had seen better days. They felt safe, like Kevin, when I touched them.

I took a quick shower that I hoped was enough to get most of the black soot out of my hair. It ran off of me in heavy rivulets, which left a ring in the tub that I felt compelled to clean up when I was done. The tile shower had been so nice and clean before I'd stepped into it.

Kevin was showered and changed as well, waiting for me with three of the large, old whiskey barrels from the storm cellar. "I think these will hold all of it. I have the pickup lined up in the delivery area. That way I can fill up the barrels and move them with the hand truck into the big freezer in back."

As ideas went, it sounded like a good one. We rolled

the barrels to the side of the inn where trucks unloaded supplies. I ignored the feelings I got from the barrels— nothing too distressing beyond workers who were un- happy with their jobs anyway. At least no one had ever been buried in one of them as had happened in a few Duck legends.

Kevin had huge hand scoops that normally were used for flour and other commodities. We used them to get the gold out the truck and fill up two and a half barrels. Kevin capped them and hammered the solid wood tops in place. Then he used the big, red hand truck to move them into the freezer. My hands were freezing and I smelled like old whiskey, but at least the job was over. The sun was com- ing up at the orange horizon when we were finished. I pulled the delivery door shut again as Kevin closed and locked the freezer door.

"Coffee?" he asked with a yawn. "I have a delivery at seven this morning for that party tonight, and I still need brandy for the peaches. I don't think sleep is an option."

"Sounds good, thanks." I forced my tired, painful body into the kitchen. After a few minutes, coffee was perfum- ing the air with its rich fragrance. Kevin brought in a blue- berry coffee cake, and I got two cups, cream and sugar.

We'd only been sitting down for a few minutes when Gramps came bursting into the warm kitchen, demanding to know what I was doing. "Where have you been all night, Dae? Your bed wasn't slept in—you're wearing *his* clothes. You smell like old whiskey. Ah, honey, this isn't the way to handle this thing with your father. And Kevin, you aren't the man I thought you were to take advantage of her pain this way."

I took out another coffee cup, too tired to get excited about his tirade. "I'm in pain all right, but not the way you're thinking." I explained about Agnes and the gold.

He sat down next to me to hear the rest of the story, managing to grab a piece of coffee cake at the same time. "That's incredible! You know, I heard something about that on the police scanner last night, but I ignored it. Sounded like your typical road-rage situation."

"Have they found the car?" Kevin asked him.

"Yeah. About like you'd expect—abandoned, stolen, owner in New York or some such. No idea who was driving it, and it was wrecked. Where's the gold?"

"In the back." Kevin nodded in that general direction.

"Want to see it?" I offered.

"No thanks. I'd rather have another slice of that coffee cake. Did you make it yourself?"

Kevin gave him a cursory recipe for the cake. Gramps nodded and continued eating. After swallowing his last mouthful, he asked, "You think someone was gunning for Agnes again, like the fire? Or were they trying to get at the gold?"

"How would anyone else know about the gold?" I asked him.

"How indeed?" Gramps chuckled. "These things have a way of making the rounds. Your friend Bunk knew about it. I'm assuming that Roger fella you've been going on about knows. Since Vicky and Celia found out, I'm surprised most of Duck wasn't out there helping you dig."

I hadn't thought of that. Kevin and I found out accidentally they were getting the gold last night, but dozens of other people could have known.

"Everyone also knows Agnes and her daughters are staying here with me," Kevin added. "If they really wanted them—or the gold now for that matter—there wouldn't be much we could do."

Gramps laughed out loud at that one. "I bet there's plenty you could do! Don't be modest with me, young man!"

Kevin offered me more coffee, but I declined. I was ready to float away as it was. "I'm tough," I told him. "If you have some secret FBI counterterrorism thing you can do to end all of this, feel free to use it."

"I'm afraid there's no surefire way to prevent someone from getting at you if they really want to," Kevin explained. "You saw what happened out at the island."

"That had to be a well-trained group," Gramps concluded. "The people who went through those security men out there wouldn't have given up with a few smacks to Agnes's bumper."

"Unless whoever did it came from within Bunk's organization," I said. "I'd say Bunk was prepared for what happened since he got away so quickly. He knew what to expect from Roger."

"Agnes is sitting on a lot of gold," Kevin observed. "Enough to make anyone think about taking it from her. Even Dae and I were making plans to fly down to the Caribbean with it before Agnes's incident."

We all laughed at the idea, but realizing all that gold was now at the Blue Whale made me nervous and I didn't even live there. "Be careful," I cautioned Kevin as Gramps and I were leaving in the golf cart a little later. "I think I know what you mean about people going crazy over gold."

He kissed me and frowned. "You be careful too. Whoever was out there this morning might have seen you there."

"I will. I'm only going to the shop anyway. Do you need any help with your dinner tonight?"

"Not once I get that brandy. See you later."

After showering again (would I ever get the soot out of my hair?) and changing into some of my own clothes, I bundled up warmly and headed down to Missing Pieces. The cold walk woke me up a little, but I was still ex-

hausted. I headed to the Coffee House and Bookstore for
a large mocha that I hoped would get me through the
morning.

There was light ice on the water's edge along the Duck
Shoppes boardwalk. The brown water plants were crusted
in it where the gray water from the sound lapped at the
land.

Shayla and Trudy were both closed this morning—
they were lucky they could plan for their customers with
appointments.

A few stray walkers came into the shop around eleven.
They were tourists from Nashville down here for a week.
I've never seen anyone more surprised that the Outer
Banks has cold weather. Apparently, they thought going
toward the coast meant warmer temperatures.

They looked around but didn't buy anything. I sat behind the counter and watched them reject my treasures.
Sometimes it could be pretty sad.

Around lunchtime, Mrs. Euly Stanley called to tell me
she'd found her ancestor's diary. She was very excited
because there were some things in the text that made her
believe the woman from the locket I'd located for her was
Theodosia Burr.

"I'm going to bring it and the pendant in around five,
if that's okay, so we can compare your miniature to what
I have. It's so fascinating, Dae, thinking we might be related to Theodosia. You know, I never believed Alexander
Hamilton didn't provoke her father, Aaron, into killing
him anyway. See you at five!"

I hung up the phone with a sigh. I couldn't think about
Theo Burr's missing heritage without thinking about Max
and his favorite dream. I was frustrated that we might be
closing in on that dream faster than we were on Max's
killer. Despite the chiefs and the SBI looking for evidence

to link Bunk to the recent deaths, I didn't believe he was responsible. Someone was still out there, possibly looking for another person to kill.

Given what had happened to Agnes in the last few days, it was looking more and more like Bunk was right about Max being accidentally killed in place of his wife. Or maybe the killer had wanted to get rid of them both.

Roger knew his way around Duck. Bunk said he had his spies. The attack on Agnes was proof of that. He was watching her. No doubt it was the gold that motivated him—Bunk's *and* Agnes's.

How long would he wait, and how far would he be willing to go? The thought made me shiver. No one would be safe at the Blue Whale while Agnes and the gold were there. I hoped Gramps was right and Kevin could take care of himself in this kind of situation. But I knew I wouldn't feel better about it until the gold was in a bank somewhere and Agnes and the girls had their own place again.

Tim Mabry surprised me with a visit right after I'd grabbed a sandwich and fries from Wild Stallions. He was unusually quiet, even calling me *ma'am* a few times. This was odd for him on so many different levels that it was almost frightening to listen to him.

"The chief wanted to know if you'd come out with me on Duck Road and show me exactly where everything happened last night, Dae. It shouldn't take too long. He asked Agnes and the girls, but they were kind of beside themselves still. Not much good at giving a statement."

"Sure. It's been pretty quiet here. Has the chief found out anything new yet?"

"Not since we located that stolen SUV." He took off his flat-brimmed police hat. "What were all of you doing out there at that time in the first place?"

I didn't want to lie, but the whole truth might not be best either. "Kevin and I went to help Agnes get some of her stuff from the house. I think she didn't want people seeing her out there going through what was left."

He brought his fist down on the cabinet top near me and made me drop a French fry. "Dammit, Dae! This is exactly why I didn't want to see you and Brickman together. The man leads a different life than the rest of us. Look at the things you've been through since you started dating him—kidnapped and taken to an island, almost killed alongside the road at a time you should've been home in bed like other people."

"Tim, Kevin had nothing to do with any of those things."

"I knew you'd defend him! And I didn't mention you were almost blown up!" His rampage continued.

"Those things would've happened whether I was dating Kevin or not." I didn't bother mentioning that Kevin and I *weren't* dating when the museum exploded.

"They wouldn't have happened at all if you'd been dating *me*! I would've made sure of it."

I sighed. "I'd heard you were already seeing someone else."

"It was only a few days. She's seeing someone else now." He shrugged. "We were too different, according to her."

"I'm sorry. What way did she say you were different?"

"She wanted to smoke marijuana, for one thing. I told her I'd have to lock her up."

"Oh."

"Yeah." He cleared his throat and put his hat back on. "I always come back around to how good you and I would be together and how we're wasting our lives on other people."

I tossed away what was left of my sandwich. It would be better to get this over. "We don't really have anything in common either, Tim, except that we grew up together."

"How can you say that?" he demanded. "I love fishing. I'd like to own a charter boat one day. I like watching sports on TV, and I'd rather take my golf cart out than my patrol car."

"With those qualifications, I think one of those online dating services would pair you up with Gramps, not me. I'm ready to go if you are."

Tim drove us slowly down Duck Road, seeming to enjoy holding up traffic behind him. I pointed out the highlights of our trip from the Blue Whale to Agnes's house and back again. He pulled over so I could get out and show him the black skid marks where the SUV spun around to go back and hit Agnes again. He ignored it when I told him that Kevin had gone back to help Agnes escape her car.

"This is some bad case of road rage," he said, writing all of it down. "I've never heard anything like it. It's not even summertime."

"I know." I didn't go into my suspicions about the incident being more than road rage. I knew the chief wouldn't want to hear what I had to say on the subject. No point in getting Tim in trouble for my theories.

We retraced the route from the point where we'd all climbed into Kevin's truck. I was pretty sure I could've walked faster than Tim was driving. At least it wasn't cold in the patrol car.

I caught sight of something bright pink resting in a clump of dead grass on the side of the road—Celia's cell phone. "Stop a minute. I think I see something."

Tim stopped, and I got out to retrieve the phone. Celia would be happy to see it, I thought, and she could talk to her boyfriend again. I was a little reluctant to touch it, but I didn't have much choice. Besides, I reasoned with myself, it could hold a valuable clue.

When I picked it up, the phone didn't reveal much other than the fact that it had been purchased at a local convenience store. It was one of those pay-as-you-go kinds. I saw the hand with the green-blue ring picking it up from a counter. No doubt it was Roger now.

But why would Roger buy a phone for Celia? Could he be her secret boyfriend?

I looked at Tim and wished I could tell him how important the phone might be. This could be the definitive clue that broke the case. If Celia was tipping Roger about everything that was going on, it all made sense. I couldn't wait to tell Kevin about my find.

Tim drove slowly down Duck Road again and pulled off when we reached the Duck Shoppes parking lot. We sat in his police car for a moment while he filled out paperwork and I silently urged him to hurry. The trip hadn't yielded anything interesting for him.

"Well?" I asked, impatient to be done with it.

"I don't know. It looks like you said. Too bad we didn't catch the driver last night."

"That would've been interesting," I agreed.

"So what kind of stuff did you all pick up from Agnes's house?"

"Mementos, a few personal treasures, whatever she could find that wasn't destroyed by the fire. I'm sure it was hard for her to lose Max and then her home."

He was writing in his notebook. "You've been seeing some of Celia and Vicky too, right?"

"A little," I responded, confused.

"Have you heard either of them talk about having a boyfriend?"

I shook my head. This right after him telling me we belonged together. "Celia seems to be dating someone."

He handed me the paper he'd filled out. "My cousin Cindy is getting married, and I'm looking for a date for the wedding. You know how Mom gets if I show up alone. Sign here if you agree with the statements."

I read my words in his handwriting. "I'm not sure about Vicky. Want me to ask her?"

"I'm not your kid brother, Dae. I can ask her myself."

"Okay. I was only offering. You don't have to bite my head off."

"Sorry." He took the statement sheet I'd signed. "I get a little frustrated sometimes when everyone takes me for granted. Good old Tim. Always there when you need a date but not a relationship. I have needs too, you know."

"You'll find someone right for you," I assured him.

"I already have—but you want someone else."

He let me out in the parking lot without offering to walk me upstairs. "Thank you for your assistance." He nodded politely.

"I'll see you later, Tim."

On my way up the ramp to the boardwalk, I glanced at Celia's phone. Curiosity got the better of me and I opened it. I had to make sure it was Celia's, right? There were dozens of calls from early this morning—one almost every minute starting at midnight. That was probably when Agnes drove them out to the house. All the calls were to the same number. Most of them were too short to have even been answered by the person at the other number. A few had lasted longer.

There was something very familiar about the number she was calling. I didn't know how I'd know Roger's number but it seemed that I did. I started thinking about how many ways this could go bad for Celia. I tried calling

Agnes a few times to warn her but there was no answer and her voice mail was full. I thought about calling Chief Michaels, but without any real proof, what could he do?

I hoped for Celia's sake that Roger was as infatuated with her as she was with him. Maybe she'd be safe until I could figure out what to do next.

I waved to Trudy as I passed Curves and Curls. She had an appointment today after all. I picked up a few UPS packages left outside my door and noticed, as I stood up, that the door to the shop was not quite closed. I was sure I'd locked it before leaving with Tim.

Probably Gramps, I thought, since he had a key too. But maybe not. Usually I don't worry about whether or not the door is locked. Of course, Tim checks it every night after I leave. The police check all the businesses in Duck. Still, given everything that was going on, I didn't feel quite safe.

I put the packages back down so my hands would be free. Not that I expected to fight off some burglar, but it seemed like a good idea. I pushed the door open carefully and stopped short when I saw Brad Spitzer sitting behind the counter.

I suddenly remembered where I'd seen the phone number on Celia's phone. It wasn't Roger after all.

Chapter 23

"Hi, Dae! I hope you don't mind me stopping by. I was down here meeting with Chief Michaels and thought I'd see if you had time to do your thing." Brad's smile was genuine and friendly.

I wasn't sure what to do next. Knowing Brad was Celia's boyfriend, the one she'd probably told about going to get the gold, raised all kinds of issues. Could he have been the driver who crashed into Agnes's car? That thought led to another—was it possible Brad could also be the arsonist who burned the house in the first place?

Running out the door, screaming, was an option. But then I might never know the truth. Not that I planned to openly confront him on any of it. But there was a small chance I might see more than he anticipated when I looked into his head.

"Sure. That should be fine." I was as friendly and open

as I could be. I had to make him trust me. "There haven't been many customers today anyway."

"Good! Now, how do we do this? You made it sound easy, but there must be more to it. There always is, isn't there?"

I laughed—it sounded too loud and forced. I closed the shop door and reminded myself to be natural. "Not really. It's either in your head or not. It's not complicated."

"You said we had to hold hands."

"That's right. You have a good memory. We'll sit over here on the sofa and take a look. What is it that you're missing?"

He got up, waited for me to sit down, then joined me on the burgundy sofa. "As I explained, it's something that my father left to me. But I can't seem to find it."

I nodded hoping I didn't seem as uncomfortable as I felt. In the meantime, my heart was racing as I considered all the possibilities. Could Brad be Bunk's son? He seemed to be in his midforties. That would fit into the time line Bunk told me about. Had Brad been the one who killed Max and then tried to kill his own father?

"How does this work?" Brad asked. "Can you see everything I'm thinking?"

"No, of course not. All I can see is what you've lost. You have to hold a picture of it in your mind. I should see where it is from there."

I didn't dare ask him what he was looking for. What could I say to get him to confess that wouldn't sound suspicious?

"Give me your hands." I put mine out. They were shaking a little and cold.

He put his warm hands in mine. "You're freezing, Dae, and trembling. Are you okay?"

Too late, I saw the unusual green-blue ring worn by

Roger. As my hand came in contact with it, a burst of emotion blinded me to everything else. I saw Brad on the island, following the men he'd paid to kill the security guards so he could get to Bunk, his father. Brad saw the ring on the dead man's hand, took it, cleaned the blood off and put it on his finger. Then he dumped Roger into the sea. *That's why I hadn't seen him.*

This proved conclusively that Brad was the killer—at least the one who killed the men on the island. It didn't prove he was involved with Max's death. Despite being totally disgusted touching that ring, I knew I had to play him along for a while.

Just remember that phone calls on Celia's cell phone don't mean anything unless you can tie them together with everything else. I closed my eyes and let myself move into his head.

At first it was dark and disorienting as always. I couldn't see anything that had substance or form. I had a reason for making sure that what I was looking for truly belonged to the seeker. My abilities didn't know the difference between true ownership and false. I could see stolen objects as well as things that belonged to the person. I'd made the rule to protect myself.

"Don't you need to know what you're looking for?" Brad whispered.

"No. As long as you know and can focus on it, that's all that matters."

And that seemed to be the case. I saw the gold Kevin and I had shoveled into the barrels stored at the Blue Whale. I gasped a little at that. Fortunately, the things I saw were usually not apparent to the seeker. Kevin was safe for now.

But seeing the gold in his mind convinced me even more that Brad was responsible for everything that had happened in Duck since Max's death. He was familiar enough with the area to use the cannon from Corolla so Sam would be blamed for the Duck museum explosion. Being an arson investigator probably helped him formulate the plan to fire the cannonball at the propane tank.

"Are you getting anything?" he asked.

"I think so." I had to string this out and hope an idea to trap him came to mind. At that moment, though, I felt nothing except terror. If he realized what I knew about him, this could all go bad very quickly. "What you're looking for is heavy, right? Something very valuable."

He shifted position a little, but when I dared a glance, his eyes were still closed. "That's right. Can you tell where it is?"

"I think whoever has it recently moved it. Do you know anything about that?"

"You're right! Someone moved it all right. And it wasn't hers to move in the first place. She had no right keeping it from me."

I swallowed hard. This was all well and good having him confirm my suspicions, but how would I convince Chief Michaels that Brad was the bad guy? The chief was still after Bunk Whitley. I needed something tangible that only Brad might know—something that the chief would realize only the killer would know.

"Your father—he's from around here, right?"

"Yes. He doesn't live here now, but he's originally from Duck."

"Your mother died very young." I felt like Shayla with her tarot cards. "Your father abandoned you after she died."

"Exactly! He never loved her—he never loved me. All he's ever loved is that gold. That's why I should have it.

He owes me. My older sister wants it but I have news for both of them—over my dead body."

He'd confirmed a mixture of facts, but it was still not enough to make a case for Chief Michaels. Did I dare go any further with this? Could I tell him where the gold was hidden without jeopardizing Kevin, Agnes, Celia and Vicky?

I wanted to give Celia a hard slap for making this worse than it was already. What was she thinking, going out with this guy she barely knew and telling him everything he needed to know?

I reminded myself that the important thing was for us all get through this in one piece. When Celia found out she'd been dating her own uncle, that would be punishment enough.

The idea of telling him what he really wanted to know became the best answer I could see out of the situation. I couldn't sit here all day guessing things he could relate to. I had to find a way for him to show his hand. My plan might be risky but it seemed the only thing that might work.

"What you're looking for is at the Blue Whale Inn. I think it might be part of the museum items being stored there." I added in the last part so he wouldn't suspect that I'd taken part in moving the gold. "You should be able to walk inside and get it."

I gave him plenty of details about the lobby, the front door and the circle drive. My plan consisted of piquing his interest enough that he'd take the bait and go for the gold. When he left to retrieve his prize, I'd get on the phone with Agent Walker and Chief Michaels. They'd be at the inn waiting for him before he even got there.

Brad opened his eyes and looked at me. "This is incredible! Once we get through this, we can work on another project—something else valuable my father left behind."

"Great!" I took my hands back, glad to separate myself from him. "Let me know how it goes."

"Sure! How much do I owe you?"

"I don't charge for this. You're welcome to buy something from the shop if you want to help the cause." It was all I could do to keep talking away, praying he'd get tired of it and leave.

Instead, he took a pistol from his jacket pocket and pointed it at me. "After we get the gold, I'll be glad to buy something from you. Get your jacket. You're coming with me."

"Wait a minute!" I feigned anger—I was really terrified. "I found your answer. Why are you doing this?"

"I know you're connected here, Dae. I can't take a chance on you giving me away before I get what I deserve. I've worked too hard to get to this point—harder than I needed to, I guess. Do you have any idea how difficult it was getting that cannon from Corolla and setting it up next to the museum here so no one would notice it? And all the time, I could've just asked you. I didn't need to go through so much to take dear Agnes out of the picture and leave the gold for me."

I knew from listening to Gramps and his law enforcement friends that it wasn't a good thing when a killer decides to unburden himself to someone. That meant he didn't plan for me to be around long enough to share the information with anyone else. It was a sobering thought. How did such a good plan go so bad so quickly?

I put on my jacket, wishing I could think of some way to let someone know what was going on. Obviously he wouldn't let me use the cell phone. Mrs. Euly Stanley wasn't due until five—three long hours away. I could be so dead by then.

I reached for a tissue, knocking over a few personal items I kept on the counter, then quietly set Celia's phone on the counter behind the cash register. I didn't know if that would mean anything to anyone who saw it, but I couldn't think of what else to do.

"Okay." He pushed the gun into my side and walked close beside me. "We'll close up for the day and be on our way. No strange moves or friendly conversations on the boardwalk. We walk straight down to my car and get inside like friends. Okay?"

"Okay."

"I'm not going to hurt you, Dae, unless you don't listen to me. After I get what's mine, you're free to go."

"Okay."

He laughed. "We're getting along just fine, right? I don't know what made me think you were such an arrogant little bitch before. You're sweet as pie."

I didn't reply to that. We stepped outside the shop together, and I locked the door behind me. Brad kicked the UPS packages out of the way. I watched them scatter across the boardwalk—too scared to care. I realized that I might never come back here again.

We walked past Curves and Curls. With the gun pressed in my side and Brad's breath on the back of my neck, I didn't wave to Trudy. I didn't even look her way. I was too busy trying not to panic, trying to think of some way I might be able to survive this. It didn't seem likely, but there was always that possibility I'd be able to escape or convince him to let me go.

We went down the boardwalk together—no one stopped to talk or even noticed we were there. It helped him that there were so few shoppers in the cold. If this had been summer, I might've been able to catch someone's eye and let them know there was a problem.

But not today. Today we walked into the parking lot and got in his car. He had me drive while he held the gun. I felt as hopeless and trapped as a dolphin in a net.

"We're gonna take it nice and slow," he said. "We're not in any hurry. Drive down to the Blue Whale and nothing fancy, please. I don't want to shoot you and draw attention to what we're doing. That would be bad for both of us."

I started the car and thought about putting my foot down hard on the gas. The car would fly through the parking lot—and at this angle, hit a group of teenagers leaving the shops. That wasn't a good tradeoff. But there had to be something I could do.

"How did you find out you had this talent, Dae?" He made polite conversation as we turned onto Duck Road.

"I found things for my mother and my grandfather."

"So you started doing it when you were just a kid, huh? I'm surprised some good-looking, sweet-talking young man didn't grab you and take you out of here. I can imagine you could make some money for someone."

I resisted the urge to jerk my head away from him as he touched the side of my face. "I've always known the difference between right and wrong. No one could sweet-talk me out of that."

"Slow down here and swing around the side instead of going to the front." I started to protest his directions, and he smiled. "I've been staking this place out for a while. There's a delivery entrance over there. I think we'd be better off going in that way, don't you?"

I couldn't keep silent anymore. He was probably going to kill me anyway. "Too bad your father didn't leave the Blue Whale for you, Brad. Is Brad your real name?"

"I wouldn't want this piece of junk anyway." He chuckled. "And Brad *is* my real name. I'm sure you know by now that my last name isn't Spitzer. That was my mother's name."

"Is there enough gold to satisfy what you want?"

"Maybe. If you can help me find what the old man hid on the island. What he gave my *sister*, Agnes, is barely enough to pay the mercenaries I hired to kill dear old Dad. He got away—again. He's good at running. But you and me, we might be able to find his stash. That's more than most people could spend in a lifetime. Lucky me, Dad never liked banks."

By this time, we were facing the open delivery door. Kevin must still be waiting for his dinner delivery. It made it easier for Brad to get inside. He'd have to rely on me to tell him where to find the gold, but even if I lied, it wouldn't take him long to go through the inn and find it.

"Let's go inside and see what we can find." He turned off the engine and put the keys in his pocket. "I think you said it was in front, right?"

It occurred to me that if I tried to walk him through the inn, Kevin might catch on and his life would be in danger too. I couldn't risk that. I decided to tell him the truth by the time we'd reached the loading area. I'd just opened my mouth to speak when Agnes, Celia and Vicky came through the door from the inn.

"Brad!" Celia smiled and ran toward us. "I saw your car pull up!"

"This is your boyfriend?" Vicky asked.

"Don't fight, girls," Agnes said. "We're back here for one reason only."

"To try and steal my gold again, sister dear?" Brad spit out the words as he shoved Celia to the side. "Don't even consider it. You got to play with it for a while. Be glad I can't charge you interest on the loan."

Agnes looked at me as though she expected me to have the answers. "What's going on? Why is he calling me his sister? I thought he was the arson investigator."

Brad laughed. "Arsonist, arson investigator, and your half brother. It seems our mothers shared a love of bad men who liked gold. He killed them both. We have that in common too."

Agnes looked almost as baffled as Celia, who was on the floor, crying. I pointed to the freezer door. "The gold is in there. Take it and get out of here."

"Smart place to hide it. Let's take a look." Brad went to the freezer door, leaving me behind in his eager anticipation. He picked up a crowbar that was close at hand and pried off the lock Kevin had put on the door. "Whiskey barrels! Now that *is* fitting!"

He was partially in the freezer, staring straight ahead as he walked toward the barrels. I remembered what Kevin had said about the lure of gold. It was now or never.

I ran to the door and slammed it shut with Brad inside. At the same instant, a dozen or so SBI agents came out of nowhere with their guns drawn. Chief Michaels led his team of Duck police officers in from the back door.

Agnes and Vicky had joined Celia on the floor—all three were crying. I leaned against the side of the freezer when I saw Kevin running back from the kitchen. It was over. Everything was going to be okay.

It was a sunny, warm day two months later as a large crowd gathered at Elizabeth Simpson's house. Today was the dedication of the Duck Historical Museum. I was wearing a new blue dress with a matching hat. This was a different look for me, but I felt like I'd grown into it over the winter. I felt more mature, more certain about where I was going and what I was doing. I wasn't sure why a hat represented that, but it seemed the right accessory to wear. I was giving the dedication speech and a surprise to a couple of Duck heroes. The day sparkled around me as I caught sight of Kevin coming my way.

The Rescue at the Blue Whale, as the event had come to be known, was a simple enough feat. It could all be blamed on the Duck grapevine and the fact that everyone knew what everyone else was doing.

Trudy didn't see Brad's gun that day on the boardwalk when I was sure my life was over. Instead, she thought I was going out with him and two-timing Kevin. She called Shayla to tell her I was snuggling up with Brad. Shayla called Kevin to tell him I was cheating on him.

Nancy called Chief Michaels when she saw me with Brad. She told him she'd seen something suspicious, maybe a gun, worried that Brad had gone off the deep end with his need to blame me for everything that had happened.

Kevin had called Chief Michaels and, together, they'd decided something was definitely wrong. The police convinced Agent Walker to join the party, and the rest was the Rescue at the Blue Whale.

Thank God for nosy neighbors! If it wasn't for them, I wouldn't be here to dedicate the museum on this fine day, looking my best and smiling bright enough to outshine the sun.

Brad Spitzer Whitley had been indicted for murder, arson and firing a weapon of mass destruction—the cannon. He admitted that he got Max to wait for him in the museum with the promise of his DNA matching Theodosia Burr's. He thought Agnes would be there too after observing what took place when the schoolkids visited the museum. He primed his cannon hidden in the scrub trees near the museum, took aim and fired.

He was in prison awaiting trial, but I didn't think we'd hear from him again in our lifetimes. Agent Walker said there were other warrants for him, including a murder warrant for Sam Meacham's death.

Nothing I said about that could dissuade him. He didn't believe either my theory that Bunk's henchman Roger had killed Sam or Bunk's story that Sam had accidentally drowned. I wasn't sure if it mattered anyway since Roger was dead. And one more indictment against Brad didn't really matter.

Then there was the matter of Theodosia Burr Alston. Not as important as solving a murder, maybe, but very important to Duck.

It was going to take time to convince skeptical historians from the rest of the United States, but we were convinced we had all the proof we needed to declare that Theodosia lived and finally died on the Outer Banks. She left behind many descendants and a diary about her life. We'd even gone and visited her grave. There was talk of making it a Duck historical monument.

There was a very nice, anonymous donation given to the historical society, in gold, that had purchased many things needed for the new museum. I knew Bunk was responsible for it, and I wondered if I'd ever see him again. Despite myself, I was glad he was still alive. He could fill in those gaps in our history someday, I reasoned. But the truth was I knew he had more to tell me about my own life.

Agnes and the girls had recovered from their ordeals and managed to find a new home, which meant they'd moved themselves and the gold out of the Blue Whale.

They planned to sell off the land their house had stood on and live full-time on a forty-two-foot sailing yacht.

They were at the memorial service full of smiles and tears while they heard at least twenty people tell about their memories of Max. He was buried in the Duck Cemetery with a special monument that was created to look like the old museum.

There was nothing said about Celia's involvement with Brad. It was mostly too stupid to mention. Celia and Brad got involved during one of his frequent visits to assure her mother that everything was being done in the arson investigation. He was handsome and sympathetic, and at least pretended to be interested in her. There was no way for her to know that he was keeping her close to get information. She was a direct line to everything going on.

If Agnes could forgive her youngest daughter for almost getting her killed, there was no one else to complain. Celia had thought telling Brad about the gold would make her more desirable. In that respect, she'd made the same mistake many of her sisters have made since the beginning of time.

I approached the podium at the appointed time and said what I had to say about Max and how much he was missed. There wasn't a dry eye in the crowd, so I thought I must've done a good job. Afterward, I gave special medals of honor to Kevin and Luke Helms for their bravery in saving Agnes's life. There was a rousing round of applause for our heroes. I was very proud to be dating one of them, especially since it was Kevin.

It was after midnight at the Sailor's Dream Bar and Grill near the old docks in Duck. I watched a man wearing blue jeans and a torn T-shirt as he closed the door and locked up for the night. He was medium height and build with sandy-colored hair. He dropped a bag in the trash can near the back door, whistling an old rock song as he got in his battered pickup and drove away.

This was as close as I'd let myself get to my father.

NEW FROM NATIONAL BESTSELLING AUTHOR

Madelyn Alt

Home for a Spell

Indiana's newest witch, Maggie O'Neill, needs a
new apartment. But when she finally discovers a
chic abode, Maggie's dream of new digs turns into
a nightmare: The apartment manager is found dead
before she can even sign the lease. And Maggie finds
herself not only searching for a new home—but for
a frightfully clever killer.

penguin.com

Madelyn Alt

No Rest for the Wiccan

Maggie O'Neill reluctantly volunteers to care for her bedridden, oh-so-perfect sister, Mel, but strange spirits threaten to divert her attention. Then a friend of Mel's loses her husband to a dreadful fall, and the police call it an accidental death. Maggie's not so sure, and sets her second sights on finding a first-degree murderer.

penguin.com